Persistent Intruder

Kay Brooks

Published by Kay Brooks, 2018.

PERSISTENT INTRUDER

First edition. January 18, 2018.

Copyright © 2018 Kay Brooks.

ISBN: 978-0999600634

Written by Kay Brooks.

To Jett and Summer Smith, my first two grandchildren

PROLOGUE

HE STOLE AWAY FROM THE HOUSE in the darkest hours before dawn. Ignoring the bedside lamps, he had simply risen when the alarm clock sounded, dressed, and walked away. His suitcase was already in the car.

Extinguishing the parking lights on the sleek black Ferrari, he intuitively followed the glow of the lights that lined the two-mile driveway. He hugged the shadows, avoided the cliffs that dropped off the other side of the drive. Off the mountain he had made his home.

He was tired of sneaking out, screening his movements, and being denied the luxury of enjoying any freedom. Rather, he hid away. Allowed his work to consume him; drive him to higher levels of achievement.

She was becoming a menace and needed to be stopped. Always emailing him, following him, meddling in his life. His concentration waivered with fleeting thoughts of killing her himself. Even if he somehow managed to get her out of his life, would it ever be normal again? He took a deep breath to calm his nerves and checked his mirrors for the darkness. He needed to get away without being detected.

The main road was up ahead and he slowed the powerful engine so that it purred quietly as he inched his way along the drive toward the stone arch at the entrance. His heart pounded when he saw the glow of lights approaching his drive. He braked and waited.

Would the car continue past the drive? Turn in and meet his car nose to nose? Or would it stop, park on the other side of the road, and wait in the shadows just as he did?

He didn't realize he'd been holding his breath until the car sped past. He gripped the steering wheel and took a deep breath to calm his nerves. Doesn't mean the driver won't turn around, his paranoid thoughts reminded him. He moved toward the entrance and then

1

turned left onto the highway. His eyes strained to look ahead and watch the rear-view mirror at the same time.

He was desperate to get away. Even if only for a few days, he needed to be around people. Sane people.

The full moon lit the road as he approached the curve in the highway. Seeing no lights ahead or behind him, he turned on his headlights and shifted the car into action. As if escaping the demons of the night, he sped down the road at seventy miles an hour and slowed only when the interstate sign appeared ahead of him.

It wasn't until he saw the first blush of the rising sun that he felt a reprieve. The horizon offered relief.

CHAPTER 1

NATALIE STOVER GULPED WHEN SHE stepped onto the elevator and saw that there was another occupant. She moved to the far corner, turned and waited for the doors to close.

"I'm harmless," deep voice spoke matter-of-factly from the opposite side of the elevator.

"Excuse me?" She turned to stare at the man leaning against the mirrored wall, his arms crossed in front of his chest. She was here for the writer's conference. Not to pick up a man.

Still, she couldn't help but admire the jeans and blue-and-grey striped shirt. He even smelled good, she thought as she picked up the scent of the new men's fragrance she recalled admiring on her last shopping spree. A romance writer, she had been looking for the perfect cologne for Adam, her current hero.

Ceiling speakers piped an instrumental tune as she stared at his reflection in the mirror. When her eyes met his brown ones, her chin went up a notch. It was obvious from the interested twinkle that he had made an intimate appraisal of her as well.

She watched his lips twitch. "I said I'm harmless," he repeated. At her blank stare, he spoke slowly. "You hesitated when you got on the elevator."

"That's because you startled me. I didn't see you at first." Her chin went up another notch as she directed her attention to the operation panel with smooth buttons, the occupancy notice and inspection report. He may have been trying to assure her, but his arrogant attitude left much to be desired.

"Sorry." He tipped his head back to watch the number ten glow on the panel.

He didn't sound sorry, Natalie thought as she cut her eyes in his direction. He looked familiar. She turned her head and discretely studied his profile in the mirror. Knew she'd seen that handsome face

3

before. Olive complexion, full mouth, and mesmerizing dark brown eyes flitted on the edge of her memory. "Oh, no," she whispered, suddenly realizing where she had seen him.

He glanced down at her, distracted by her comment.

She took a deep breath and tried to ignore him. Pretended to search her pocketbook. Looked anywhere but at him.

"Forget something?" he inquired too politely.

"What? Oh...no," she repeated as she let go of the purse that hung from her shoulder. She recalled his picture on the back cover of the newest horror novel she had processed just last week. Although a published author herself, Natalie still supported herself by working in the cataloging department at a college library. Her stomach did a somersault when she realized that this man had written the book that had sent chills down her spine.

He continued to look down at her. "Are you sure you're okay?"

Natalie looked up at him and saw the frown that creased his high forehead. She opened her mouth to answer, but nothing came out.

"Oh, no," he mumbled, parroting her favorite phrase.

Natalie watched him cast a desperate glance at the emergency stop button, as if preparing to flee the second the doors opened. She winced and felt her cheeks flush. "I'm sorry," she finally spoke, "it's just that I suddenly recognized you and was taken by surprise."

"I was afraid of that."

"Brian Cato?" she asked, extending her hand. "I'm Natalie Stover." He stared at her hand, obviously hesitant about making body contact, which Natalie could readily understand. He was probably used to having fans invade his privacy all the time. "Although I'm not as prolific as you, I've published three romances."

"Romances, huh?" His lips twitched for a second time. His hand enveloped hers, the contact setting off a warm tingle throughout her body. She wondered if he felt it too.

"Yes," Natalie replied, waiting for the sarcasm. It wasn't uncommon for people, especially men, to sneer at the romance genre despite the fact that romances were the hottest selling titles. Besides, why would a *New York Times* best-selling author be impressed with her meager success?

"I've read some good ones lately. What are your titles?"

Her eyes grew wide. "You read romances?"

"A few," he said as humor replaced the boredom in his eyes. "Keeps me posted on what appeals to my female readers."

The elevator jolted seconds before the metal doors opened. It wasn't until Natalie turned to exit that she realized he was still holding her hand. She frowned up at him when he gently squeezed it. Swallowed nervously and held her breath when she found him staring at her lips.

He smiled. "Happy writing." He released her and followed her out of the elevator.

Natalie watched him walk away, then found the directional signs to the hotel's front lobby, dining room, and rest rooms. Heading in the direction of the dining room, she realized she was following in Brian Cato's footsteps and hoped he wouldn't think she was stalking him.

Natalie sighed moments later as the hostess seated her in the small booth. Dinner at last she thought. It had been a long day and she was famished.

"If you'd been here thirty minutes ago, we wouldn't have been able to seat you," the woman said. "It's almost closing time and this writer's conference has kept us running all evening."

"I'm not surprised." Natalie chuckled. "Writers love to munch and gab, I'm surprised you got them out of here this early."

The Dark and Stormy Writer's Conference had been a popular mystery writers' retreat for twenty years. Although a romance writer, she wanted to add some suspense to her stories and looked forward to the weekend ahead. To add to the suspense, the keynote speaker was an added mystery. She'd already checked her registration packet. Studied the names of the two hundred attendees to see if anyone famous jumped out at her. Nada.

Natalie glanced over the menu and immediately sensed that someone was watching her. She peeked over the top and her eyes clashed with Brian Cato's dark brown ones. He sat facing her across the room.

She looked around and saw that there was only one other couple in the entire dining room. And they were getting up to leave.

Wonderful, she grumbled to herself. Here she was in this big dining room, alone with Brian Cato. It was more than obvious during their ride in the elevator that he preferred to be alone and if she could, she'd accommodate him—unfortunately, she was hungry too.

She understood his desire for privacy, but if it weren't for her and his millions of other fans, he wouldn't be where he was today. He was just going to have to share the big room with her. Having decided on the chicken pasta, she closed the menu then strummed her fingers beside her water glass, trying without much success to look everywhere but at Brian Cato.

He, on the other hand, looked far from nervous. In fact, he seemed to be enjoying the situation as he openly stared at her.

Alluring, Brian thought as he watched the light of the chandeliers reflect off the auburn highlights in her long dark brown hair. She looked down, around, anywhere but at him. If he had known she was coming to dinner, he might have invited her to join him, despite his recent vow to steer clear of women. He'd certainly had his fill of them lately. Still, his gaze drifted back to Natalie, drawn almost against his will to her narrow oval face, full lips, and high cheekbones. Serene was the description that came to mind as he recalled her relaxed smile and soft conversation with the hostess.

He smiled. She'd said she was a romance author and wondered if they were steamy ones. He recalled her tall slender body and sapphire blue eyes. She might have exuded calmness in her floral print dress, but he had felt a spark when they shook hands.

Funny how long slender fingers could be so mesmerizing, he thought to himself, as he watched her wrap them around the glass of water, carry it to her lips. Suddenly he had visions of those fingers moving across his body.

The sparkling diamond dangling from a narrow chain around her neck drew his attention to the cleavage of small breasts peeking from the V of her top. He remembered admiring the long slender legs and red toenails visible from her open-toed heels. He was surprised he had noticed so much about her in such a short time and remembered it so vividly. He watched her smile at the waiter as he arrived with her salad and was again impressed with her calmness. He wondered what might have happened if she had smiled like that in the elevator. They certainly wouldn't be sitting at two different tables.

The more his eyes feasted on her, the tenser she became. She was doing her best not to look his way. He smiled. Maybe she needed something to relax her and signaled for the waiter.

Moments later, the waiter returned with a bottle of white wine and two glasses. After sampling the wine, Brian signaled for the waiter to fill the other glass and watched her eyes grow round in shock when the waiter stepped towards her table.

"For you, from the gentleman at the other table."

When she accepted the wine glass and looked his way, Brian raised his in a silent toast.

After they were both their meals arrived, Brian stood and sauntered toward her table. He was sure the blush of her cheeks was from nervousness, not the wine.

"It's silly for us to eat alone, don't you think? Maybe we can munch and gab together. Would you like to join me? Or may I join you?"

Natalie stared up at him. "Do you always eavesdrop?"

"Of course. It's rule number three in the writer's handbook. Now, which will it be? Me join you, or you join me?"

"Why don't we toss?" She reached for her purse.

"Here," he pulled out his double headed nickel, "use mine. Heads I move, tails you move." In a matter of minutes, he had shifted everything from his table to hers.

"So," he put his napkin in his lap and reached for his wine, "I couldn't help but notice the welcome signs in the lobby. Are you here for the Dark and Stormy Writers' Conference?"

Natalie smiled. "Yes. I've been looking forward to this conference for months. I enjoy the networking, critiquing, and sharing ideas at conferences. They always inspire me, and I definitely need it now."

"Oh?"

She shrugged a shoulder as she scooped some pasta. "Been having a little writer's block these past few weeks. I'm sure you don't have that problem."

"What makes me any different from you? I've written fifteen books, but I still need to come up with fresh, innovative ideas if I want to continue to be published."

"I enjoy writing my romances, but I want to try something different. A longer more suspenseful story. Even Dixie, my agent, suggested that I add a little mystery to my novels. That's why I decided to come to this conference."

Brian smiled, cocked an eyebrow at her "Ah, romantic suspense. Steamy romantic suspense?"

"Well," she reached for her wine, "I'm not a prude. I add some spice but leave a little to the readers' imaginations."

"Good idea." He raised his glass to her. "These days many of the authors think the more graphic the story, the better." His eyes sparkled as he sipped his wine. "Personally, I enjoy the foreplay."

"I've noticed that. About your books," she quickly added, then dropped her gaze to her plate.

"Have you started it?"

"Excuse me?" Natalie blinked, almost choked on her chicken.

Brian thought her panicked look was priceless. His mouth twitched. "The mystery. Have you started it?" he repeated, his expression innocent.

"Oh!" She expelled a breath. "Yes. Yes. I've pretty much plotted the story but suddenly it just wouldn't flow." She reached for her wine and took a generous swallow. "Then on the drive here my imagination went into overtime and as soon as I settled in my room, I couldn't do anything else but write. I wrote over twenty-five hundred words in little over an hour. If my stomach hadn't reminded me that I needed to eat, I might still be sitting up there."

"Happened to me more than once."

The conversation stalled, and Natalie became nervous. "So, what made you decide to write?"

Brian smiled. "My Dad was an architect, designed houses. When I was a teenager, I did the narrative for the designs and before long, several of the clients said my descriptions made them want the plans.

Then in my junior year, my English teacher, Ms. Painter, offered to critique some mysteries I'd written. She gave me the names of some publishers, but the rejections rolled in.

I continued to write in college and still no takers. My girlfriends were always talking about the latest romance they'd read so I decided to give it a try. Of course, I wrote under a pen name and finally sold one. Then another. After my third romance, I pulled out my mysteries, tweaked them, added some darkness and sold them too.

My only regret is that my father never lived to see my success."

He smiled at the waiter who laid their bills on the table. "I think it's time for us to move on," he suggested as he picked up both tabs.

Natalie lay her hand on top of his. "I think one of those belongs to me."

"I don't mind," he said, registering the static charge that surged through his body. Her voltage had jumped since their encounter in the elevator. On a scale of one to ten, it had to be an eight this time, and all she'd done was touch him. He wondered what it would be by the end of the evening.

"But I do." She cast him a determined stare, while her hand remained on his.

Thirty seconds felt like five minutes and Brian was impressed. In the past, women welcomed his paying for their dinners. He couldn't help but admire her streak of independence. Weighing the fire behind the statement, he shrugged a shoulder. When her other hand reached for her purse, he continued. "There's one stipulation."

She narrowed her eyes. "I'm almost afraid to ask."

"Take a walk with me. It's still fairly early, and I'd like to check out the entertainment."

Natalie hesitated, and Brian could almost read her thoughts. He was sure that deep down she wanted to say 'yes' but things were probably moving a little too fast for her. After all, they'd met only two hours ago. Even with the mellowing effect of the wine, he wouldn't blame her if she said 'no'.

Then she looked him directly in the eyes and smiled. "Okay. For a little while."

"Good." He slipped both tabs with his credit card into the pouch and handed it to the waiter. "You take care of the tip and I'll buy the drinks."

Natalie's mouth fell open in surprise. She started to complain but he was already following the waiter. "Drinks," she exclaimed. "I agreed to take a stroll, maybe listen to the entertainment, but I have more writing to do."

Brian kept walking but signaled for her to follow him.

Several hours later, writing was the furthest thing on Natalie's mind. Having talked writing all during dinner, she and Brian found they shared other interests—music and dancing. It wasn't until the band had played its last song that they realized how late it was. Brian offered to walk her to her room.

They rode the elevator in silence, appreciating the quiet after the loud music. His hand rested at the small of her back as they walked down the long hall toward her room. She nervously wondered what would be an appropriate good-night. Smile and a handshake?

It had been two years since her divorce. A long time since she'd been with a man. And Brian Cato wasn't just any man. He was a celebrity. What would he expect? What did she expect?

She'd danced in the arms of a man she barely knew. From the first slow dance, they'd leaned into one another as if lovers. He'd murmured the words to the songs making her light-headed. Conversations became whispers and shared looks made her tremble.

Her pulse quickened when she stopped outside her door and turned, extended her hand. "Thank you for a fun evening." She smiled up at him. "I thoroughly enjoyed it."

"Me too." He returned her smile, took her hand, and stared deeply into her eyes.

Natalie panicked and looked away. If he could read her thoughts, he'd know she didn't feel as casual about him as she was pretending.

Brian's eyes shifted to her lips and he realized he wasn't ready to say good-night. As much as he distrusted women, he couldn't understand the feelings of desire that overwhelmed him. They had just met. How could she have mesmerized him in such a short time? Then he saw the warmth in her eyes turn to concern and realized she wasn't ready to go any further. He appreciated that she didn't throw herself in his arms as other women had done. He turned her hand over and leaned down to kiss the palm before moving to the inside of her wrist, and then her cheek.

"Very slick," she whispered.

"Thank you," he murmured near her ear. "I'm thinking of using it in my next novel."

He appreciated the dimple in her cheek when she chuckled softly. But when she finally looked up at him he saw the banked desire in her eyes and realized he needed to get away from this woman. Fast. It had been a long time since he had felt desire for a woman.

"Happy writing," he said over his shoulder as he did an about-face and walked toward the elevators.

Natalie nudged the drapes aside and gazed down at the parking lot outside her room. She'd been in a fog since Brian had left. For twenty minutes, she'd done nothing but walk around the room, listening to the hum of the heater and muted conversations in the hall. It was too late to sample the complimentary chocolates.

She sat at the desk and stared at the bright screen of her laptop. The corner of her mouth turned up in a smile. Excitement raced through her as she recalled dancing in his arms, sharing slow sensual smiles. She felt so alive and knew sleep was a long way off. Her hands rested on the keypad. She needed to incorporate these sensual feelings into her story. Breathe some life into Adam and Cecilia's relationship.

The sudden ringing of the telephone startled her. She looked at the digital clock and saw it was almost midnight. Who could be calling her this late?

"Natalie," a familiar deep voice spoke before she could even say hello.

"Brian?"

"I want to see you tomorrow."

"Tomorrow?" she whispered, her pulse accelerating.

"Yes. I thought I could walk away, but I want to see you again."

"Well, I don't know when. I'll be busy at the conference all day tomorrow and then leaving on Sunday," she said softly.

"I'll hook up with you somehow. Just say you'll see me."

"I might not be very good company. I doubt that I'll get much sleep tonight."

He laughed. "You find me that attractive?"

She chuckled. "Actually, it's my hero. He's suddenly making my heroine nervous."

Brian laughed. "I guess I'll just have to try harder tomorrow."

Brian Cato smiled as he lay back on the bed, his hands behind his head. Sneaking away had been worth it. He might have been a little apprehensive about coming, but Natalie Stover had certainly made it worth it. He'd enjoyed talking to her, watching her easy smile and soft eyes glow with excitement. Even the way she said his name just now, stirred something deep inside. He'd known lots of women, but none intrigued him as much as Natalie Stover did. So quickly.

She relaxed him with her quiet ways. She'd simply let him talk, and seemed to understand his frustrations with the constant interruptions and harassment from the media. Like him, she preferred the private side of writing.

But she'd had spirit too. He grinned as he recalled their disagreement over the dinner tab. She was obviously a woman who valued her independence, and he could appreciate that. A little. He still liked to have control, but also understood a woman's need to look out for herself.

She might be shy, but the author in him detected traces of a sensual woman he was sure he'd find underneath. And he fully intended to search. All evening her smooth, lilting voice and classy perfume had enticed him to move closer, listen to every word she said. And the harder she tried to tone down her actions, the sexier she became.

He recalled the swish of the dress against her slim hips when she'd moved ahead of him onto the dance floor, remembered fantasizing how her long legs would feel wrapped around him in bed.

He hadn't tasted her lips. But there was still tomorrow.

It was her shyness that intrigued him the most. She didn't try to push herself on him as, so many women did when they realized who he was. She'd been hesitant about dancing but once he'd cajoled her onto the floor, she started to relax and enjoy herself. He smiled. If he didn't watch it, she could become an obsession.

He wondered where she lived. They had discussed writing, but nothing personal. It was like she went out of her way to respect his privacy by not talking about her own life. He reached for the conference packet and searched for the list of attendees and their addresses.

Fredericksburg, Virginia. He was sure some major Civil War battles had taken place there. And he vaguely remembered visiting a college near there a few years ago. Not that far away from the mountain. He just might have to do a little more research there. Soon.

Two hundred miles away, cool green eyes searched the perimeter of the house. It had been quiet ever since Brian's friend, Max had left late this morning. She kept looking for movement within the house, but there was none.

She snuck toward the back of the house and approached the laundry room window she knew would be loose. Brian and Max didn't know she'd been in the house several times while they had been away.

She dislodged the screen, lifted the tape holding the pane of glass and set it aside. Reaching inside, she unlocked the window and climbed in. Landed on top of the drier, jumped to the floor and slowly made her way into the kitchen. The house was quiet. Too quiet. Her whole body flushed with fury when she opened the door to the garage and saw that both cars were gone. How had she missed him? How had he managed to sneak away?

She stomped through the house, snatching things she knew he had touched. She clutched them tightly as if they could tell her where he was now, but slammed them back into place as they failed to provide any clues.

Climbing the stairs to check his bedroom, she brushed her hand across the unmade bed. That was so unlike him, she thought as she made it up for him.

Her brows snapped together and her jaw clenched when she discovered his suitcase was missing in his closet. She scowled, angry that he had managed to slip away. She prided herself on knowing every little move he made.

She raced down the hall to Max's room, discovered that his suitcase was also missing.

She scowled. How had they both managed to slip past her?

She went into Brian's office and searched the desk. Nothing. No notes, no tickets, no messages. Not even a manuscript.

Then she saw the little slip of paper in the trash can. There were lots of numbers and it appeared to be a room confirmation. For a hotel in Philadelphia.

She smiled. Looked like she would be going on a little trip as well.

CHAPTER 2

SATURDAY MORNING DAWNED BRIGHT AND early for Natalie. She'd programmed the coffeemaker as her wake-up call and knew she would need the caffeine to get her moving since it had been after one in the morning before she'd settled down.

Normally, she would have preferred to sleep a little longer but this morning she made an excited dash across the cold tiles in the bathroom for the shower. Today was going to be a good day. She just knew it. The conference would be packed with information and she would see Brian again.

She wondered when and how he would get in touch with her. He knew she'd be at the conference all day. Would he leave her a message? Call her? Or just show up at the door?

She skipped breakfast, using the extra time to edit what she wrote last night. Her writer's block had disappeared, she thought as she reviewed the scenes, emotions, and conversations that had flowed through her fingers onto the laptop.

Thirty minutes later, she smiled at the computer, then frowned when she noticed the time at the bottom of the screen. She had ten minutes to get to the conference. She grabbed her key card and conference packet and made a mad dash out the door.

You shouldn't have worked so long this morning she scolded herself. The conference doors were already closed, and she'd be lucky if she found a decent seat. She yanked the door open and collided with a hard form that stood on the other side. Almost fainted when that hard form turned around.

"I was just looking for you," Brian whispered.

Natalie was shocked and then breathless. "What, what are you doing here?" she stammered. "I thought you'd be writing or researching."

He smiled and winked. "First things first."

"And now," The conference coordinator's voice echoed from the podium. "The moment you've all been waiting for...our surprise keynote speaker. All his suspense and horror novels have appeared on the *New York Times* Bestseller list. His newest book is being made into a movie for television. Ladies and gentlemen, please welcome Brian Cato."

"Walk with me," Brian said as he cupped her elbow and nudged her toward the podium. "I think I see a seat near the front." Amidst the applause, Brian smiled as he escorted Natalie to the empty chair on the front row and continued up to the podium.

"Good morning." He gave everyone a broad smile.

Natalie stared straight ahead. How could she be so stupid? She should have figured it out last night. Why else would Brian Cato be here but to keynote the writer's conference? After the way he had escorted her in, she was sure her cheeks matched the red turtleneck sweater she had chosen to wear.

When she finally tuned in to Brian's speech, she noted that he was discussing his persistence with writing. How he ignored the mountain of rejections and pushed on until he was successful

"But with success comes more work. Harder work. You're constantly challenged by your editors and readers to create bigger and better stories. Your mind is always wondering, *what if.* Before long, your characters take over and you begin seeing the story through their eyes. Begin to think, feel and react like them." He paused and cast a glance in Natalie's direction. "Such as when your hero meets his heroine for the first time. He doesn't just see a woman. He experiences a sensual awareness of her. His heart pounds. His fingers itch to run through the long brown hair that drapes over her slender shoulders, flows down the back of her bright red sweater. He sees the gold earrings that adorn her small ears. The bright blue eyes that sparkle with merriment. He imagines kissing her soft full lips while his hands caress her slender body. Imagines her long legs wrapped around him."

Brian paused a moment. Watched everyone start squirming in their seats, some fanning themselves, other grinning at one another. Natalie was the only one to stare straight ahead with a shocked look on her face. He was sure she realized that he had just described her and hoped she wasn't too upset. He meant it as a compliment.

Brian grinned. "I realize it might be getting a little warm in here, but the point I'm trying to make is that you don't just sit down and write. You let the imagination go. You experience and see the story through your characters. That makes it more believable to the editor and your readers and keeps the rejection slips out of the mailbox."

Natalie started to relax as he continued to talk. He had a way of making you feel as if you were the only other person in the room. As if he was talking to you one-on-one. Several times he looked her way, once even winking when he made a joke, causing more than a few heads to look her way.

If she could crawl to the side door and disappear Natalie would have done it. She preferred to be a fly on the wall that observed, not the focal point of everyone's creative imaginations.

Despite her initial embarrassment, she joined everyone in the standing ovation at the end of his speech. His message had been vivid and sensual with one obvious goal. To stir everyone to continue their writing. She looked around and smiled at the woman next to her that voraciously clapped.

"Wasn't he great?" the woman asked her. "He's so handsome. I wish I was twenty years younger."

Natalie laughed. She had to agree. Who wouldn't appreciate a good-looking man dressed in a purple and gray plaid shirt, bright purple tie, and dark gray pants? He had such charisma she was sure he could convince anyone they could write a best seller.

They took a break and she watched the women crowd around him, seeking autographs on books, conference programs, even napkins.

After the break, everyone broke into workshops. She attended a promotions panel discussion and didn't see Brian again until later that afternoon when he held an intensive plotting workshop.

The workshop itself was open to all the attendees, but the one-on-one session that followed was open to the top five of twenty registrants to submit ten pages for comments. Hers was one of the finalists. Brian had agreed to critique and discuss each of the anonymous entries.

As he closed his discussion, Brian said, "Now, I'd like to talk with the five finalists privately. Just to offer my thoughts and words of encouragement to improve your writing."

Once again, fans sought his autograph or thanked him for the lecture. Finally, there were six occupants in the room. Five anxious women, Natalie included, and Brian. He called out each title, and spent about fifteen minutes with its author, pointing out the good and ideas for improving the bad.

Then it was just Natalie and Brian in the room.

Brian stood and smiled as he sat on the edge of the table. He had observed her throughout the day and now watched her stand and walk toward him. He wondered if she had studied ballet, her movements were controlled, poised, and graceful. Despite the long, intense day it occurred to him that she calmed him with her soft blue eyes.

"Somehow, I have a feeling you knew that one was mine," Natalie said as she stopped in front of him.

"I suspected last night," he finally spoke, "but wasn't sure."

He reached for her hand, and held it between his. Her voltage once again thrilled him.

"I decided to save the best for last. Would you prefer to discuss it over dinner? Is this the mystery you mentioned last night?"

"Yes."

"Good." He stood, gathered his papers, and stuffed them into his briefcase. With a hand at the small of her back, he silently steered her past the rows of chairs toward the elevators.

Natalie was beside herself. Was he really going to make her wait till dinner?

"Well?" she finally asked as the elevator doors closed. "Is that all you're going to say?"

Brian punched the number for her floor before he grinned down at her. "I like it. Although I have some suggestions, my gut tells me it's a winner."

"Really?" A thrill of excitement jolted her. She felt her cheeks flush as she looked up at him. "You really think so? You think it might be a bestseller?"

"Nothing less." He draped his arm across her shoulder, hugged her tightly. "How much have you done?"

"Five chapters. But the rest is well plotted. Just a matter of finding the time to get it finished." She smiled up at him.

"Good." He gave her another hug. "You have two hours to relax before our dinner date. How about a repeat of last night?"

Natalie froze, her stomach flip-flopped as he leaned down, their faces inches apart, his eyes intent on her mouth.

If only the elevator doors hadn't opened, Natalie thought ten minutes later as she fell back on the bed. When the bell had sounded, and the doors opened, Brian quickly dropped his arm. Fortunately, no one was waiting for the elevator and she'd been spared more embarrassment. Brian had simply walked her to her door and said he would be back at seven thirty.

Natalie stared up at the ceiling. She was waiting to be put through to Dixie Elliott, her agent. Dixie had left a voice message on her cell phone which she had turned off before going to the conference. Now she fidgeted as she waited for Dixie to pick up. Dixie had been her strongest advocate and her dedicated persistence had paid off. They were amid negotiations on another book as well as the mystery she was working on. She couldn't decide whether to be excited or apprehensive.

"What's the verdict?" Natalie asked as soon as she heard Dixie's voice.

"They bought it," Dixie exclaimed. "And they're interested in the mystery as well."

Natalie's laugh bubbled out. "Really? I can't believe it!" First Brian had given her high marks on her submission, and now the editor was interested in the finished product. It seemed her dreams might be coming true after all. "What about royalties?"

"Same as before."

Natalie smiled, remembered why she had hired Dixie in the first place.

Myra is editing the manuscript as we speak but wants to see the mystery A.S.A.P. How's the conference going?" Dixie asked.

"Wonderful. You'll never guess who the keynote speaker was."

"Madalyn Connors." Dixie named the newest, best-selling mystery writer.

"Even better. Brian Cato. And he actually likes my story."

"Fantastic." Dixie knew about Natalie's submission for a critique from the mystery guest. "While you're at it, why not get him to put you in touch with his editor?" she joked. "I heard some scuttlebutt that Myra might be moving on. Need to be prepared."

"Well, he did ask me to dinner later. I'll see what I can do."

When the call ended, Natalie wandered over to the window to stare down at the empty pool and sighed. It had been a long day. A long, exciting day. Full of mixed emotions. Brian had said she'd have two hours to herself, but she knew it wouldn't be to write. Nor to take a nap. She found her bottle of wine in the little fridge, reached for her robe and headed for the bathroom. A nice relaxing soak with the jets was what she needed.

Natalie settled in the tub and rehashed the excitement of her day. First, there had been the surprise of learning that Brian was the keynote speaker, then the embarrassment of his sexy description of her, followed by the pride and excitement as he had praised her manuscript. The man himself was an emotional roller coaster.

His eyes locked with hers whenever they were in the same room. He had a great rapport with everyone that attended the conference but there was something different about the way he looked at her. There was always a twinkle and, a couple times, mischief when he winked or smiled at her.

Her back still tingled where he had touched her on their walk to the elevator. It was almost a caress when he pulled her closer as they drifted past people in the halls. Her heart skipped a beat as she relived their closeness in the elevator and his parting comment that he looked forward to tonight. Last night had been fun. But they hardly knew one another. What would tonight be like?

His description of her during the morning session indicated that he was more than a little aware of her. More than a little interested in her. And his hands on her shoulders and small of her back had been possessive. How would they feel tonight as they danced? When he walked her to the door?

She cast a nervous look at the phone and for a moment seriously debated cancelling the date altogether. He was a little too potent for her. But he held her critique as ransom. She wanted to know what he had to say about her writing. How could she resist meeting him for an evening of dinner, dancing, and pleasant conversation?

The glass of wine and soak in the tub helped relax her. She finished her makeup with a final touch of her mascara, she smiled at her reflection and headed for the closet. She knew which dress she would wear and was glad that she had thought to pack it. Bought on a whim during her last shopping spree, it would be just right for her night of celebration with Brian. Although the flowing black georgette mid-calf skirt had caught her eye, it had been the gold and black floral top with its spaghetti straps that had cinched the sale.

She felt feminine and seductive. Two gold hair clips held her hair away from her face and gold filigree earrings dangled from her ears. She was stepping into her heels when Brian knocked at her door. Adding one more dab of perfume, she gave herself a last look-over before opening the door.

Brian' s bold perusal told her all she needed to know.

He didn't look so bad himself she thought admiring his coal black suit, crisp white shirt and pewter gray tie. Handsome.

"Beautiful," he murmured before reaching for her hand. He turned it so he could kiss the inside of her wrist. Natalie worried that he felt the rapid pulse she knew had spiked. "Did you get a chance to rest?" he asked minutes later as they rode the elevator down to the dining room.

"Not really. I was too excited about my newest sale." When he gave her a quizzical stare, she grinned and continued. "I had a call from my agent and she informed me that they bought my fourth book." She raised her hand and crossed her fingers. "They're also interested in the mystery proposal I sent with it."

"Congratulations." He squeezed her hand and grinned. "Now we have something to celebrate."

Natalie smiled up at him. She knew he was sincere. Only a writer could understand the joy of selling a book, and although he was published many times over, she knew he shared her happiness.

Brian was glad he had reserved a secluded booth. After speaking at the conference, everyone recognized him. Much as he appreciated their admiration, he wanted a private evening with Natalie.

They started with a dry sparkling wine. "Here's to a successful new genre and book."

Natalie smiled. "I still need to finish it."

"I find that having deadlines keeps me focused. I assume you're still working. Will you be able to do that and continue working too?"

"I'll have too. Hopefully this won't be any different from the others. I might have to juggle in more time for research."

"I was going to ask about that. Your topic is interesting. The Prohibition era?"

"Yes, it was a difficult time. Even wine suffered." She smiled as she sipped her wine. "You don't see too much fiction about that time era and I thought I'd work in a little history."

"Smart. I do the same." Brian leaned forward, his finger brushed hers. "Readers want to learn something too."

Natalie's heart skipped at his touch and she tried to keep her thoughts coherent. Away from the intimate touch. "I double-majored in history," she said, clearing her throat, "so I know a little about the times."

Brian smiled. "Planning to work in some bootlegging and gambling?"

"A little. I have a personal reason for writing the book."

"Some skeletons?"

"Well, I have family ties. Not to the bootlegging but law enforcement."

"Really?"

"I have a great uncle who was a Town Sergeant at the time. He was murdered in 1935 and they never found who did it."

As the evening progressed, Brian found himself leaning closer and closer to Natalie while they discussed her manuscript. Although plots and characters always interested him, he was more interested in the woman herself. He would much rather ask her about her job, where she lived, when she wrote. Who she was seeing.

"After Sam and I divorced, I concentrated on my writing. That's how I was able to finish the other two."

He smiled. "So, I don't have any competition at the moment?"

"No. Just my writing."

Brian was fascinated with the way her eyes sparkled like sapphires, and her easy smile expressed her happiness.

The wine relaxed her and Natalie wondered if Brian's leg brushing against hers under the table was intentional. Or was it wishful thinking? *Whatever..* She really didn't care, she was happy. With her writing. With Brian. With life in general.

Although the evening was a repeat of the night before, the mood was different. Their conversation was much quieter and their looks more intimate. Instead of dancing every dance, Brian appeared to be interested only in the slower songs as his caressing hands molded her body to his.

After the last song had been played, and they were leaving the lounge, he pulled her close to his side as they rode the elevator back to her room. She rested her head against his shoulder.

Once again, she was ready with her card key. Once again when she turned to say good-night, he took her hand and turned it over in his. But this time, he lingered longer with each kiss as his tongue brushed first her palm, then the underside of her wrist.

Brian watched her complexion turn rosy and he felt her pulse quiver. He heard her gasp when he brushed the soft skin of her shoulder and neck. Breathed deeply of the perfume that had been intoxicating him all evening. He nipped her right ear and grazed her cheek before his mouth settled on hers.

When she opened her mouth to murmur "We shouldn't -" his tongue slipped between her lips as he molded her to his hard, aroused body.

He lifted his head and stared into her eyes, then her lips. "You've bewitched me."

"Brian," Natalie whispered, raising her lips to his once more. She found that she preferred his kisses to talking.

When some rowdy guests walked by, Brian pressed her against the door. His back shielded her from the stares and hid their identities. "May I come in?" he whispered in her ear.

Natalie stared up at him. Her head was spinning, her breathing labored and her body consumed with desires he had awakened. It had been so long. There had been no one in her life since her divorce from Sam two years ago.

Surely Brian wouldn't take advantage of a woman who was alone. Charm her for his own pleasure. Seduce her because he was bored. He was so much more experienced than she... She was sure he never lacked female companionship and had to wonder why he'd chosen to spend time with her.

She saw the smoldering desire in his eyes that was a twin of her own cravings. Her heart pounded, nerves trembled, and fingers ached to touch him. She held her breath, swallowed and took the leap for passion.

"Yes," she responded without thinking. She fumbled with the room card and stepped inside. Dropped her purse on the dresser and felt an unexpected shiver of excitement. The click of the door behind her shut out the outside world. Secured them within their newly discovered world of passion. Anxious, uncertain, and afraid of what to expect, Natalie glanced in the mirror at his reflection behind her.

Brian remained near the door. He watched her, noted her tense, uptight body. She was nervous, he thought, and smiled to himself when her hand fidgeted with the hair brush on the dresser. Did she consider it a possible weapon?

He hadn't missed her hesitancy, and realized he would have to move very slowly. As much as he wanted her, he needed her desire even more. He stepped behind her and watched her in the mirror. "You're so very beautiful."

Natalie took a deep breath, almost succumbed to the warmth which radiated from him. It would be so easy to lean back against him and give in to the heat of the moment. Still, an ounce of uncertainty lingered in her mind. "We barely know each other," she whispered, her gaze still locked with his.

"Not true, my love... we've known each other forever." His husky voice sent shivers of desire up and down her spine.

Despite her nervousness, she couldn't resist smiling. "Is that from one of your books?"

He didn't return the smile, but a flicker of surprise lit his dark eyes. "No. I think it came from my heart."

That does it. Natalie closed her eyes and relaxed against the solid wall of his chest. He was doing serious damage to her composure.

Brian leaned down and brushed his lips along the side of her neck. His hands moved softly down her bare arms to reach for her hands. He felt her shiver when his teeth nipped her neck.

"It's been a wonderful evening," he murmured in her ear. "Your conversation was stimulating, your dancing provocative." He kissed her cheek. "And your kisses, intoxicating. So, intoxicating," he turned her in his arms, "I don't know that I can stop," he said before his mouth covered hers once more.

Natalie moved her hands across his broad shoulders and deepened the embrace, fueled the sexual tension that had been smoldering throughout the day. Her fingers tingled with a need to touch him. Her mouth became moist, savoring the passion of his kisses. The rising hairs on her arms and nape shivered with pleasure. She craved to be touched.

Passion engulfed them as their bodies, not their creative minds reacted to one another. And not imaginatively, as authors, but in the most basic of ways.

Natalie's knees weakened, and Brian's chest rose and fell with rapid beats as desire consumed them. Flamed a need to be at the very center of the other. To feel everything possible.

"It works both ways," she whispered between kisses. "I've never felt like this."

"I want you, you know that. I need you" He said, his breathing harsh in her ear. His mouth covered hers, urging her lips apart.

Natalie ran her fingers through his hair and succumbed to desire. That word—need – triggered a reaction. She too needed. Needed to feel desirable, beautiful, worthy of attention. Lost on the emotional roller-coaster, she allowed her caution to be swayed by the madness of the moment. Natalie pressed against him, feeling his hardened arousal against her stomach. She trembled with each caress of his hand and moaned when she heard the zipper of her dress, felt cool air at her back followed closely by his warm hands as they brushed the spaghetti straps down her arms.

When her dress fell to their feet, Brian lifted her, carrying her to the bed. He lay beside her, kissing her deeply. The heat of his aroused body warmed her as he quickly unbuttoned his shirt and tossed it aside. She felt his hand caress her breast before his mouth captured the hardened nipple.

Natalie felt as if she'd become one of her heroines. She gasped when his lips returned to hers while his hand moved down her body. She experienced the raging emotions, intense feelings, and erotic sensations she had written and dreamed about. She never imagined that it could be like this.

She squirmed in reaction, enjoying the tug within the very core of her body. Her hands moved over the corded muscles of his back, loving the hard feel of him.

He stared into her eyes while his leg settled between hers. "Something about you called to me the minute you stepped onto that elevator," he murmured softly. He removed the clips from her hair and ran his fingers through it, splaying it across the pillow before his mouth settled on hers once more.

There were still too many clothes between them; too many items to stifle the heat of their desire for one another. They shed their remaining clothes quickly, tossing them across the room.

That was better, Brian thought as he gazed down at her bare breasts, then kissed them while his fingers moved down her body, found her moist and ready. He hummed when he felt her immediate climax.

"Brian," she breathed when he kissed her once more.

He felt her hands caressing him, pulling him closer. His heart swelled, then pounded when she touched him intimately. He usually took pride in his ability to sustain his desire, but never had a woman created such an instantaneous reaction in him.

He rested atop her, his elbows on either side of her head. His eyes moved over her face taking in the swollen lips, glazed eyes, and flushed cheeks while her hands continued to move up and down his back.

Natalie studied his eyes trying to look deeply into his soul. She had never experienced such exquisite pleasure. *How does he really feel about me?* She doubted for the briefest of moments. *Was this a mistake?* a little voice whispered in her heart.

His expression softened. "I know this sounds crazy, Natalie, but I've never felt for another woman what I'm feeling for you."

His gentle reassurance comforted her. Her doubts melted away as she pulled his head down to hers, a hair's breath away from her lips. "I feel it too," she breathed as he thrust forward, his mouth swallowing her gasp of pleasure.

Brian never realized the heaven that awaited him when he'd wondered how her legs would feel wrapped around him. He only knew it would be painful when he had to say good-bye.

CHAPTER 3

BRIAN REACHED FOR HER SEVERAL times during the night and each time they returned to the world that fulfilled their bodies' cravings and bound their souls more tightly.

Near daybreak, their private world was shattered by the shrill ring of the hotel room telephone. His eyes opened wide and he stared at the ceiling, forced his body to relax. He glanced at the phone. Had he dreamed it? He felt Natalie's sleeping form snuggled closely beside him. Exhausted from their lovemaking, she didn't move when the phone rang a second time.

On instinct, Brian reached for it, mumbling a hello as he sat up—and suddenly realized this was not his room, not his bed, not his telephone. He shouldn't have answered it.

His fears were confirmed when there was a moment of silence on the other end before the click of disconnection.

Brian broke into a cold sweat, stared into the shadows of the predawn room. Could it have been a fluke? A mistake? Was it possible that some jerk may have called the wrong number? Or some kid was being annoying?

He turned to watch Natalie sleep, oblivious to what had just occurred. Although he would have preferred to remain in bed and kiss her awake, he knew he had to leave.

Return to his own room. Check out the possibilities. Make some calls of his own.

After dressing in the shadows, he searched for a notepad to scribble a note reaffirming their date for breakfast, and laid it on the pillow beside her head.

His eyes softened as he stared down at the woman who had brought him more passion than he'd ever known. The sheet just covered her bare breasts as she lay on her back, one hand across her flat stomach and the other resting on her hair which was splayed across the pillow. There was a relaxed, contented expression on her face as she smiled in her sleep.

A matching smile curved his lips as he recalled their lovemaking. She had returned every caress, kiss, and gesture, measure for measure.

He leaned down to kiss her cheek and she stirred, making a purring sound. If he hadn't already dressed, he would have stayed and had her purring double time.

She murmured his name before turning on her side to return to her fantasy world.

Brian nuzzled her cheek and turned to leave. If he didn't get out of here, fast, all his good intentions would be a wasted effort.

Natalie awoke at the third ring of the telephone. She'd put in a wake-up call last night before realizing Brian would seduce his way into her bed. She decided she would much rather spend the day in his arms.

She returned the receiver to its cradle and smiled. Stretching her leg in search of Brian's warm one, her eyes flew open when she found a cold bed instead. Turning her head, she saw the note he'd scribbled and reached for it.

"Don't be late—breakfast at eight . . .B.C."

"A poet he's not," she murmured, groggy from lack of sleep.

Much as he'd said he preferred a private breakfast in bed, they both had commitments and responsibilities on this final day of the conference.

Making her way to the shower, she winced at the strained muscles and sensitive places on her body that hadn't seen action like last night in over two years. Deciding on a Jacuzzi bath instead, she arranged the jets to soothe the sore areas and lay back to relive the memories of last night.

How had Brian managed to accomplish in two nights what Sam never did their entire marriage? Instead, Sam offered belittling and sarcastic comments about her lack of sex appeal, made her skittish to start any sort of relationship with another man.

In one night, Brian had torn down the fortifications and made her feel like a desirable woman again. His kind words, stimulating conversation, and gentle hands had created havoc in her mind, caused her to ignore her sensible self and succumb to the frivolous, erotic side of love. From the very beginning, he had given her a special look that made her insides melt.

The moving bathwater ceased as the timer jingled from across the room. She needed to get moving anyway she thought as she quickly dried herself.

Today's dress was casual, so she set the jeans, black sweater, and black ankle boots aside before packing the remainder of her clothes.

She checked out before meeting Brian for breakfast and had just enough time to put everything in her car.

With only a few minutes to spare, Natalie made her way to the dining room.

She followed the hostess to a table, returning the smiles of some of the women she recognized from the conference yesterday. She began to feel a little embarrassed as she wondered what some of them might be thinking having seen her and Brian together last night.

She was no groupie who would sleep with her idol at the drop of the hat. That might have been what happened, she scolded herself, but it certainly wasn't her normal reaction to a man.

"Thank you," she spoke to the hostess, "Someone should be joining me, shortly."

While she waited for Brian, Natalie found herself eavesdropping on the conversations around her. Many of the women were complaining about being awakened in the night by a crank caller.

"Whoever it was, they didn't say anything," she heard one say, "just hung up as soon as I answered."

"Mine sounded like a woman," another said. "When I refused to say anything, this gruff voice demanded, 'Who's this!' as if I were the one making the crank call."

"Well, whoever it was," spoke another, "I gave them an earful."

Natalie leaned a little closer as one of the women asked, "How?"

"Did you whisper obscene words?" another giggled.

"Better than that," she chuckled. "We used to get calls like that all the time, and when my husband was alive, he kept a whistle beside the phone. I guess I've kept up the habit, because I had one with me and gave whoever it was an ear full."

Natalie smiled to herself as she listened to the other women laugh.

Obviously most of the women in the room had the same problem as several from another table commented they wished they had had a whistle. Many had been too scared to go back to sleep for fear that someone might be casing the hotel.

"We could develop this into a brilliant mystery if we all put our heads together," another of the group said jokingly.

Natalie found herself chuckling to herself as each of the tables decided to use the thirty minutes they had before the conference session and started to see which one could come up with the best plot.

Brian stopped in his tracks when he spotted the figure seated near the main check-out counter of the hotel. He raised a hand to hide his face, made an automatic turn into the nearest open door.

He shouldn't be surprised. Not after that phone call in Natalie's room. He had called Max as soon as he'd returned to his own room.

Max Donovan, his secretary, bodyguard, cook, and friend, had confirmed that she'd disappeared and could have followed him.

Sure enough, she was here, sitting in the hotel lobby.

Brian looked around and realized he had wandered into the gift shop. He saw roses of every shade and variety and stepped up to the counter to place an order.

"**A**re you sure you don't want to order something?" The waiter asked for a third time.

"No, thank you." Natalie glanced at her watch. "It's almost time for the conference to start and I really should be heading down there. If you could just bring me my bill for the coffee, I'll be out of your way."

"You wouldn't by any chance be Natalie Stover, would you?" The waiter asked when he returned moments later.

"Why, yes, I am."

The waiter breathed a sigh of relief. "These were delivered fifteen minutes ago, but we weren't sure who Natalie Stover was." He handed her a long, white floral box.

"Oh, my," Natalie said as she removed the lid and stared at the six red roses. She opened the card and saw the note.

"*Thank you for last night. Something unexpected has come up. I'll call you...soon. B.C.*"

Natalie stared at the note. Her heart clenched at the rejection. Nothing Sam had ever said to her hurt more than the sharp dejection that swept through her as she read his words. Was it really a one-night stand after all? Never had she felt so used. So, abandoned. So, hurt.

How could she have been so wrong about Brian? How could she have experienced such passion and not recognize the signs of a philanderer?

"Thank you," she handed the waiter a ten-dollar bill which more than took care of her tab and his tip.

When he started to protest, Natalie shrugged and swept out of the dining room, and continued all the way out of the hotel.

Forget the conference. I have to get out of here! She wanted to get on the road. Back to her normal routine. Back to Fredericksburg.

She tossed the box of roses into the nearest trash can, never saw the dark brown eyes that watched from the black Ferrari nearby.

One week later, Natalie's telephone was ringing when she returned home from work. Normally she loved coming home to her townhouse. It had been her salvation after the divorce. Sam had given up his share in the settlement and she had spent three months redecorating it...removing anything that reminded her of him.

Not too big, not too small. It was just the right size for her. The front door opened into a small alcove that led to the living room. An open kitchen and dining room sprawled across the back of the townhouse. There were two bedrooms and a bath upstairs. She had converted the spare into an office for her writing.

Even the neighborhood was good. Everyone was friendly but not in an overbearing way. Being located ten minutes from the library, her place of work, had been the best perk.

She tossed her pocketbook onto the sofa and debated whether to answer the phone. Several times she had held out, only to regret it afterward when Dixie left scathing messages.

These past few days since the conference had been murder on her nerves. She'd snapped at her co-workers, begged off from her usual tutoring meeting with Heather Brown, and for the first time she hated her job.

Today hadn't been any better. She'd arrived in time to see the delivery man stack eight boxes of books beside her desk. After sorting them and cataloging half of them, her head began pounding. Since she knew she wouldn't accomplish much more, she decided to take advantage of her accumulated sick days and came home to go to bed.

The telephone rang a fourth time and she still refused to answer it.

Her writing had also suffered. The enthusiasm she'd felt at the conference had evaporated and for the first time she had to force herself to write. Whenever Brian hadn't interfered with her thoughts, she struggled to scribble a page, scene, and finally another chapter.

The only way she had managed to get through the grisly murder scene was imagining Brian as the victim. That had seemed to solve the problem because having exorcised him from her thoughts, she was now ready to tackle the next chapter.

"Natalie." Brian's voice came from across the room.

Natalie gasped, turned a complete circle. She wondered if he just might be the ghost of her victim coming back to haunt her.

"I know you're there." His voice came again. "They said you left work an hour ago. That you'd complained of being sick."

Natalie stared at the answering machine. He was on the telephone.

"We need to talk," he continued. "I realize I must have hurt you, but something really did come up. Please call me." He recited his phone number. "I'll be here all evening. And if you don't call, I'll call every hour on the hour until you do. So, either return my call or get ready for a long night."

"Don't be too sure of yourself," she muttered at the machine. She grabbed her purse and headed back out the door. Her headache seemed to have evaporated. She might have planned to do some research tomorrow during her break at work, but tonight was as good a time as any to start.

Four hours later, she returned home, exhausted but pleased with her effort. Her anger at Brian had driven her to research and plan the next three chapters. All she needed was the time to get it on the computer.

She glanced at the answering machine. The number five glowed on the machine. She listened to Brian's messages, each successive one sounding more frustrated.

The phone sounded again and on the fifth ring, Brian's voice kicked in.

"You're obviously a very stubborn woman. I like that, but two can play this game. You're setting yourself up for a major fall though because I fully intend to win. Consider yourself warned."

Natalie heard nothing more from him that night.

Two days later she received a special delivery with the midmorning mail. It was a case of canned chicken soup and a *"Hope you're feeling better"* balloon attached to the box. She hid it under her desk as she tried to ignore the amused smiles of her co-workers who heard about it.

That afternoon, as she cataloged the last of a shipment of books, the Federal Express guy dropped another package on her desk. It was addressed to her and turned out to be Brian's newest best-seller which he had autographed just for her. *"Am confident that one day you too will be a best-selling author. B.C."*

"I've got to show this to Emma," Marie Carson, a fellow cataloger and good friend, said as she grabbed the book and started up the hall. Average height, with jet black hair, creamy skin and bright sky-blue eyes, Marie had been her rock during the divorce from Sam.

Natalie didn't see the book for another hour as everyone in the office had to drool over it.

She was annoyed with the way Brian had turned her peaceful life into a circus. As if dominating her thoughts during her writing hours wasn't enough, he now had to make his presence known on the job too.

What next? How could she stay mad at a man who went to so much trouble and expense to keep reminding her of him?

She half-way expected to find something on her doorstep that evening, but nothing awaited her. Nor did he call, and she began to think he might have been bluffing after all.

The following morning, the meditation tapes arrived.

"*Mood music to write by,*" was the attached note.

The next day, she received a case of computer paper and pens with another note. "*Just so you know, I plan to critique what you've written...soon.*"

The following afternoon, she returned from lunch to find a large flat box atop her desk. There was also a crowd waiting for her to open it.

She lifted the lid and stared at a shiny silver garbage pail lid with a toy sword. "*The battle is coming,*" was scribbled on one of his business cards.

"What battle?" everyone asked at once while they stared at her waiting for the answer.

Natalie sighed as she shooed them away instead.

Thank goodness, it's Friday. She shut the door to her office hoping to prevent any further interruptions. Maybe the weekend would bring her some peace of mind.

The new week brought more irritation in the form of co-workers stopping by her office just to see if she had received another package. Fortunately, nothing else arrived.

At six o'clock on Wednesday evening, the telephone rang.

Natalie debated answering it, wondering if it was Brian. He might have mellowed her, but she still wasn't in the mood to be nice. Curiosity won out as she answered on the third ring.

"Natalie Stover?" she heard a strange, deep voice speak on the receiver.

"Yes."

"This is Frank Goldstein, the editor of *The Fredericksburg Times.* I understand you have just sold your fourth book and I'd like to do an interview for our forthcoming "Community Notes" section."

"Why me?"

"It won't be just you. I'm focusing on local citizens who have achieved success and have already interviewed people in the arts, literature, and music field," he explained.

"But how did you find out that I'm published?" she asked suspiciously.

"I happened to notice your recent book in the bookstore with a "local author" sticker on it. When I asked the manager, she gave me your contact number. Would you be interested in being included in the article or not?" he asked, sounding impatient.

"I'm not sure," she hesitated. Only Marie and a few of her friends knew she was published. She had even had some questioning looks when everyone read Brian's comment with his autograph.

Until she sold her best-seller, she had planned to keep her second career a secret. She wondered if she was ready for her friends, coworkers, and neighbors to read about her success.

And what if they did find out? They could either ignore it or congratulate her. It sure would do Sam some good to learn of her accomplishment. Put him in his place.

She decided to take the chance. "Okay. I guess so. Yes."

"Good. Would it be possible for you to meet me at the Battlefield Park reception area this Saturday? Around one o'clock? We can do the interview and then I can get some pictures."

"Sure. I'll be glad to. Should I wear anything special?"

"No. Anything casual will be fine. I'll see you on Saturday."

Natalie replaced the receiver. She sat back and stared at her laptop on the sofa across the room.

The impact of what she had just agreed to do hit her. After the article, her life would be an open book. She would no longer be an inconspicuous citizen doing as she pleased. She might even become a recognizable celebrity.

And with notoriety would come an obligation to do more as she was sure her friends and colleagues would expect it of her.

And if the article went well, would she still be able to write to her heart's content, sell it, then move on to another project? She reached for her cell phone. Maybe she should give Dixie a call.

The phone on her desk rang before she could locate Dixie among her contacts. When she answered, she was greeted with silence.

"Hello?" Natalie spoke once more.

Still no one spoke.

This is ridiculous, she thought. "Hello," she repeated, "is someone there?"

Again, there was an eerie silence. Natalie was becoming impatient. She knew someone was on the line, she just knew it.

"Brian, is that you?"

There was a click at the other end and the connection was broken.

Frigid emerald eyes squinted at the piece of paper. She now had the woman's telephone numbers at home and at work. She had tapped Brian's line and listened to his attempts to talk to the woman. It would be a matter of time before he called her cell and then she'd have all the numbers.

Her hand fisted then she grabbed the pen and broke it in two. Threw it across the room. It angered her that he was spending so much time courting the tramp and not focusing on his writing. It was up to her to make sure the woman didn't want any more of his calls.

CHAPTER 4

BRIAN ARRIVED IN FRONT OF Natalie's townhouse complex only to see her leaving. Lucky he had come when he did. He decided to follow her and simply join her when she stopped. She mingled with the traffic, taking her time to reach her destination.

When she pulled into the parking lot of the battlefield museum, he continued past, thankful that the tinted windows hid his identity. He hoped she wouldn't recognize his personalized plates.

He parked several rows over from her car and watched her lock her car.

Once again, he was struck by her beauty as she moved gracefully toward the picnic area. Her white turtle-neck sweater reminded him of a winter snowflake as it stood out in the cloudy overcast day. The jeans and black boots made her long legs seem endless.

He watched her walk toward a painted mural of the Fredericksburg Battlefields and speak to a tall, blond man. He would have been jealous had she not just shook the guy's hand in a business-like manner.

They chatted a few minutes, then walked across the parking lot toward the long stone wall that bordered one side of the lot. They settled near a pin-oak tree and talked. Natalie spoke more than the guy.

Must be an interview, Brian decided. The man seemed to ask questions and wrote down her responses.

He remembered his first interview after his first book was published. That woman had asked more questions about his personal life and took hundreds of pictures.

He watched as Natalie's reporter took several pictures of her on the stone wall. One pose impressed him the most and he decided he'd ask Max to get a copy for him.

His fingers itched to run through her long brown hair as it drifted in the wind that suddenly gusted across the area.

Thunder rumbled, mirroring his own mood as he became mesmerized by the smiles she shared with the reporter. And when she removed the dark brown sunglasses, he was parked close enough to see
the soft sincerity which shone as she stared back at the camera.

When the clouds grew darker, the interview was brought to a
rapid close. He watched her shake hands with the reporter again,
pocketing the business card he gave her before making her way back
to her car.

Long after she had pulled away, Brian remained where he was
parked, deciding on his next move. He'd driven all morning and seeing her made him want her more.

Natalie had just changed into her worn jeans and faded sweatshirt
when the doorbell chimed. Not expecting anyone, she checked the
peephole and couldn't believe her eyes when she recognized the man
standing outside her door.

She leaned her forehead against the door, debating what to do.

Just when she had finally worked him out of her system, she
moaned silently. She'd managed to get back into her writing routine
and there he stood, big as life and twice as handsome.

So much for making up for lost time by writing into the evening.
While her heart pounded with excitement, her mind screamed, *Be-
ware!*

What should she do? Did she want to see him? Did she want to
add more pain to her already aching, but mending heart?

She jumped when the doorbell chimed again.

"Natalie, I know you're there."

You can do this, she told herself. She rubbed her damp palms
along the legs of her jeans, squared her shoulders, and opened the
door. The smell of his sexy aftershave reminded her of the last time

they were together, and she briefly considered shutting the door in his face.

They stared at one another in silence.

A roll of thunder shook the building. The storm that had been brewing the last thirty minutes of her interview with Frank Goldstein had finally arrived.

"May I come in?" Brian asked.

The combination of his deep, compelling voice and dark intense eyes nearly undid her. He had uttered those very words the last time they had been together, and she'd gotten more than she bargained for.

If she allowed him inside her townhouse, would it be a repeat performance? Cold anger began to swell inside her, giving her the courage and control she needed.

The thunder rumbled once again and the skies opened.

Silently, Natalie stepped back and let him inside.

A gust of wind had the balloon he had sent her bobbing against the ceiling at the far corner of the living room. The garbage pail lid rested in the box on the end table below the balloon.

Was this the battle he had referred to? Was she ready for a showdown of anger, hurt feelings, and mixed emotions?

She squared her shoulders. Yes, she decided she was ready. She would give him a piece of her mind and then kick him out. Before she could open her mouth, he spoke.

"Have you eaten any of the soup yet?"

She simply glared at him. He stood with his hands stuffed in the pockets of his jeans. The sparkle in his eyes destroyed the meek image he tried for.

She crossed her arms beneath her breasts, her nose spiked up. "Not yet," she finally responded.

Thunder rumbled once more, and Brian looked toward the heavens.

"It's a good day for soup and sandwiches."

"Is that a request?"

Brian shrugged. "I left home early. Didn't have time for lunch."

Natalie impatiently tapped her foot on the floor. The man had some gall. It was all she could do to restrain herself from choking him. Did he think he could just waltz back into her life and calmly ask for lunch?

She groaned when her own stomach growled. The interview with Goldstein had taken longer than she had expected, and she realized she herself had missed lunch.

"What do you want?" Natalie asked as she turned and headed toward the kitchen.

Brian breathed a sigh of relief as he watched her leave the room. *So far, so good.* He could understand her anger, and was thankful she hadn't kicked him out. *Not yet, anyway.*

He followed her into the small kitchen but remained near the door, out of throwing distance in case she had a temper.

"You," he said.

Natalie whipped around, raising the can of soup and aimed it at him. Her eyes were like ice chips. "You've got some nerve, Brian Cato. What's the matter? Have you gone through your list of groupies and looped back to me already?"

He laughed, which seemed to infuriate her even more.

"My list of groupies?" he repeated, genuinely amused. "I'm sorry, Natalie," he held his hands up in surrender, but that's so ludicrous. If you only knew how much of a hermit I am, you'd laugh too."

"Well, I'm not laughing so get on with your explanation." She looked at the clock on the wall above him. "You've got two minutes before I throw you out."

God, she's gorgeous when she's mad. Brian thought with admiration. He stifled his amusement when he saw her fingers flex around the can of soup. "I thought you were letting me stay for lunch?"

"I didn't say that." She glanced at the clock on the wall. "Now you've got a minute and a half."

Brian realized teasing her back into a good humor wasn't going to work. "I'm sorry I stood you up for breakfast, but I got an emergency phone call and had to take care of something important."

He felt a twinge of guilt at the half-truth. It was true. Sara had found him and made the call he'd answered in Natalie's room. And her unexpected appearance in the lobby, he certainly deemed an emergency. All he could think about at the time was getting Natalie as far away from Sara as possible.

Natalie emptied the soup into the pan. When she put the pan on the stove and turned, he saw that her eyes had lost some of the iciness. "More important than our breakfast date?"

He could hear the near-capitulation in her voice and plunged even further into the sea of semi-truth. "It was an illness."

Natalie suddenly felt like an insensitive idiot, concerned only with her own feelings. She took a deep breath and leaned against the counter.

"I didn't stop to think it might be something like that. I... When you didn't show up for breakfast, it just made everything seem like a sordid one-night stand." She paused, her hands gripping the counter behind her. "The roses were lovely," she said softly.

Brian breathed a sigh of relief. It had worked; he would worry later about explaining why he'd kept the full truth from her. He moved swiftly to her side, trailed a thumb down her cheek and tipped her chin up so he could see into those killer eyes.

"Sweet Natalie... I understand why you got upset, and I'm sorry it happened. Will you forgive me?"

"If you'll forgive me."

Brian felt horrible but there was no way in hell he was going to tell her the truth now. He pulled her close, hugged her tightly. He had missed her. "There's nothing to forgive. I was the one that let you down. Can we just forget the whole thing and start over?"

Natalie rested her head on his chest and sighed. "Maybe." She didn't want to give in too quickly.

She felt the strong rapid beat of his heart and the delicious warmth of his body.

Brian embraced her again, lost in his fantasy where he was peeling her snug jeans from her slim hips and lifting the sweatshirt to find those enticing breasts.

"Will he be alright?" she asked.

"Who?" he asked, his voice thickening.

"The person who was ill."

"I don't think there's any hope," he replied in an emotionless tone.

Something about the way he answered struck new doubt in Natalie's mind, but his finger under her chin was lifting her head to look at him. His mouth found hers and she was lost.

Three hours later, they were arguing about her manuscript.

"This can't be right," Brian said.

"What do you mean? It's a love scene."

"Natalie, they're in a closet. That's not possible."

"Yes, it is."

"Have you tried it?"

"No, but I used my figures in a scale model."

"Excuse me?"

"I have some action figures. I use them when I want to try out a particular scene and am not sure about where the hands should go."

"And?"

"And, one day I accidentally fell into my closet when I was cleaning up. At the time, I thought that would be an interesting setting for a love scene. I filed it away in my journal. Then when I found Adam and Cecelia hiding in the closet, I thought this would be a wonderful twist. I stood in the closet to get a feel for what would happen."

"But have you actually done it in a closet?"

"Of course not. Have you?"

"No, and I find it hard to imagine," he chuckled. "Firstly, there isn't enough room, and secondly, Adam really wants to choke Cecelia. Not make love to her."

"Exactly," Natalie agreed. "But the cramped quarters make him more aware of her and rather than choking her, he ends up seducing her."

"I still can't believe it." Brian grabbed her hand and pulled her off the sofa. "Let me see this closet."

"Now Brian," she tried to pull her hand away, "I didn't intend for it to be acted out. The readers will have to use their imagination."

"But suppose someone tries it," he challenged. "Would you want it on your conscience if some lovers actually suffocated trying to act it out? I can see it now," he paused, raised his hand as if depicting a newspaper headline, "Family of asphyxiated lovers sue author. C'mon, let me see this closet."

He stopped in the hall and opened one of the doors. There were too many shelves.

He pulled her up the stairs to her bedroom. Paused outside the door with the full-length mirror. It was a walk-in closet.

"Somehow I don't think it was this one either. Too much room. Which one was it, Natalie?"

"The guest bedroom," she sighed.

"Let's see it. Ah," he chuckled. "We've found it."

There before him was an average size closet with a few small boxes on the shelf and several coats and dresses hanging from the rack.

He lifted the manuscript pages and began reading.

"According to this, Adam is standing here," he said as he stepped inside the closet. "Cecelia has run in after him, and is leaning against him." He placed the manuscript on the shelf above his head.

"Like this?" He reached for Natalie, pulled her into his arms.

"Yes," Natalie muttered against his chest. It was more confining than she'd imagined.

"And because someone had come into the room, they had to close the door." He closed the door. "Very interesting," he whispered in the darkened room.

Natalie tried to push away, but there was little room to spare. "You have to remember that they had been getting on each other's nerves all day. The last thing on Adam's mind is making love."

"But in such close quarters, what else comes to mind? After all, it's dark, I can hear your rapid breathing, and we need to be quiet because someone is lurking on the other side of the door. You also smell wonderful." He whispered in her ear. "I have this irresistible urge to move closer and kiss away your fear."

"But I'm not scared," Natalie chuckled, trying to push away from him.

"But Cecelia was," Brian taunted. "You said so."

"Okay, she's scared," Natalie found herself giggling.

"And being a typical man, as you describe Adam, he never lets an opportunity pass, so he tried to steal a kiss, even though he had heard the intruder leave the room."

"You seem to remember a lot after having read it only one time."

"Love scenes intrigue me," he murmured as he pulled her close. His mouth easily found hers in the dark.

Natalie thought about resisting, but Brian was a too experienced. Too intoxicating. Too seductive. And within the darkened niche of hushed intimacy, she succumbed to the sensual pull of his charm.

"**I** can't believe we did that," Brian said an hour later as they lay in Natalie's bed.

Somehow, he managed to open the closet door and carry her to her bedroom where they enjoyed another tempting session in more comfort.

"Are you sure you didn't try it in the closet before today?"

"Positive," she moaned as she turned and rested her head on his chest.

"You okay?"

"Wonderful," she moaned again, then giggled. "I wonder where all our clothes landed?"

"Have no idea. Do you want to try the closet in here? It's definitely bigger."

Natalie lifted her head and stared down at him. His ego had definitely mended.

Much later, they grilled chicken on her gas stove, and after sharing in a quick clean-up, returned to bed for more critiquing of her manuscript. Brian wore his boxers and Natalie his shirt.

First, Brian focused on her murder scene, remarking that it was very realistic. He debated asking her if she'd been thinking of him when she wrote it.

When he was unable to find any more love scenes to act out, he suggested several possibilities.

When there was no more story to critique, they dressed and relaxed in front of the fire with a glass of wine.

"Do you have any family?" Natalie snuggled closer as they lay on the sofa.

"No. My parents were older when they married. I came along even later. Neither lived long enough to see me succeed as a writer."

"I'm sorry. It's a shame you don't have anyone to share your success and happiness."

"Almost had a wife once," he ran a finger up and down her arm.

Natalie hoped he would elaborate, but he remained silent, taking another sip of the wine instead.

"And I hope to have a son before too long."

Natalie gulped some wine then pulled away. Set the glass on the table and stared at him. "Oh?

"Yes. I'm negotiating with a woman to be my surrogate."

"A surrogate?"

"Um-hum," he pulled her back into his arms, kissed the top of her head.

"I'm surprised. Why not the conventional way?"

"That's the way I want it. No strings. No attachments."

"And what if she doesn't want to give the baby up?"

"She won't have any choice. The agreement will be that she'll sign over all maternal rights before I agree to the insemination."

Natalie pulled away once more, stared at him. Some woman must have really hurt him, she realized. She wished he would tell her what had happened but respected his desire for privacy. It was a shame that he preferred the cold, clinical approach to childbirth as opposed to the more exciting happiness a couple shares as they create and watch their child grow within the mother's womb.

"And what if it's not a boy? Will you be happy with a daughter?"

"It will be a son."

Natalie was stunned. "Does that mean that if you have a daughter, you intend to abort her? Cast her aside? Brian," she exclaimed, "that's so cold."

"Natalie, there's a procedure that selects the sex of the child. It's what I want."

"Still, it seems so impersonal. What kind of life would your child have without a loving mother?"

"Are you saying I won't love my son?"

"No, I'm not. But as a writer, I know you need your time to write and you can't just put a child on the shelf until you have the time to take care of it. A child needs constant love, nurturing, and under-standing. All the things that make them a person. Twenty-four hours a day."

"When I have my son, I intend to cut back on my writing," Brian pulled her close once more. He stared into the fire. Her questions made him face some truths he wasn't sure he wanted to acknowledge right now. Could he raise a son by himself and write too? Would he need a woman after all? A nanny, perhaps.

As much as he would have liked to spend the night with her, Brian decided it would be best if he returned to his hotel. "I'm expecting a call a little later and need to look over my notes first." He reached for his cell phone and called for a taxi.

"Where's your car? I thought you drove."

"I did," Brian answered without thinking. "Ah, I drove to the hotel but then the check engine light came on, so I had a mechanic check it out. They're supposed to have left it at the hotel. I came here in a cab."

"But why didn't you tell me?" she remonstrated. "I don't mind giving you a ride."

"It's late, and I don't want to have to worry about you."

"I'm a big girl, Brian. I think I can manage to drive myself back here safely."

"I'm sure you can," he chuckled, "but this way I won't have to worry."

Several minutes later, they heard the taxi outside.

Natalie followed him to the door. Since it was still raining, she flipped the switch for the porch light to give him some illumination in the rain.

Brian leaned down to give her a quick good-bye kiss, then opened the door and raced down the sidewalk toward the waiting cab.

Natalie watched the taxi drive away then realized she was standing in the dark. She stared at the light switch which was turned off. I know I turned it on, she thought to herself.

Several blocks away, Brian asked the driver to turn into a parking lot. He paid the fare and waited for the cab to leave. When he knew he was alone, he walked to his car and drove to the hotel. If Sara were following him, he didn't want her to know where Natalie lived.

CHAPTER 5

DARLING, I'M SO SORRY I missed you at the Mystery Writers' Conference in Philadelphia. By the time I managed to get a room, you had already checked out. Maybe I had your room? Number 1575? All my love, Sara

Brian re-read the email for the fourth time. Max had found the letter on the porch this morning then scanned and emailed it to him earlier this afternoon

It was one o'clock in the morning and sleep was the furthermost thing on Brian's mind. He checked for any emails from her but found none. He was tempted to delete Max's email but knew he needed it to document how she had once again ignored the judge's restraining order. She was not to come within five hundred feet nor to make any contact with him. This wasn't the first time she'd disobeyed the court document. Despite his precautions, care, and vigilance, she had still tracked him to Philadelphia.

She obviously enjoyed taunting him. Showing him how easily she could locate him. Why did he think he could possibly have fooled her this time? Her saucy reference to the room he had registered using an alias proved how resourceful and persistent she was—and how low she would stoop.

He was sure she had called all the rooms that Saturday evening. Tracked him to Natalie's room.

He paced the floor while his stomach burned. Suddenly the quiet room felt claustrophobic. He wanted to open the doors to the balcony and let the cool breeze inside, but knew he couldn't. If she had managed to follow him to Philadelphia, she could possibly be here in Fredericksburg as well.

She could have been downstairs when he returned to the hotel. Even though he had been cautious about not parking near Natalie's townhouse, he might have been a little sloppy casing the area before parking at the hotel. He should have been more observant.

He dashed across the room and closed the heavy drapes. She knew he was a night-owl and if she were here, watching from outside, his lights could help her pinpoint his room.

He returned to his laptop. No, Brian sighed, he wouldn't delete the email. He'd keep it as a reminder that his life would never be normal again. She was his cancer. A thorn in his side. As long as she was alive he was destined to be a recluse.

He reached for his cell phone and called Max Donovan. "I know it's late, but I'm pissed. Really pissed."

"I was too when I found the broken window this afternoon."

"Where?"

"The laundry room. After I sent the email I took a walk around the perimeter of the house. Bugged me that as cautious as we were about the conference, she still found out."

"I didn't even make arrangements on the land line." Brian said.

They knew that she often tapped his phone. Ever since Max had discovered her footprints in the mud, they had been cautious. A couple times, Max had managed to send her off on wild goose chases.

"Nearest I can figure, she must have come in that Saturday after I left." Max said. "Must have found the receipt."

"Actually, I recklessly threw it away." Brian said. "Should have burned it. And now that I think about it, I remember finding the receipt was on top of my desk when I got home. And of course, we can't prove that she was the one to damage the window or that she came inside."

"No. But I have another idea."

"What?"

"A dog."

Brian was silent. A dog meant responsibility. Feeding. Training.

Max was on a sabbatical from the Secret Service where he had served with the branch that protected the President. A sharpshooter, he and his team travelled ahead of the President and scoped sites of planned visits. After fifteen years of working twenty-four hour shifts and travelling on short notice, he was taking some time off before joining the investigative team.

He and Brian had been roommates in college and when it became apparent that Sara wasn't going to stop harassing Brian, Max offered to move in and act as a buffer to her unwanted attention.

"I got a call from one of my Secret Service buddies. Another buddy got taken down and his canine partner isn't adjusting."

Since the seventies, when the Secret Service created the K-9 Division, they had paired dogs with handlers. The dogs became a part of the handler's family but worked to locate drugs, explosives, and firearm German Shepherds were the first breed used, but lately they had switched to Belgian Malinois.

"Bo's been trying to work with the dog but it's going to take more time than he has. Thinks the dog needs to be retired from active duty."

When Brian remained silent, Max continued. "I can work with him. You won't have to do anything. He could certainly alert us anytime she might be outside the house. Maybe even drive her away."

Brian reconsidered. "Okay. Do it. The sooner the better."

Brian lay on the bed and stared at the ceiling. Despite deciding to get the dog, sleep still eluded him. He couldn't relax. Would a dog really make a difference? Would he ever be rid of Sara?

The sound of a woman's laughter in the room next door reminded him of Natalie. The surprise gift of companionship he had received in Philadelphia. The ray of sunshine in this weekend's storm.

He continued to stare at the ceiling, visualizing Natalie and her soft blue eyes, gentle smile and quiet demeanor. She had given him a glimmer of hope that maybe life could be normal again. That maybe he had found someone who understood his erratic writer's life. That he might possibly have found a woman interested only in him and not his success.

He recalled her excitement at the conference, laughter on the dance floor, and moans of ecstasy as they had come to know each other that weekend in Philadelphia.

Until Sara had shattered the dream with her early morning call. He vividly remembered the anger he had experienced when he saw her sitting in the lobby. It was all he could do to think rationally and send Natalie the flowers instead of meeting her for breakfast.

He closed his eyes, remembered watching Natalie throw the roses in the trash. He didn't blame her. He could well imagine how she must have felt. But he couldn't help it. It was for her own good. He had hated not being able to explain in person, but he didn't want to jeopardize her safety.

He would never forgive himself if anything happened to Natalie because of him.

He hoped his calls, messages, and gifts had softened the blow. He smiled as he remembered the fun he'd had plotting and then ordering the obnoxious gifts.

Even Max had commented that the old spring seemed to have returned to his step.

And this afternoon. In the closet. He had no idea making love could be so stimulating. Spontaneous. Spine-tingling exhilarating.

Damn, he sat up, rested his elbows on his knees. He was now faced with a repeat of Philadelphia. Once again he had to decide whether to risk seeing Natalie or leave. He knew if he pulled another disappearing act, she would never forgive him.

He recalled reading her murder scene and could almost feel every blow. If she could wield her temper like she did her words, it would take him forever to make amends.

He raked his fingers through his hair. Deep down he didn't want to disappear again. He wanted to see her. Talk to her. Make love to her.

On the flip side, he didn't want to jeopardize her career. Or happiness. She had great potential and he knew it was a matter of time before she would be competing for his fans.

She was too trusting. If she was going to succeed in the published world, she needed to be more observant, cautious, suspicious of people and events around her. Once your name was out there, your privacy disappeared.

He pushed off the bed and paced in the dark. He was damned if he'd let Sara ruin his chances for a good life. But where was she? Was she here? If so, what would she do? Would Natalie's life be in danger?

He didn't want Natalie to think he was only interested in her body. Two of the three times they had been together, they'd ended up in bed. He wanted to do things with her, go places.

He stopped in his tracks. Maybe if they met in a public place...

Natalie drove up to the KFC kiosk and ordered a bucket of chicken, macaroni salad, and biscuits.

"Let's make a day of the battlefields," Brian had said when he called an hour ago. "We'll get some chicken and have a picnic lunch somewhere."

She snuggled deeper into her purple cardigan sweater when she pulled up to the window to pay. Yesterday's storm had ushered in a cold front and the March winds were blowing in full force today. He obviously hadn't checked the weather before suggesting a picnic.

And when would Brian catch up with her? He had simply asked the location of the nearest KFC and said he would meet her there. Didn't even give her a chance to offer to pick him up.

How was he going to get here? Another taxi? She wondered what could possibly be wrong with his car. Surely, as successful as he is, he's driving a dependable, even expensive car. But he did say something happened on the way, she reminded herself. She had started to ask where it was being serviced, hoping that it was with a reliable mechanic, but he hung up so quickly, she never got a chance. Come to think of it, she didn't even know where he was staying.

I hope I don't start acting this strangely when I'm successful.

The passenger door swung open and a man climbed in. Before she could scream or jump out of the car, he had grabbed her hand.

"It's me."

It was Brian's voice. When she took a good look at the man beside her, Natalie realized that if it weren't for his cologne, she never would have recognized him. He was dressed in jeans, a dark turtle-neck sweater, and wore a New York Yankees baseball cap pulled low over his sunglasses.

"Brian! You scared me," she covered her pounding heart. "Where did you come from?"

"Over there," he pointed to a beige Prelude parked near the back of the lot. He handed her two twenties. "Your chicken's ready."

In a daze, Natalie handed the money to the cashier.

"Instead of dirtying your car," Brian said, "let's go in the rental." If Sara had followed him, Brian didn't want her knowing what kind of car Natalie drove. "No sense using your gas to give me a tour," he said after he settled behind the wheel.

"We might have to picnic in the car," Natalie said. "Little windy, don't you think?"

They started at the Fredericksburg Visitor's Center museum where Natalie had done her interview the day before. She ran inside, grabbed some pamphlets and maps of the battlefield routes.

"You know, you Yankees might have won the war, but they took a beating here in eighteen sixty-two. General Burnside had the advantage, but Robert E. Lee and the Confederate Army stood tall behind the sunken wall."

Brian stopped at the pedestrian crossing next to the National Cemetery and she pointed up to the multi-leveled hillside. "Over fifteen thousand Union soldiers are buried up there."

Brian cut his eyes to her. "What makes you think I'm a Yankee?"

"Well your cover bio says you live in Pennsylvania." She glanced at his hat. "And you're wearing a *Yankees* hat."

"I grew up in Colorado. Settled in Pennsylvania after I sold my third book. The Civil War isn't my favorite time-period; I have no partiality for either side."

"Well, today will definitely be a history lesson. Fredericksburg is among the most famous battles of the Civil War. In fact, the Battle of Chancellorsville took place about five miles from here and is considered the greatest victory of Robert E. Lee's military career. He was outnumbered two to one but still managed to push the Union soldiers back across the Rappahannock."

"How do you come to know so much?"

"I carried a double-major in college—Library Science and History. And being from Fredericksburg, the history of the war has been instilled in me."

"You went to college here?"

"Yes. And being local also helped me to get the job." She pointed toward the left at the light. "Let's go across the bridge to Chatham."

They braved the winds and walked the grounds of the eighteenth-century plantation home that overlooked the Rappahannock River. It also offered a splendid view of the city.

"Chatham served as Union headquarters and a hospital during the war." Natalie explained. "It was also ransacked, but restored. Many notable people have lived here—and they all had famous ties. It was built by William Fitzhugh who was a cousin to Thomas Jefferson. He was also a good friend to George Washington and served with him in the Continental Army. Fitzhugh's daughter married Washington's adopted grandson. And their daughter married Robert E. Lee."

"Small world," Brian laughed. "Two famous generals in two different time periods."

"Abe Lincoln, Clara Barton, and George Marshall have also stayed here. Even authors like Walt Whitman and Washington Irving."

"I'll have to come back for another visit and add my name to the roster."

"You should see this place during Garden Week." Although the gardens were presently bare, she explained that in a little over a month it would became a quilt of color, scents, and flowers. "For my tenth birthday, my father called in a favor and five of us had a tea party here." She pointed to the far side of the lawn. "We sat over there at a little table in our long dresses and felt like princesses."

"Your birthday is in the Spring?"

Natalie nodded. "May. May tenth." She smiled, then shivered.

Brian put his arm around her shoulder and steered her toward the parking lot. "Maybe we need to be heading back to the car."

They followed the path of the war until early afternoon.

Remaining in the car, they stopped to read the markers or view the panels depicting battles that had been fought on that very site over a century ago.

Brian hinted at the atrocities of parts of the Southern way of life to which Natalie heatedly reminded him that it was the Yankees who ravaged the land far more than the Confederates. When she proceeded to enlighten him on other Yankee misconceptions, he laughed, raised his hands in defeat.

They had worked their way back to the city and Natalie couldn't resist commenting "would you mind telling me why we're going around in circles?"

"We're not going around in circles."

"If we aren't, then that jogger has been running all over town. He ought to be pretty winded by now," she pointed out dryly.

"Just checking to see if you know where you're going."

"I live here, remember?"

They turned onto Lee Drive and Brian noticed a picnic area sign. They'd been going in circles because he'd had an uneasy feeling that they were being followed.

"Maybe we should take a break. That chicken's been tempting me." He followed the arrow toward the picnic area but continued past the parking area and tables, and backed into a spot under some trees that faced the main road. This let him observe each car that came into or drove past the picnic area.

"We can eat in the car. Much warmer."

Natalie laughed. "Definitely." She reached for the thermos of coffee and cups. "It's a good thing I brought this along. March is so unpredictable around here. Sometimes it can be like spring, but occasionally we're covered by a foot of snow."

Brian leaned over to kiss her. "Good cuddling weather," he murmured.

"Considering all of the sites we've seen, have you come up with any spine-tingling plots?" At his blank look, she continued. "Did you come to Fredericksburg to do some research or just to see me?"

"Maybe a little of both. Always looking for new plots though."

"I noticed you watching the mirrors a lot." She opened the bucket of chicken. "I can understand being a conscientious driver," she joked, "but down here in the South, we move at a slower, safer pace."

Brian raised an eyebrow, gave her a crooked smile. "It never hurts to be cautious. You on the other hand need to be a little more careful." He reached for a piece of chicken and saw her frown. "Your door? At the drive-thru? Shouldn't they have been locked? I could have been a crazed maniac, for all you knew."

"I can't help it if my doors unlock automatically when I pull to a stop. Besides, you weren't," she smiled, handing him his fork and the container of macaroni and cheese. She wished she'd remembered to bring some plates. They'd simply share the food from the container.

"Maybe not this time but next time might be different," Brian remarked brusquely.

Natalie had been joking but saw that he was very serious. In fact, he didn't return her smile, glared instead.

"And what about Philadelphia?" He continued. "When you stepped onto that elevator? It might not have been me."

"True, but I certainly don't have any control over who uses such public places."

"You shouldn't have been alone," he grumbled. "Not at that hour."

"It wasn't that late, Brian. Besides," she sat back to nibble her chicken, "if I hadn't been alone, would you have had dinner with me?"

"Probably not," he sighed. In this world of crazy idiots, Brian hated to think that someone would harm her. "Natalie, I don't mean to scare you. I'm just asking that you take care. You're too trusting, and I'd hate for something to happen to you."

"Where is all this coming from? Why the sudden mood change? I thought we were having fun."

"I've been thinking about that newspaper article."

"What about it?"

"You yourself said you weren't too enthused about doing it."

"Not at first," she agreed as she reached for more macaroni and cheese. "But he was very professional. There were no personal questions. He was more interested in how I got started and what I've done since becoming published."

"But he took your picture. You'll be recognized."

"Brian, my picture is on the back cover of my books. Besides, maybe I'd like a little recognition. Let everyone know about my writing achievements."

"Once you become a celebrity, your life isn't your own anymore."

"Maybe, but the way this town is, next week someone else's face will be getting all of the attention."

"I hope so." He watched a gray car drive past the entrance for the third time. "Just promise me you'll be more careful."

The gray car turned around and headed toward the picnic area. Moved slowly past some vacant slots in the line of parked cars and continued around the circle. Toward them. His heart pounded, and his stomach burned. Would it keep going or stop beside their car?

He'd have to act fast if it was Sara.

Natalie leaned toward him to toss her fork into the trash bag on the back seat. The next thing she knew, Brian was leaning forward, pressing her against the seat, and kissing her. She was so startled she couldn't decide whether to push him away or pull him closer.

He tasted of chicken and when her mouth opened to comment on his spontaneous show of affection Brian took advantage and carried the kiss to another level. Unable to resist, she returned his embrace, wrapping her arms around his neck to pull him closer.

Fleeting thoughts of her eight-year marriage to Sam invaded her senses. There had never been these whimsical moments of intimacy. In fact, Sam rarely showed affection and she had often wondered why he even married her. Although it had hurt at first, she'd learned to accept it.

Brian was so different. She enjoyed being in his arms, running her hands across his strong muscles, smelling his clean scent, tasting the mixture of coffee and chicken. She murmured and snuggled closer, encouraging him to continue.

She heard the engine of a passing car and remembered they were in a parking lot. Although the brim of his baseball cap prevented anyone recognizing them, Natalie was still conscious of the fact that they were in a public place.

Natalie stroked the back of his neck, and he relaxed. He lifted his head, his mouth inches from hers. They stared at one another. She looked warm and content while he tried to hide a sudden feeling of desperation.

God, he didn't want anything to happen to this woman.

Ice cold jade eyes watched from the gray car parked across the lot. She and Brian had been playing cat and mouse since leaving the KFC.

She knew he was looking for her yellow Volkswagen. Like him, she had switched vehicles and wondered what he would think if he were to go back now and find her Volkswagen parked two cars away from his classy Ferrari.

And who was this woman that was leading him astray? First in Philadelphia and again this weekend. He should be writing. The woman was derailing him from his fast-approaching deadline.

Small hands gripped the steering wheel as she watched them kiss. It hurt to see him betray her, but she would remain strong. She wouldn't let it disturb her. They would work it out. They had to. So much was at stake.

He would be hers once again. He would come back. He always did.

There had been others. This one was too pretty. Too meek. She knew he preferred strong women. Like herself. Women who would stand up for themselves.

She watched them leave and quickly ducked in case he glanced her way. He might not recognize the car, but he would definitely know her if he saw her.

She heard the car move past and peeked over the dash, watched him turn right.

She smiled as she followed them. He would soon be hers once more.

CHAPTER 6

"I'M WHAT?" NATALIE EXCLAIMED IN shock.

"You're pregnant."

Natalie gaped at the doctor. "Dr. Smith, I came in here for my routine check-up. I can't be pregnant. I haven't," she stopped when she thought about Brian. "Oh no. I mean, that's impossible. I'm not really seeing anyone. And all those years I was married to Sam, I never got pregnant. I just thought—It just can't be—"

Yes, it could. She and Brian had used no protection. How could she have been so careless? She stared at the ceiling. "Are you sure? Really, really sure?" she groaned.

"It's early, but all of the signs are there. Bloodwork verifies it. Didn't you just say that you'd been feeling sluggish?"

"Yes, but I thought it might be the flu. Several of the women at work have been out sick."

"Well, yours is the nine-month strain." He smiled as he took her hand, helped her to sit up. "But you're strong, healthy and I don't foresee any problems. Next time you come in, we'll do more bloodwork and should be able to pinpoint a more specific delivery date. Right now, I'd say early December, but it's a little too soon to tell."

Natalie decided not to mention that she could probably name the date she'd conceived. A certain Saturday night in March, in Philadelphia. At a writer's conference. With the keynote speaker. She was sure of it. She should have known better.

"Natalie?"

What would Brian say?

"Natalie?"

How would he react?

"Natalie, are you okay? You're not going into shock, are you?"

Natalie focused on Dr. Smith and tried to smile. "Probably. I'm just surprised, that's all."

"I realize you and Sam are divorced. Hope it won't cause any problems for you."

Oh, major problems, she thought to herself. She'd be one of those single mothers she sometimes complained about. How could she have been so stupid?

"No," she spoke out loud. "I just figured there'd be no children. Guess I was wrong."

"What about the father?"

What about Brian? What would he say? She recalled his discussion about having a son. It appeared he wouldn't be needing a surrogate mother after all. *Or would he?*

"Natalie?"

He'd said he wanted a son, but no mother.

"Natalie?"

Suppose he tried to take the baby away?

"Natalie," Dr. Smith gripped her hand. "Are you sure you're okay? I'm going to give you this sample sedative."

"But, I thought you weren't supposed to take medicines when you're pregnant. No wine. No smoking. Not that I smoke. I do enjoy wine though."

"It's okay. This is a mild one. You may have some trouble sleeping and I want you to take it only if you become restless or can't relax. Some new mothers react this way at first."

"I'm sure I'll be okay. It's just been a shock, that's all."

"Just in case." He handed her the sample box with the prescription. "I've also noted some suggestions for vitamin and calcium supplements. It's important that you take care of yourself. For the baby's sake."

"I understand."

"Now," he headed toward the door, "if you have any questions, be sure and write them down and we'll discuss them at your next visit.

By the way," he paused before opening the door, "I saw the article about you in the paper. Congratulations on both counts."

After scheduling her next appointment, Natalie headed out of the office. Funny, she thought, the walk to his office hadn't felt this long.

Pregnant. The thought hit her as she stepped into the sunshine. How could she have allowed such a thing to happen? She'd been so focused on writing and getting her next book published. How was she going to fit a baby in her busy schedule?

There'd been no baby with Sam, so she'd assumed she wasn't destined to be a mother, resigning herself to a life with no children.

She paused at the curb to let a car pass, then crossed to the entrance of the parking deck. Natalie smiled at the young couple that pushed a stroller from the opposite side of the street. Couldn't resist peeking into the stroller and seeing the sleeping infant.

A baby. What would Brian say?

What would everyone say? Dixie. Her editor. Her friends. Her co-workers.

After the fiasco with Brian's gifts, many on the staff hinted at meeting her famous admirer. What would they say when she told them she was pregnant with his child?

If she told them. She certainly wouldn't tell them right away. The college wouldn't necessarily frown on pregnancy, but she was almost embarrassed that she had let it happen.

No, she'd keep this little secret to herself for a while. She was still coping with everyone's reactions to the newspaper article. Most had been congratulatory, but a couple of them were angry that she hadn't told them about her pastime.

She jingled her keys as she headed toward the car, then frowned. Something didn't look right. She walked around to the other side and groaned when she saw the flat tire.

Today just wasn't her day.

Wasn't it only two weeks ago that she'd had them rotated? She kicked the offending tire, then opened the trunk for the jack and small donut spare. It was brand new, she fumed. Now she'd have to have it replace. And have them check the other three tires, she reminded herself.

She was grateful that she hadn't been driving when it had gone flat. It was a whole lot easier changing it in the parking lot than on the side of the interstate.

Later that evening Natalie collapsed on the sofa and stared at the gas logs in the fireplace. She'd been chilled all day and hoped she wasn't coming down the flu on top of everything.

Her hand rested on her stomach. Pregnant. Her life would never be the same.

She'd have to switch the guest bedroom from office to nursery and hoped her townhouse would be big enough for the next few years.

Then get busy and finish her book because there was a lot that needed to be done. Buying furniture, clothes, and other essential baby items. Even maternity clothes for herself. Painting.

And what about after the baby was born? Would she be able to quit her job at the college and stay home with the baby? She enjoyed her job, but a baby would most definitely change things.

Maybe she could write full time and be a stay-at-home mom. She'd need another book under her belt. A successful one at that.

She recalled Brian's mentioning that he planned to cut back on his writing when his son was born.

She would have to hustle. She certainly didn't have the bank account to support herself and a child like he did.

She went to her desk in search of her datebook. Where was it? She kept it in this middle drawer, but when she opened the drawer to the right, there it was. *How did it get there?*

Natalie opened it to December. Dr. Smith had said December and nine months from that night at the March conference was December tenth. That date was already circled because it was the release date for her fourth book.

Wow. In addition to working overtime to finish her current project and get ready for the baby, she'd have to start planning the promotions for her new book as well.

Dixie had suggested updating her press package with new pictures. She'd have to do it soon before she gained too much weight.

She glanced at the calendar once more. Christmas. Her baby would be a Christmas baby. She smiled as she remembered her Christmases as a child and sighed when she realized her parents would never see their grandchild.

In fact, her baby would have no family but herself. An only child, her parents had been killed last year in a head-on collision with a teen who had been texting and driving. Maybe the settlement would be finished by the time her baby was born. She would much rather have her parents, though.

She looked for their picture on the mantle and saw that it had fallen over.

The shrill ring of the telephone startled her and she hesitated answering it. There had been several hang-ups the past few days.

It could also be the garage. Al had said he would call when he found out what caused her tire to go flat.

She looked at the caller ID. "Number unavailable" The hang-ups had also been unavailable. Could it be Brian? He had called her several times on her cell phone since his weekend visit two weeks ago.

She decided to pick it up on the fourth ring.

"Written any good love scenes lately?" A familiar male voice asked. "I still have fantasies of our session in your closet."

"No," she chuckled. "They are back to fighting. Actually, I haven't been able to focus these past few days. Really need to get the muse going again."

"Feeling under the weather?"

Natalie's mouth dropped open. Did he know she'd been to the doctor? Did he sense something was wrong?

"No! No, I'm fine," she murmured a little too stiffly.

"You sound preoccupied. Are you sure you're okay?"

She wanted to scream, "I'm pregnant with your baby," but knew she couldn't.

"I'm fine," she answered instead. "You on the other hand sound pretty chipper."

Brian laughed. "I guess I am. Just had a call from my lawyer."

"Oh?"

"He's arranged a meeting with the surrogate mother I was telling you about. It's scheduled for next week and if all goes well, she'll have the procedure that evening."

"Wow," Natalie exclaimed. "So quick." She thought about her own baby. Should she tell him not to bother? Sure, they were seeing one another but what guarantee did she have that their relationship would continue? Last? And would he be willing to share custody of their child? "Are you sure this is what you want?"

"I want a son."

"Yes, but—"

"No buts. I'm almost thirty-eight. If I don't do it now, I'll be too old to enjoy him. When he's twenty, I'll be pushing sixty."

"You keep saying him. Brian, what if it's a girl?"

"It won't be. The doctor explained how it's done and how I can choose the sex."

"Wow. For your sake, I hope you're right."

She rubbed her own stomach. He never mentioned love in all this. The way he'd talked about his plans with the surrogate...no emotion. Just determination to have a son the easiest way possible. What about love?

Once again, Natalie debated what to do. If she mentioned that she could be carrying the son he so desperately wanted, would his feelings change? Or would he negotiate with her? Offer her money for the child she carried?

And what about her? Would he allow her to see the child? Care for the child? Love the child?

No. She couldn't tell him and risk losing the baby. If he wanted a son through some sort of business arrangement, let him do so. She would have her baby and keep it.

I'll have to stop seeing him, she realized. End a relationship that had seemed so promising.

Besides enjoying each other in bed, they also shared a passion for writing. Critiquing each other's works, tossing around plot ideas, even mapping out scenes.

"Did you get my letter?" Brian interrupted her thoughts.

"Letter?"

Her visit with Dr. Smith had discombobulated the rest of her afternoon; she'd forgotten to check the mail.

After dropping the tire off and having her spare replaced, she had rushed back to work, but accomplished very little. And as soon as she arrived home, she'd collapsed upon the bed and taken a short nap.

"I sent you some tickets."

"Tickets?"

"To the Virginia Museum in Richmond. I'm doing a reading there. Next weekend."

"Next weekend?" She flipped her calendar back to this month.

"Yes. It's a special Museum benefit with limited seating. Since I am the program, I sent you my tickets."

"Yours?"

"Yes. Does your phone have an echo? You seem to be repeating everything I say."

Just like she zoned out at Dr. Smith's office, she thought. She jumped up and walked across the room. She certainly couldn't have him becoming suspicious. "I'm fine," she answered crisply. "When is this event?"

"Next Saturday. Like I said, I've sent you my tickets, so you can get in. I'll explain that you're my guest and they'll be expecting you."

Should she go? She felt her flat stomach. It was early in her pregnancy and she certainly didn't show but she would be nervous all the same. Would he guess?

"This may be the last time I'll be able to see you for a few months."

His words were unexpected. "Oh?"

"Yeah, my publisher is sending me on a tour. After the Virginia Museum function in Richmond, I leave for D.C., then New York, Chicago, and across the rest of the country."

"Wow."

"They're putting a lot into promoting my latest and if I can't see you next weekend, I don't know when I'll see you again. So...can you make it?"

Natalie debated with herself for a minute. Unless she spilled the beans, there could be no possible way he would guess she was pregnant. And maybe after three months or so, the spark will have evaporated to a point that they were simply friends.

"Natalie?"

"Okay," she decided. "Where and what time?"

"Everything is in the letter. Just be sure and bring the letter with you. They won't let you inside without it. And if you don't receive the letter, call me on my cell." He repeated his cell number before ending the conversation.

Brian leaned back in his chair, and stared at the mountainside. He frowned as he glanced at his watch. Little dark for six o'clock, he thought. Must be some storm clouds moving in.

A smile replaced the frown as he replayed his conversation with Natalie in his head, glad she'd said she would see him this weekend. She'd seemed a little preoccupied though. Surely she'd tell him if there was anything wrong.

He reached for his schedule and checked to see if he could squeeze a day out of the weekend for her. *Too much to do.* The proposal for his next book was due on Monday. Wednesday was his meeting with the lawyer and the surrogate and then the reading at the museum on Saturday. And since he was leaving Sunday for the tour, he needed to organize and pack more than usual.

Brian heard a knock and looked up to see Max standing at the door.

Max held up an envelope. "Another one arrived this afternoon. Seems she has changed perfumes."

"I wish she'd change victims."

Max chuckled. "Would certainly make life easier. Since you were here, I thought I'd let you open it."

Brian sniffed the letter and his heart stopped It was Natalie's perfume. Was that a coincidence? How could Sara know?

He reached for the letter opener and thunder rumbled outside as the blade slipped across the top of the envelope.

Darling, It has been nice seeing the lights on at the chalet once again. I'm sure you are preparing for your deadline and the tour. I've had some plot ideas, but every time I call, it seems the phone is busy. It's so frustrating when I want to share my ideas. And speaking of calls, do you by any chance know who has this number, 555-373-1455. It's always busy too! Love, Sara

Brian stared at the number on the paper. His stomach muscles tensed. He felt the heat flush his face and his ears roared as he fought dizziness as he recognized the dark undertones of her message. Crumbling the letter, he threw it across the room.

"That bad, huh?" Max asked.

"Read it for yourself."

Brian paced to the window and stared at the blackening skies. He wondered if they were really rain clouds or the clouds of doom that seemed to hover over him these past two years. What would it take to get her out of his life? Or would he never be rid of her?

How could she possibly think that he would even consider any of her ideas? How did she manage to trace Natalie's telephone number?

His hands fisted. The thought of Natalie being in danger made him sick. He turned back to Max who was shaking his head.

"When was that note delivered?" Brian demanded.

Max shrugged his shoulder. "Sometime this afternoon. I actually found it on the front step when I returned from town."

"She knows Natalie's telephone number." He turned back to stare into the night. "And her perfume."

The thesaurus he had used earlier had fallen off his desk. He kicked it across the floor. "How does she find out all this stuff? I've been so careful where Natalie is concerned."

"Hell if I know." Max answered. "Either she's got the phone tapped again or she followed you to Fredericksburg."

Brian wanted to choke her. No matter what he did, how cautious he was, she always managed to find out his deepest, darkest secret. "How long before the dog gets here?"

"Another week or so. When I saw Sara's latest stunt, I decided to give Bo a call. Said the paperwork's done; just a matter of processing everything."

Twenty feet below, sage colored eyes stared up at Brian and smiled. He looked so wonderful. Tired, but wonderful.

He'd probably gotten her note by now. It wasn't on the front stoop when she checked. She was sure he'd want to talk about her ideas. It was a shame the promotional tour was coming up, but she planned to be by his side. She was good for him. He needed her encouragement.

She shivered, leaned closer to the tree, trying to shield herself from the rain. It was getting colder and she was exhausted. It had been a long day. She should be leaving, but was still drawn to the warm golden glow of his office light. Seeing him there was so wonderful. She saw his frown and wanted desperately to comfort him. She could be strong for him.

At least that woman wasn't there. He hadn't seen her for two weeks which was a good sign. Maybe he was tiring of the woman already and was ready to return to her once again.

She smiled her Mona Lisa smile. She could get into the house anytime she wanted. Despite his ever-changing security codes, she always managed to get past the security system. They had repaired the window in the utility room, but she would find another way.

There had been no security system at the woman's townhouse and it was a piece of cake getting inside. She'd taken her time walking around, touching her things. Moving her things. She wondered if the woman had missed her perfume yet. Or if Brian had recognized the woman's perfume on her latest letter.

She was sure Brian would be calling her soon. She couldn't understand what was taking so long.

Three hundred miles away, Natalie jumped when her telephone rang a second time that evening.

"Ms. Stover, this is Al."

"Yes, Al, how are you?"

"I'm fine, but it's you I'm worried about."

"What do you mean?"

"Have you parked in that parking deck before?"

"Only when I have an appointment."

"Do you know whether they've had problems with any of the other cars there?"

"Not really, why?"

"Do you by any chance have any enemies?"

"Enemies? Al, you're scaring me. Why all the questions?"

"Your tire wasn't defective. Someone punctured it."

CHAPTER 7

BRIAN WATCHED NATALIE MAKE HER way across the marble floors of the museum lobby. Seeing her in the flesh, he realized how much he had missed her these last few weeks.

He'd seen her when she arrived but was hesitant to make his presence immediately known. He wanted to observe her; appreciate her beauty softened by the dimmed lighting of the exhibits.

The egg-shell blouse accentuated her small shoulders. It was draped over the mid-length black skirt that spiked just above her knee in front and dipped to mid-calf on each side. She looked classy. Sophisticated. Beautiful.

She'd combed her hair into a severe bun at the base of her long neck. Pearl earrings adorned the ear lobes he'd nibbled several weeks ago, the low V neck of the blouse hinted at temptation but revealed nothing.

He'd watched more than one male head turn in her direction.

She seemed nervous, frequently looking over her shoulder. Was she anxious? Uncomfortable being alone? Or was she searching for him?

Brian stepped out of the shadows and made his way to where she strolled nervously from exhibit to exhibit. She stopped to admire a sculpture on display in the middle of the room, then gravitated toward the gem collection off to one corner. He knew she was interested in gems and crystals. He'd noticed the stones scattered about her townhouse. She'd claimed they gave her energy and inspiration for her writing.

He reached into his pocket to rub the stone he'd picked up for her yesterday. It would be his parting gift.

Natalie stared at the beautiful gems, reminding herself of the different powers each held. Her favorite was the amethyst, not only for its rich purple color, but because she knew it was known to lift your spirits and help in the meditation process. She had several at home.

She gazed at the sapphire and diamond ring on her finger. A family heirloom given to her by her mother, she'd only recently learned that sapphire was the gem of destiny and diamonds were known to help you achieve wealth and prestige. She smiled. No wonder it was her favorite piece of jewelry.

A man's long fingers slid a delicate pale blue and white stone across the top of the glass display next to her hand. It sparkled, beckoning her to pick it up.

"For you," Brian spoke into her ear.

Natalie's spine tingled at the sound of his voice as she felt the warmth of his body behind her and breathed in the scent of his cologne. Realized how much she had missed him.

She turned her head, smiled up at him. She couldn't help but appreciate the way he handsomely filled out the black tuxedo and crisp white shirt.

"I found it yesterday in a shop near home."

"It's very beautiful." She lifted the stone.

"For a beautiful lady," he murmured, leaned forward to kiss her cheek. "Do you know what it is?"

"Moonstone?"

He nodded. "Sometimes called the humanitarian stone. They say it can also help you find love."

Natalie blushed. "I believe it's also called the traveler's stone. It is supposed to give you luck when travelling over water under a full moon." She laughed. Did you get one for you to take on your tour?"

"Actually, I got myself a pearl."

"A pearl?" Natalie looked up at him, surprised at his selection.

He smiled, brushed a fingertip along her cheek. "To remind me of you. Feminine, loving, bashful, supportive, and always a lady. Always saying the right thing."

"Brian, you're embarrassing me."

"But it's true." He reached for her hand and tucked it under his elbow, led her toward another exhibit.

More people were arriving and he wanted to make the most of his time with Natalie. From years of experience, he'd learned that by steadily moving about, people tended to leave him alone.

"How did your appointment with the surrogate go the other evening?" Natalie asked. With her own baby uppermost on her mind, she'd been concerned for him as well and had decided that if things went well for him, she wouldn't feel so guilty about keeping her news to herself.

"Not good."

"What happened?"

"I called it off."

Natalie's stomach did a somersault. She was glad in one sense, but worried too. Now that his plans with the surrogate mother had fallen through, what would he do if he found out about her pregnancy? Would he try and take her baby away from her?

"I'm sorry," she managed to say despite her pounding heart.

"I'm not. Max did a background check and didn't like what he found."

Natalie stopped, frowning up at him.

"Last year she signed a contract with a California couple and then skipped town," he explained "They lost thousands of dollars. In fact, if Max hadn't had her investigated, she might still be conning other couples. She thought that by travelling across the country, no one would find out. Right now, she's in a holding cell in Philadelphia."

"I'm so sorry," she repeated.

Brian sighed. "Now you know why I don't need a woman in my life."

"Not all women are like that, Brian."

"Maybe, but that seems to be my luck."

"I guess this means you'll have to put your plans on hold? Or are you already looking for another surrogate?"

"I've decided to wait until my tour is over." His gaze cut down at her and added, "Not unless you'd consider doing it."

Natalie gasped out loud, felt the blood drain from her face as she cast a dumbfounded expression his way. Did he already know? Was he baiting her?

Brian saw the shock on her face. "Natalie," he squeezed her hand, "I'm kidding. That was a sick joke and I shouldn't have said it. I don't know what came over me."

As he apologized, a tall, lanky woman appeared at Brian's side. She smiled at him.

"Mr. Cato, I believe we're ready to start. If you and your guest would like to follow me, we'll begin seating everyone."

She led them up the stairs to the second level toward an elegant reception room with high ceilings and columns. Large circular tables were arranged throughout the space, and Brian and Natalie were seated at one near the front where a podium stood on a small platform.

Brian would do the reading following the dinner.

Seated side by side, they waited for everyone else to find their places. Three other couples shared their table.

Brian reached under the table for Natalie's hand and gave it a slight squeeze. He smiled when she looked at him. "I'm glad to see some color in your cheeks," he whispered. "For a moment there, I thought you were going to pass out on me."

Natalie smiled weakly. She was still reeling from the shock that he might have found out about her baby.

Finally, everyone was seated, and the salads were being served. There was a hum of conversation throughout the room and Natalie did her best to participate, but it was obvious that the other occupants at the table were interested only in Brian and the selection he had planned to read.

"I was re-reading one of your earlier novels last night and just couldn't put it down," an older woman gushed.

Brian smiled.

"Where do you get the ideas for your stories? I can't imagine them coming from personal experiences. Dear me," she fanned herself with her fork, "it's a wonder a woman would be able to stand it if you actually lived like that."

There was a strained hush at the table. It was one thing to compliment an author but to insinuate or hint at a weird lifestyle was gross ignorance. These petty insinuations about his home life were another reason he preferred the private side of writing.

"Fortunately for me," Brian cast a cold glare at the woman, "there are no women in my household. And if there was, she'd have to accept me for what I am."

"Oh," the woman replied, cast a glance in Natalie's direction. "I'm sure–"

The shrill tone of the fire alarm cut through the awkward silence. The blaring ring sent chills up his spine as he tried not to imagine what, or who, might have triggered the alarm. He quickly glanced toward the back of the room and watched Max disappear through the doors to the security office. He and Max had made a thorough walk through of the museum earlier in the afternoon and knew every entry and exit in the place.

People stared at one another in confusion, trying to determine if it was a false alarm. Some people rose from their tables and started to leave while others ignored the noise altogether.

A security guard entered and waved everyone back to their seats. He made his way toward their table, spoke to the woman who had seated them. After a brief conversation, she walked up to the podium.

"I'm sorry for this inconvenience, but everything is really okay. There's no fire, nor are there any burglars. It seems someone tried to come in through an unauthorized entrance and while we try to track down their whereabouts, we hope you'll continue to enjoy the dinner and entertainment."

Brian looked toward the back of the room and saw that Max had returned. Max shook his head insinuating that all was okay and left with the security guard.

Brian was sure he knew what had caused the disturbance.

That burning sensation that only Sara could trigger flared in his stomach. She was here. Waiting. Hiding in some restroom, huddled behind an exhibit, or even seated among the guests.

He looked across the room. There must be over a hundred people here. She could have disguised herself. She had done it before.

Brian debated his next move. Until he was sure of Sara's whereabouts, he needed to remain calm but detached with Natalie. He wanted Sara's attention focused on him, not Natalie.

He glanced in Natalie's direction and saw that she seemed to have accepted the guard's explanation and was eating her salad.

He was beside himself with worry. He knew he needed to do something. Should he leave or stay? How could he protect Natalie? Obviously, he couldn't leave; he had a commitment to speak. But if he stayed and Sara thought he was paying too much attention to Natalie, it would put her in harm's way.

Drawing from past experiences, he withdrew into himself, concentrating on the chapters he had chosen to read. If he was being observed, no one would have the slightest idea that the beautiful woman seated beside him was dearly important to him and drove him to distraction.

Natalie leaned toward Brian. "Glad it's nothing serious," she whispered. She frowned when he turned to speak to the man on his other side without responding. As he continued the conversation,

Natalie realized Brian had gone from hot to cold. It was crazy, but it seemed as if he was ignoring her.

Natalie managed a stiff smile as the waiter took her empty salad plate.

Brian's cold shoulder was like a slap in the face. So much for the moonstone he had given her.

Her heart ached with this sudden change.

It was as if the fire alarms had shattered the mood of the whole evening.

Awaiting the next course of her dinner, Natalie rested her hand on her stomach, visualizing the baby growing inside her. To think that she had felt guilty about keeping the news from him, knowing how much he wanted a baby. Now she was glad she hadn't told him. The man seated beside her now wouldn't hesitate to call in his lawyers.

No, she hugged her stomach once again. She'd made the right decision. Nothing would come between her and her baby.

He hadn't looked at her since the fire alarms went off. Natalie was glad she hadn't told Brian where she was staying; she was beginning to regret having come in the first place. If he continued to shut her out, she might just slip out while he spoke and head back to Fredericksburg.

When everyone was served their desserts and coffee, Brian moved toward the podium. The lights were dimmed, and a spotlight shone down on his dark head. He settled on the stool behind the podium. His reading material was already there and after making a brief introduction, he opened the binder to the first page.

Natalie tried her best to listen, but the rich dinner wasn't sitting too well with her. She wasn't sure whether it was because of her pregnancy or nerves. All she knew was her stomach and her heart hurt.

Seeing Brian at the podium brought back memories of his speeches in Philadelphia where he had flirted openly with her, even winked at her on more than one occasion.

Tonight, an entirely different man was performing. He didn't have the warm sparkle in his eyes or the ready smile. Instead, he appeared very serious, almost stern. And he looked everywhere but at her.

She might as well not even be here for all the attention he was giving her. Suddenly she realized her meal wasn't going to settle at all.

She rose and moved slowly but purposefully along the wall toward the back of the room.

Several men stood in the back, but she ignored them. Anxious to get away, she hurried past them, not even looking up when one held the door for her and followed her into the hallway.

"Are you okay?" he asked.

"Yes," she whispered, hurried toward the restrooms at the end of the hall. She barely made it through the door before her stomach began retching.

Ten minutes later, Natalie rested her head against the cushioned back of the love seat in the restroom lounge. She dabbed her face with a damp paper towel and closed her eyes to rest a minute. *I've got to get out of here.*

She heard the door open and sensed someone walk past her. Totally exhausted, she didn't bother to even open her eyes to see who had entered.

All she wanted to do was revive herself enough so that she could walk out of this bathroom. Out of the museum. Out of Brian's life.

Brian tried his best to concentrate on reading the words in front of him. He was worried. He'd watched Natalie leave the room and couldn't blame her. He understood her wanting to get away from him, but he was trying to protect her. He wished he could have slipped her a not or something. The only consoling thought was knowing that Max had followed her out of the room. Some time ago. Now he was concerned that she hadn't returned. Nor had Max.

Vengeful green eyes watched Max follow the woman out of the Museum.

She was angry. Not only because she'd missed Brian's reading, but she hadn't been invited. The nerve of those people telling she couldn't enter without a special pass.

Why hadn't Brian seen to it that she received one?

She smiled. Despite all their efforts, she had managed to get inside anyway. Snuck in through the kitchen only to be caught by one of the security guards. Simply because she didn't have a name tag. And when she had run from him, she escaped through a fire exit door.

She laughed as she recalled watching all the security people, Max included, race around the parking lot searching for her. She'd simply hidden behind the boxwoods and then snuck back inside through the kitchens once everyone had settled down. They obviously thought they had scared her away.

How had that woman managed to get inside? She even sat beside Brian at the dinner, she fumed. It should have been her, not that woman.

She pulled the dark wig off her head. It had been bothering her all evening, now she had a splitting headache. She looked in the mirror and straightened her hair. Smiled as she recalled walking past Max in the halls. He'd never even recognized her.

When she stepped into the bathroom and saw the woman sitting on the sofa, it was all she could do to keep walking past her and not grab her. But the other woman hadn't even seen her come in—her eyes had been closed. Sara had waited in one of the stalls until the woman left, then followed her.

She was surprised to see Max also follow the woman to a hotel down the street and wondered who was seeing whom. Maybe she needed to send Brian another note.

After watching Max leave, she was tempted to go inside and have it out with the woman. Before she could step off the curb, the woman was coming out again. She spoke to the valet at the door. She was carrying a suitcase and another large object which she quickly stuffed in her car when the valet pulled up.

Either she was leaving to meet Brian or going home. She smiled. Maybe she'd just follow and give everyone a big surprise.

"Are you sure she's okay?" Brian demanded as soon as they settled in the Ferrari. The reading was over, he'd autographed a mountain of books, and was in the mood for a fight.

Max nodded as he turned the car onto the busy street. "She was in the restroom for about ten minutes. When she finally came out, I thought she looked pale so when she just headed out of the building, I followed her to be sure she was okay. She went to her hotel."

"But what about her room?"

"That too." Max chuckled. "I grabbed a fruit basket, charged it to your account, and delivered it to her. Said it was compliments of the hotel." He laughed. "She looked a little startled, but when I scanned the room, everything appeared okay."

"You're sure?"

"I'm sure. Her suitcase was on the bed. I guess she was unpacking."

Brian threaded his fingers through his hair and rested his head against the headrest.

He was exhausted. First there was that false alarm. Then he had to ignore Natalie, never mind the effort it took to be nice to that snobby woman at his table.

He had a splitting headache.

He reached for his cell phone. "What room is she in?"

He needed to talk to her. Apologize for his behavior. Try telling her what's going on.

Just when things had been going so well, he fumed as he waited for the connection.

"What do you mean she's not registered there!" he demanded minutes later.

CHAPTER 8

NATALIE WAS SICK FOR SEVERAL days after the trip to the Museum.

She drove back to her townhouse, fell onto the bed and slept through the next day.

Using Monday and Tuesday as sick days, she visited Dr. Smith who told her she had a touch of the flu combined with the fact that her body was still adjusting to being pregnant.

By Wednesday, she felt like a human being again.

It helped that it was a beautiful day. The cherry blossoms were in full bloom and there was the scent of hyacinth everywhere. Heading up the steps to the main entrance of the library, she almost collided with Andy, one of the student aides who was leaving for his next class. It suddenly occurred to her that she would miss working here if she quit after the baby is born.

She'd been here five years. This job had been her sanity during the divorce.

She had friends here. Especially Marie, the social butterfly who encouraged her to get out and have some fun. Prove to Sam that he had been wrong about her.

Always smiling and optimistic, it seemed Marie never had a bad day.

Natalie pulled on one of the heavy exterior doors. Next year would be the college's centennial celebration and she was sure the library was one of the first buildings on the original campus. The heating and electrical had been updated but the wooden floors and ticking grandfather clock were reminders of the past. Overhead lighting had been updated with bright florescent bulbs, but lamps scattered atop long wooden tables offered a cozy setting for quiet study and research.

Twenty years ago, they had built a glassed-in foyer to conserve energy. Posters and flyers of upcoming events covered the glass.

Natalie waved to Colleen who was scanning books at the large wooden front desk that faced the entry. She admired the sheen of the magnificent counter that was the hub of the library, the place to come when students checked out or requested resources from the stacks. Use of the library was growing, and she was thankful that they had automated the collection years ago, providing much faster service.

Framed archways on either side of the main room led to reading rooms. Reference books and long reading tables were on the east wing. Computer terminals and study carrels on the west wing.

Directly behind the Main Desk were two doors that led to the stacks where the bulk of the library's collection was housed. She had made many trips up and down the spiral metal steps to the subject oriented levels. One of those levels housed the classics and popular fiction titles where she had shelved Brian's newest book several months ago.

To the right of the front doors, wooden stairs led up to the second level where a balcony overlooked the main room. Below those wooden stairs were doors that led to the offices and library science classrooms in the basement.

Natalie headed down the steps to her office in the basement of the East wing.

She sat at her computer, reading over the email messages that had come in during her absence. When she reached for a pen to jot a note to a colleague, she noticed that the pencil holder wasn't where it was supposed to be. In fact, her stapler, note pad, and a picture of her parents were all three out of place.

She sat back to look around her office and discovered that her calendar had been changed as well. Instead of displaying the month of May, it had been switched back to March with a big red circle around the tenth. The first day of the writers' conference.

She recalled looking at the date when she'd tried to figure the baby's due date, but that had been in her datebook. At home. Not here in her office.

Someone had been in her office while she'd been away.

Movement in the hallway snagged her attention, and Marie walked by, carrying an arm full of books past her door.

"Marie," Natalie called out, "did anyone use my office while I was out sick?"

"No. Not that I know of." She leaned against the door frame. "Why?"

"Some of my things have been moved around."

"Humph. Now that I think about it, your door was shut yesterday afternoon, but when I knocked and looked inside, no one was here. I just left it open, like you always do. You're not missing anything, are you?"

"No. Just some things were moved, that's all."

Marie laughed as she continued on her way. "If they moved anything in my office, I'd never know it." It was a standing joke that Marie could use a class in organization. She might be messy, but whenever they had needed anything from her office, she was always able to find it. It might take her a few minutes, but she always found it.

Natalie began organizing the backlog of work and was sorting a box of new books when the telephone rang.

She hesitated, then answered, waited for her caller to speak. There was silence. When she spoke a second time, there was a click and the call disconnected.

Thirty minutes later, the same thing happened.

Later that afternoon, the telephone rang again, but when she answered it, there was just a dial-tone.

Natalie dialed the front office.

"Arlene? Have you been having problems with the phone system today?"

"No, why?"

"I've received three calls today. Two were hang-ups and the third a disconnection."

"Everything is working fine here. But I do recall getting a call the other day. Specifically asked for your office location and extension number"

"Do you remember whether it was a man or woman?" Natalie asked.

"A woman, I think. The voice was sort of muffled."

"I guess if it was important, they'll call back." Natalie said.

There were no more calls.

When Natalie returned home that evening, she noticed she had a message on her recorder.

It was from Brian. "I'm sorry I haven't called sooner. Figured you might be upset with me after the other night. But I wanted to be sure you're okay. You left in such a hurry." He rattled off some numbers. "Please ask for room seventeen-thirty. Or call my cell. I'll be here until seven. Then I have to leave for a book signing and dinner."

Natalie purposely waited until after eight o'clock and left a message that she was fine.

Later, as she was preparing for bed, her telephone rang again. Thinking it might be Brian, she decided to let the recorder take the call.

It was her gremlin from work. This time, whoever it was decided to try heavy breathing.

Angry, tired, and feeling queasy, Natalie lifted the receiver and loudly blew the whistle that she now kept beside her bed. She slammed the receiver down and unplugged the phone.

The following morning, Marie stopped by her office with a note from Sharon McAllister. The Children's Literature professor needed her to pull a list of fifteen books from the stacks so that she could use them in her class that afternoon.

"Why is she asking me to do it?" Natalie asked. "I'm a cataloger. That's what we have the library aides for."

Marie shrugged one shoulder. "All I know is that Colleen at the front desk handed it to me as I came in this morning. The woman that left it said Dr. McAlister asked her to leave it at the front desk. And it has your name on it."

"I'll do it," Natalie fumed. "But Dr. McAllister and I need to talk." She scanned the list. "My gosh, these are all on the third level in the stacks."

She marched upstairs past the front desk toward the stacks. Her shoes clacked on the metal steps as she navigated down the narrow, circular stairwell to the third level. Row after row of tall metal racks displayed the books that the library had accumulated over the years. Books filled the shelves, leaving only a few inches at best to see over the tops to the other side.

The aisles were long and narrow, and the lighting was minimal, just enough to read the titles.

List in hand, Natalie located a small book cart and headed toward the children's section. She began searching for the titles the kiddie lit teacher had requested.

Every few shelves, she smiled when titles caught her attention. She remembered her mother reading these books to her over and over when she was a little girl.

Something she planned to do with her own little boy or girl.

She heard footsteps on the metal steps and mentally counted the number of steps taken and realized whoever it was had stopped on her level. She listened for them to move toward an aisle or walk past.

Instead there was silence. Had she imagined it? She debated calling out. Could the person be searching for her?

Natalie shivered. She never liked coming down to the lower stacks. The dim lighting made it downright spooky. Her creative mind had often envisioned a murder or mugging in the eerie depths of doom.

She peeked between the shelves and saw a dark shadow. A shadow that simply stood there. Was the shadow reading a book? Following her? Trying to scare her?

She tried to get a better look, but all she could distinguish was someone in a hooded sweatshirt. It reminded her of the contacts icon on her cellphone with the rounded head and solid shape. Ambiguous; unidentifiable. She couldn't see the eyes but felt them. Someone apparently wanted to rattle her. And they were succeeding.

Natalie reached for her cell phone but remembered she'd left it on her desk. There wouldn't have been any service down here anyway. She debated leaving but since she was almost finished with the list, she quickly found the remainder of the books then wheeled the cart to the dumb-waiter, another artifact of the original library. There was no room for elevators. She transferred the books to the opening and pressed the button to transport them upstairs to the main level.

She turned and reached for a heavy book, prepared to throw it at anything that moved her way. She breathed a sigh of relief when she saw that the shadow was no longer there. She ran up the steps and transferred the books at the front desk with a note for Dr. McAllister to call her.

Natalie scanned the lobby before heading back to her office.

Brooding emerald green eyes watched the woman put the books on the back counter at the front desk. She sneered as she recalled watching the bitch search for the books. Lucky for her, she'd bumped into the professor and caused her to drop her armful of papers. And snagged the list when she helped the clueless teacher gather the papers.

She knew she had spooked the bitch. Felt the fear when their eyes briefly connected. She had watched her scramble to get the books as quickly as she could. Almost laughed when she hid in the shadows and watched her pick up the oversized book. As if that book would protect her. She could take the woman out any time she wanted.

She flicked the hood of the sweatshirt back, then scowled at a boy that stared when she moved past his table. She was used to the odd looks. Brian's appreciative eyes were the only ones that mattered. But his eyes were on someone else lately.

It wouldn't be much longer before the other woman was out of his life.

Natalie's phone rang as soon as she returned to her desk. She worried that it might be another crank call; but it could also be Dr. McAllister, so she answered—and heard Brian Cato's voice with loud noise in the background.

"Are you okay?"

"Of course, I'm okay. Didn't you get my message last night?"

"Yes, but I wanted to hear your voice again."

You didn't want to hear it the other night, she wanted to say. "Where are you? What's all the noise?"

"I'm at the airport. Between flights. Wanted to talk to you about the other night. Thought I'd have better luck catching you at work."

Natalie remained quiet. She was sure he knew she hadn't wanted to talk to him last night.

"I'm sorry about what happened at the Museum last Saturday. Those alarms really spooked me and with the reading on my mind, I guess I wasn't very good company."

"No, you weren't."

"I'd like to make it up to you."

"Don't worry about it. Concentrate on your tour."

"I'd enjoy it more if you were here."

"I'm afraid that's not possible. Brian, I hate to cut this conversation short, but you've caught me on my way out for a staff meeting. I'm sorry, but I have to go."

"Okay," he sounded meek. "But I'd like to call later."

"Whatever. Thanks for the call but I really need to go." She hung up before he could say anything else.

Natalie opened the drawer to her desk and reached for the squish ball she used in times of stress. Squeezed it hard while she stared straight ahead. She didn't know whether she was lonely and missed him, sorry that she had lied, or angry that she had felt pity for him.

Three hundred miles away, Max opened the door to Brian's mountain home and stepped inside. A large lanky mahogany and tan Belgian Milionis shepherd followed at a brisk pace, sniffing the perimeter of the front hall.

The dog's name was Fitz and Max let him meander, checking out his new home.

While Brian was away on his tour, Max had been working with Fitz under Bo's supervision. Fitz needed to become familiar with his new owner, and Max needed to learn the shepherd's commands. The dog still missed his original handler and Max knew helping him fit in would take time and patience.

Brian needed reinforcements. He wouldn't mind a companion. And Fitz needed a second chance.

With Brian on his tour that meant Sara would be nowhere around here.

Max put Fitz's bed in his bedroom. For now, they would be inseparable. He tossed Fitz's toys, old and new, on the floor beside the bed.

Fitz was only four years old so hopefully it would just be a matter of time before his old handler faded to memory and Max and Brian became his new family.

Brian was sure Natalie had cut him off. It was in the tone of her voice. She was still upset with him and he had to admit he couldn't blame her. He'd probably be mad too.

Since he still had some time before boarding his plane, he decided to give Max a call. He knew he and the dog were due back at the house today.

"How's it going?" Brian asked.

"Good. Just got here and I'm letting him settle in. Probably take him for a walk later."

It occurred to Brian that while they had talked about the dog, Max had never shared his name. "What's his name?"

"Fitz. Short for Fitzgerald." Max waited for Brian to catch on. "As in F. Scott Fitzgerald? When Bo told me his name, I knew it was a given. A dog with an author's name for an author."

"Humph," was all Brian said for a moment. "Don't guess you've seen anything of Sara?"

"No. I did a quick walk through the house when I first got here and didn't see anything out of place. Thought maybe Fitz and I would take a hike this afternoon and see if he picks up on anything."

"I know you suggested Fitz as another resource, but I'm beginning to wonder if maybe we need to beef up the alarm system."

"I've mentioned that several times. Been waiting for you to make the decision."

"Okay." Brian snapped. "I've made the decision."

"Wise decision." Max wasn't offended by Brian's curt response. He knew Brian was uptight. With a woman like Sara haunting his every waking moment, who wouldn't be?

"If you find that she hasn't been around the house, it must mean she is following me. And if that's the case, now might be the time to have the system revamped."

"I'll have it done by the time you end your tour and if she tries to make an appearance after that, we might be able to actually catch her."

"Let's just hope you're right." Brian sighed.

CHAPTER 9

NATALIE STARED AT BRIAN'S TEXT the next day. **Staff meeting go okay yesterday?**

When she didn't answer, another text chimed. **Happy birthday?**

Natalie frowned at the phone. She was busy preparing for an inventory and didn't have time for his foolishness. She turned the phone over and continued to print reports.

Still, she heard the ping of another text and couldn't resist. **You said your birthday was in May. Today? Tomorrow?**

She continued to ignore him.

Unless you tell me, I'm going to send you a dozen roses each day for the next two weeks.

It's day after tomorrow. Go away, she texted.

Two days later, she received an Anthurium plant at work. Marie oohed about the beautiful coral blooms. "Look at them. The blooms and leaves are heart-shaped. Somebody must like you a lot to send you heart-shaped flowers."

Natalie set the plant in the corner and shooed Marie out of her office.

When she got home that evening, her neighbor greeted her with a dozen salmon colored roses. "These just came. The delivery guy asked if he could leave them with me."

Her cell phone pinged as she was setting the roses on her desk. **Get my roses?**

She sighed and responded, **Yes. And the plant. Brian, it's too much.**

Not enough for having deserted you. I'm sorry. It's not over yet.

Natalie worried that he might have managed a break in his schedule and was coming to see her. She groaned when there was a knock at her door. She checked the peephole and saw a woman. "Can I help you?" She asked through the open space between the door and chain.

The woman was dressed casually and carried what looked like a large suitcase. She smiled. "I'm Michelle Gammon. Are you Natalie Stover?"

Natalie nodded.

"Brian Cato is a friend of mine and he asked me to deliver your birthday present. Did the flowers come?"

"Yes, all of them," she sighed as she released the chain and reluctantly opened the door.

Michelle laughed. "Brian doesn't do things half-way. I'm a massage therapist. Brian has had sessions with me, and he asked me if I'd drive down from D.C. to give you one as a birthday present."

Natalie gaped at her. "Brian asked you to drive over an hour to give me a massage? You've got to be kidding."

Michelle smiled. "He can be eccentric, over the top sometimes. I have my table and just need a couple minutes to set up."

Twenty minutes later, Natalie was lying on her stomach, almost asleep. Her face in the face cradle of the massage table, she stared at the floor and watched Michelle's feet shift as the woman massaged her shoulders and back. Her hands worked their way down to Natalie's lower back.

"I still can't believe Brian paid you to do this. I mean, I can understand why, you're fantastic, but I barely know the man."

"Brian is a special guy. He helped me out once and usually calls me whenever he's in D.C."

"Mind if I ask you how he helped you?"

"He's friends with my brother. I used to give them massages after their football games. When I got in a little trouble a few years back, he offered to pay for my training. Then he found me a place in a big franchise. I started my own business last year and he's sent a lot of his friends my way." Michelle patted her back. "I need you to roll over."

Natalie almost groaned when Michelle worked the muscles in her arms.

"I'm picking up a few knots. Been doing any lifting lately?"

"I'm always lifting books. Guess I need to be more careful."

Michelle refused Natalie's tip. "Brian has paid me very generously. Besides, it's your birthday."

"Please, take this and treat yourself to a dinner before heading back North. There's a delicious Mexican restaurant a couple blocks from her. Tell Gabe I sent you."

"He doesn't sound too Mexican."

Natalie laughed. "His wife's name is Alejandra."

Natalie felt refreshed as she changed in the bedroom. She headed to the kitchen when there was another knock at her door. This seemed to be her night for surprises, she thought as she looked through the peephole. This time, there was a young man wearing a chef's hat.

"Ms. Stover? I'm Ashby and Mr. Cato asked me to fix your dinner this evening." He held up a bag. "I've got chicken. He said you liked chicken cordon bleu so I've got ingredients for that, a salad and my favorite, fresh asparagus. He also asked me to bring my specialty, fudge pie for dessert. I'll even put a candle on it, if you'd like. All I need is to use your kitchen for an hour."

Natalie watched as he pounded the chicken breast, layered the ham and cheese, then rolled it, coating it with panko bread crumbs.

"How long have you been a chef?"

"Actually, I'm a sous chef at the Ironstone in D.C. but my goal is to be a personal chef. Mr. Cato always asks for me whenever he's in town."

"Did you by any chance drive down with Michelle?"

Ashby laughed. "No, but he did give me a big tip."

After eating, Natalie felt badly about her last text to Brian. 'Go away' certainly deserved to be changed into thank you' after all he had showered her with.

Thank you, she texted. **For everything. I feel like a princess, all pampered and fed.**

Ten minutes later her phone pinged. **Glad you enjoyed it. I rather enjoyed making all the arrangements.**

As the weeks passed, Natalie's life settled down and her body adjusted to being pregnant. She found herself watching for the small changes Dr. Smith had mentioned at her check-up. Her breasts seemed fuller, her stomach a little swollen. She smiled. She had a small baby bump.

Her energy level was a minus ten at the oddest times. Fortunately, she discovered that if she took a longer break in the afternoon with some fruit and a book, she could make it through the day with no one becoming suspicious.

She didn't need a new wardrobe yet, but some of her clothes were starting to get snug. The weather had turned hot and the sun dresses she wore were not only cooler but helped hide her secret.

Brian called on a regular basis and she found herself looking forward to hearing about the book signings, local television and radio appearances, and functions he'd been requested to attend.

"You're not going to believe what I have to do this week. For the Fourth of July."

"What?"

"Be the Grand Marshal in a parade."

"A parade," she exclaimed. "That's so neat. I remember marching in parades when I was in Girl Scouts."

"You might think so. It's supposed to be one hundred degrees."

"You'll have fun, you know it. Just smile, wave at everybody and you'll be a hit. I wish I could be there to see it."

"Me too. Won't you be off?"

"Only for the day. I'm planning to spend the day working on my next chapter." She was coming down the home stretch with her mystery and was anxious to see its conclusion.

"Written any good love scenes lately?"

Natalie laughed. "No, they're bickering. Ann is making a play for Adam and Cecelia can't understand why she's so jealous. Do you get any time to write?"

"A little. I have my laptop with me, but I find I have better luck dictating into my phone as the ideas hit me."

"I guess you'll be busy transcribing everything when you get back home."

"Probably hire a temp. You interested?"

Natalie laughed. "Hardly. I might be tempted to snitch a few of your ideas though."

"That'd be okay too." He was silent. "I miss you."

"I miss you too," she finally admitted more to herself than to him.

"I want to see you. Are you sure you can't meet me—"

Suddenly the line went dead. When Natalie tried to use the phone again, there was no dial-tone. It was late, and she was tired. I'll call him tomorrow, she thought.

There was still no dial tone the following morning and she called the telephone company as soon as she arrived at work. They promised to check it out and call her.

"Ms. Stover?" A student spoke from her door, handed her a note. "Heather Brown asked me to give this to you."

Natalie smiled. "Thanks." She'd been tutoring Heather in creative writing two evenings a week while the girl attended summer school and wondered if Heather wanted to cancel their session this evening. She hoped so, she was exhausted.

Natalie opened the note and thought it was odd that Heather had typed it. *Would you mind pulling these reference books for me to use after our session this evening? I'll be in class all day and need to use them for a research paper due the end of the week.*

She had done this a couple times already. Knowing Heather was struggling hard this summer with her classes and working on weekends, Natalie tried to help whenever she could.

At least she didn't have to go to the stacks, she thought as she carried the stack of books to her office. Dr. Smith had warned her about lifting heavy objects but what was she supposed to do? If she left them on the table, someone would put them away or use them themselves.

Although the books weren't supposed to leave the room, she'd used her position to sign for them and was taking them to her office, promising that Heather would return them later that evening.

The reference room was in the west wing which meant she had a long walk back to her office in the east wing. She decided to take the stairs down to the lower level and follow the long halls back to her office. Hopefully a book cart would be available in the halls.

Natalie opened the door at the top of the steps, shifted the books to her side and held onto the railing as she started down the steps. She took her time but by the time she reached the door at the bottom of the steps, her arms were tired, and she was out of breath.

She set the books on the bottom step and reached for the door knob. She'd just grab a cart from the hall or in one of the classrooms and roll them to her office.

She turned the knob, but the door wouldn't open.

That's strange. They'd never been locked before. In fact, these doors were supposed to be accessible all the time. In case of emergencies and for easy access to the rooms on the lower level.

She debated her options. She certainly couldn't stay here. No telling when someone would come through the door since only staff, volunteers, and library aides used the basement stairs.

She reached for her cell phone but quickly realized she had no signal. She stared behind her and sighed. She'd have to go back upstairs to alert security and then come through from the other side.

The stairwell plunged into darkness. *What had happened to the lights?*

Natalie's heart lodged in her throat. She grabbed the railing but remained still. The silence was eerie. It suddenly occurred to her that no one knew where she was. She hadn't even told Marie where she was going.

Maybe the entire library is out? But if that was so, the emergency lights would have kicked on. Something was wrong. She felt for the light switch beside the door and breathed a sigh of relief when the lights came on.

She still had to go back upstairs.

The lights went out a second time and when she flipped them on, they went out again. If someone was trying to scare her they were succeeding.

She heard a slithering movement on one of the levels above.

"Hello, is anyone there?"

Silence. She was beginning to think she had imagined it until she heard the sound again. Someone was slowly coming down the steps, one step at a time.

What was it with her and steps? First in the stacks and now on the stairwell.

"Hello," she called out again. "Is anyone there?"

Still there was only silence.

Each flight of steps was seven steps with a landing, turn and then seven more steps. Every other landing had an exit door to the library.

She heard the clicks of footsteps. Whoever was in here with her was on the upper level and continued to slowly come down the steps. The quietness made the echo of each step seem so much louder.

Natalie backed into the corner and she found herself counting the steps. Had her tormentor followed her from the second floor?

Four... five... six...The echo and darkness were so deceiving she couldn't decide whether the person had reached her level or the level above her.

She almost whimpered when she realized her tormentor had made the turn on the landing. But which landing? The landing to the first floor or right above her?

Whoever it was, they moved slowly. Deliberately trying to scare her.

How did anyone even know I was here? Unless they had seen her enter the stairwell.

Who had locked the lower basement door? How could they have known I'd be coming to the basement.

Anger replaced fear as she wondered if it could be a student playing a sick joke on her. But why her?

Five... six... seven... She continued to mentally track her tormentor and determined that he or she was now on the landing just above her.

Again, there was silence. Natalie held her breath. Would they go out the door to the first floor, or continue down to the basement?

Natalie stood in the dark, huddled against the basement door, one hand over her pounding heart and the other over her stomach as if to protect her baby. It was all she could do to keep quiet. It was obvious the person meant to scare her, maybe even harm her.

There was a sudden rattle of a door echoing from above.

"Good grief," someone exclaimed. "What happened to the lights?"

"I don't know. Try the switch," another said.

Natalie heard a faint click before the bright lights momentarily blinded her. She also heard the door open directly above her. Her tormentor had apparently left the first-floor stairwell.

"What sicko turned the lights off?" The first student said.

"Hello," Natalie hollered up the steps. "Is anyone there?"

"Yes ma'am," the kids hollered down to her. "You okay?"

"Yes, but the basement door is locked. Are you leaving the building?"

"Yes ma'am," they answered.

"On your way out, would you please tell the security guard that the basement door in the west wing is locked?"

"Sure thing, but are you gonna be okay?"

"Only if you hurry," Natalie sat down on the bottom step. She didn't want to tell them she was a nervous wreck. Didn't know when her heart would ever slow down.

Please hurry, she pleaded silently.

"What happened?" Brian demanded thirty minutes later when he called her office phone.

Natalie stared at the receiver. How had he found out so quickly? She had just now returned to her office and was trying to relax a moment.

"How did you find out?"

"Find out? Natalie, we were disconnected last night, remember?"

With all the excitement in the stairwell, she'd completely forgotten about his disconnected call last night.

"Oh, that," she breathed a sigh of relief. She didn't feel like telling him about her frightening experience in the stairwell.

"What do you mean, 'Oh that?' Are you sure you're okay? I tried calling you back last night but never got a dial tone. I even tried your cell phone. Did you have a storm?"

It occurred to Natalie that she had switched her phone to vibrate for the staff meeting yesterday and had forgotten to switch it back. She reached for it and saw that she had missed five calls from Brian.

"No. I don't know what happened. I reported it first thing this morning, but I haven't heard anything yet. I'm sure it was something minor and will be taken care of by the time I get home."

"I hope so. You had me worried. Promise me you'll call me when you get home. I need to go now, but you can leave me a message. And I'll talk to you later."

Natalie leaned back in her chair and stared at the phone. He certainly was getting possessive. If she didn't know better, she'd think he was concerned about her. She shook her head. That's not possible, he'd said he had no room for a woman in his life.

She placed her hand over the slightly rounded stomach as if to reassure herself that all was okay. Her eyes widened, and she laughed out loud when she felt the slight flutter. Her baby had moved.

Heather Stansbury arrived later that afternoon for her tutoring session. Natalie worked with her for an hour, suggested changes on an article Heather planned to submit to the college newspaper.

"By the way," she pointed to the stack on the corner of her desk. "Those are the books you asked me to pull."

"What books?" Heather asked.

"Didn't you send me a note asking me to pull some reference books for your research paper?"

Heather frowned when she looked at the titles. "No."

"You don't have a paper due this Friday?"

"No, ma'am."

Natalie pulled the note from her trash can. "You didn't send me this note?"

"No. Besides, if I needed you to do anything, I'd have sent you an email. Not a typed note."

Natalie stared at the piece of paper. "Then who sent me this note?"

Heather shrugged her shoulders.

They both jumped as the phone rang. Natalie quickly reached for it.

"Ms. Stover," she heard a male voice who identified himself as the technician from the telephone company.

"Oh, yes." Natalie remembered they had promised to call her. "Have you been able to fix my phone?" She asked.

"I'm here now, but it has taken a little longer than planned. Has your neighborhood had problems with burglars?"

"No, why?"

"It seems someone cut your line."

Max had been working with Fitz all afternoon. Commanding him to walk, run, and heel. He even had the dogs searching for some of his things.

He wished he had something of Sara's, so they could do a search of the mountainside. Things had been quiet. She was apparently tracking Brian.

It had been a long day. The security company had finally finished upgrading the alarm system. It had been tested thoroughly as Max re-enacted many of Sara's attempts to get into the house. He had even tried climbing in the laundry window, but the alarm sounded as soon as he removed the screen. Max was sure there was no way she would be able to get inside the house. The Sheriff's Office knew they were testing the system but after today, if the alarm sounded, it meant they needed to get here. Fast.

He decided to give Brian an update and stepped outside to use his cell phone in case they missed a bug. They had found two already. He shook his head at the extremes and expense Brian's stalker went to.

"Great news," Brian said. "You're sure it works?"

"Definitely. And it's so loud I'm sure they can hear it in town." Max laughed.

"How about the phone? Had any problems with that?"

"No. Why?"

"It's just that the last several times I've talked with Natalie, there have been problems. Disconnections."

"Want me to check things out?"

"No. You've got enough with training Fitz. I worry that Sara might be stalking Natalie. I know I was discreet when I visited her last, but she knows Natalie lives in Fredericksburg."

"Has Natalie mentioned anything strange going on?"

"No. Maybe I'm just paranoid, but there have been problems with her phone."

When the call ended, Max considered contacting the Fredericksburg police. He knew Brian was worried; heard the concern in his voice just now.

She'd been quiet the past month. He hoped that Sara had given up on Brian.

He tossed his cell phone on the table and looked over at the dog resting on the corner of the deck. Fitz raised his head and stared at him.

He had been pleased with Fitz's progress. A few days in his new environment made all the difference. The dog was more energetic, curious about his new surroundings.

He knew it was getting late but decided to try something new. He reached for the ball that was on the table beside him and dropped it on the floor.

Fitz's ears perked up, his eyes wavered between the ball and Max.

Max nudged the ball toward the dog.

It stopped inches from Fitz's paw. He sniffed the ball, checked it out, nudged the ball back toward Max.

Max tried not to shout hoorah as he nudged the ball back to the dog.

When Fitz repeated the action, Max smiled. He reached for the ball, bounced it a couple times then gave it a hard bounce, sending it down the steps and across the yard. He laughed when Fitz jumped up to chase it down.

He decided to see just how good Fitz could track him and ran inside the house to hide.

CHAPTER 10

DARLING, IT WAS WONDERFUL SEEING you in D.C. and New York. Watching all those fans crowd around you gave me a warm feeling, knowing your writing is appreciated. I'll be glad when this tour is over and you can return home to me. Where you belong. I'm sorry I was unable to hear your reading at the Virginia Museum. I wasn't very happy to be turned away, but understand the tight security. What I don't understand is how other people could attend. One wasn't even a member! Maybe you should ask Max why he has taken an interest in following her. Love, Sara

Brian studied the letter and envelope Max had scanned to him. Another email for the folder reserved for her. He couldn't even give the folder a name; just put a question mark for the title. Giving the file her name would be acknowledging her existence. Banishing them to that folder prevented her interfering in his life every time he checked his emails. Out of sight, out of mind.

He quickly scanned the other emails she had sent. How many would it take for the police and the judge to agree that she was indeed stalking him? He and the justice system had been several rounds, but emails weren't considered serious offenses unless they implied physical harm.

Would she ever tire of him? It had been over two years since she first contacted him. Well past the usual time a stalker would haunt his victim.

He had tried to let her down gently in the beginning. When he realized she was stalking him, he talked with a profiler friend who said she was shy, more likely lived alone and probably had no friends. She imagined Brian to be the man of her dreams therefore he must be in love with her too. The profiler warned that the longer the situation continued, the more aggressive she would become—and that she might turn violent.

He should have known the peace he'd been feeling these past weeks wouldn't last. She'd said she had been in D.C. and New York, and, although he hadn't seen her, he didn't doubt her word that she'd been there. He had two years of proof that she could pretty much do anything she set her mind to.

Rereading the email, he noted the date. The letter had been mailed the week after the reading at the Museum. Over a month ago. It seemed like forever despite the fact that he and Max had been busy. Maybe Max should have waited a little longer to check the mail.

The hectic tour had helped him to relax some. He'd stopped looking over his shoulder all the time, enjoyed connecting with his fans at the signings. If this was what it took, he might stay on the road all the time.

Except for Natalie. He missed her.

It never ceased to amaze him how little things about her flittered through his thoughts at the oddest times. Her perfume, her smile, their lovemaking.

He recalled the woman in Kentucky who from the back, reminded him so much of Natalie. Then she'd turned around and he saw that she didn't have Natalie's warm smile.

Brian started a quick email to Max. He was due to leave within the hour for a guest appearance on a local talk show and then a dinner party with the Mayor and Town Council. After the parade tomorrow, he would be boarding a plane back to the East Coast.

Closer to Natalie.

If he didn't know better, he'd think he was falling in love with Natalie. Couldn't be possible though, he hardly ever saw her. Since the tour had started, they had talked on the phone more than in person. But the bond was there, he reminded himself.

Yes, they'd made love but so far, their relationship was one of words. First the written words of her manuscript and now spoken words on the telephone.

Only Natalie could calm him when the tour got overwhelming. One call to her could relax him quicker than any workout or marathon writing session.

He clicked the send button and glanced at his watch. It would be six o'clock her time. She should be home by now.

He was worried about their disconnection last night. Then she'd seemed so preoccupied earlier this afternoon. He wondered if something might have happened at home or at work.

He reached for the telephone. They should have fixed it by now.

Natalie sat in her office and stared at the picture of her parents. Heather had just left, and she really should be going herself.

She looked at her watch. Six thirty. Past time to be out of here.

After Heather's denial about requesting the books and then that disturbing call from the telephone company, she'd been glued to her chair, unable to move.

Who could have cut her telephone line? She lived in a safe neighborhood—no murders or break-ins. Was it a kid playing a sick joke? A peeping Tom?

And why her? She led a quiet life. Minded her own business. Tried not to draw attention to herself. The only thing different was Brian and she hadn't seen him in almost two months.

She shivered to think that someone might have been watching her. But why cut the telephone line? It would have been different if someone had tried to break in, but nothing had happened.

Everything was intact when she left for work this morning. There weren't any broken windows or torn screens. And all the doors were locked. Maybe it really was a prankster, and someone had spooked him. Whoever it was, she hoped he wouldn't come back.

Thinking about it wouldn't make things any better, she scolded herself. Only make her more nervous and she'd had her share of scares for one day.

She reached for the reference books she'd pulled for Heather. They'd have to be returned before she left the building.

Minutes later she stopped at the front desk to check out some books for herself and noticed that the children's books she had gathered for Dr. McAllister were still sitting on the back shelf.

"Dr. McAllister hasn't picked up her books?"

"No, ma'am," the student aide said. "And they've been there awhile. We were wondering if maybe we should just put them back on the shelf."

"She asked me to pull them two weeks ago." Natalie said. "If I recall, she said she needed them that afternoon. I'd hate to have her think I didn't do it. Would you give her a call before you put the books back? And please, let me know what she says?"

All she needed was for Dr. McAllister to say she hadn't requested them.

Natalie stepped outside the library and headed toward the staff parking lot. After the day she'd had, she found she was more observant of her surroundings.

She heard footsteps. Was someone following her?

Hadn't that yellow car been waiting at the stop sign a little too long?

She waved at students cutting across the grass, but avoided eye contact.

Get a grip, she scolded herself as she made a dash for her car.

Arctic green eyes of wrath watched from the yellow car at the stop sign.

She was still upset from last night. Hurt morphed into anger as she listened to Brian telling that woman how much he'd missed her and wanted to see her.

How dare she? Brian is mine! It was all she could do to restrain herself from dashing into the townhouse and just getting rid of her then and there.

Instead, she had cut the telephone line. Now Brian wouldn't be able to call anymore.

And today, she sneered to herself, on the stairs. She wished she could have seen the fear she heard in the woman's voice. If those stupid kids hadn't come along when they did, she might have been able to scare the woman even more.

She gripped the steering wheel and revved the engine. Maybe she could take care of the problem now. She looked around. Not that many kids out. And if anyone saw it, she'd say she lost control of the car.

She almost laughed out loud when she watched the woman almost run to her car.

All her hard work was beginning to pay off. It wouldn't be much longer.

Natalie's telephone was ringing when she opened the door to her townhouse. The recorder flashed that she had missed two calls.

"Where the hell have you been?" Brian demanded as soon as she answered. "I called you at work and they said you'd left. I tried your cell and it went to voicemail. Natalie," he sounded exasperated, "where have you been?"

"At work. I also had my tutoring session with Heather." She reached for the TV remote.

"I've been calling for over an hour. Did you get the flowers?"

"Flowers?" She asked, distracted by a news bulletin.

"Yes, as in a dozen roses?"

"No, nothing came today. Brian, you shouldn't waste your money."

"I ordered them several days ago. You should have received them by now."

Natalie shivered. Too many strange events had been occurring in her life lately.

"What did the telephone company say about your phone?"

Natalie almost told him, but wondered how he would react. She didn't need him hovering. Or making any unexpected trips to see her. It was still early but her pregnancy was becoming more obvious. She was surprised that Marie hadn't said anything.

"It was nothing," she lied.

"What do you mean it was nothing? Something had to have caused it. You don't know how worried I was, especially after I couldn't get you on your cell phone."

Natalie let him vent while she tried to think of a reasonable explanation for the disconnection. She understood his being upset, but knew he'd be more upset if she told him the line had been deliberately cut.

A severe storm watch bulletin was flashing across the screen on the television and she decided to move the storm up one day.

"Brian," she interrupted his tirade, "we had a storm last night... It caused several accidents around the city." She smiled when her imagination kicked in. "One must have hit a transformer. There were a lot of people without power."

"Are you sure?"

"Yes, I'm sure," she continued her lie. "Everything's okay now, they assured me."

Brian was quiet. "Well, I hope it doesn't happen again," he finally said.

"Me too," she responded, too heartily.

It was almost time for his talk show. "Be sure and check on those roses," he said before disconnecting.

The following morning, Natalie arrived at work to find a long white box laying on the floor outside her office. She bent to pick them up and realized the door was shut.

That was odd. She always left it open. Even the janitor knew to leave it open.

She reached for the knob, then hesitated. Recalled what had happened in the stairwell yesterday. Should she open the door? Could someone be in her office?

What is the matter with you? she scolded herself. She'd never been so timid before. But then she'd never been pregnant, trapped in a stairwell, gotten prank calls, or had her telephone tampered with, a small voice reminded her.

Before she reached for the door knob a second time, she heard the door from the stairwell open. Her office was around the corner of the long hall. Someone was coming her way. Slowly. Maybe not as slowly as yesterday, but slow just the same. Natalie held her breath praying it was a fellow worker, or student, and not yesterday's tormentor.

Marie came around the corner. She was reading a sheet of paper as she walked and looked up as Natalie gasped.

"Natalie?" she asked, rushing to her side, "are you okay? You're as white as a sheet."

"I'm fine," Natalie whispered, rested her forehead against her door. "You just gave me a scare."

"I'm so sorry." Even as Marie apologized, her head tilted as she noticed the box in Natalie's arms. "What do we have here? More flowers? You're going to have to introduce me to this guy. Does he have any brothers?

Natalie chuckled. She opened the door to her office and gasped a second time, her amused relief vanishing. Someone had most definitely been in her office. Her desk was bare, its contents strewn across the floor. Her chair had been slashed, the cushions protruding from the leather. File cabinet drawers were open, and the catalogs and papers scattered about the room.

Natalie stepped forward and heard the crunch of glass beneath her feet. The picture of her parents had been smashed.

"Oh, Natalie," Marie whispered. "What happened? Who could've done such a thing?" Marie grabbed Natalie's arm. "You're white as a sheet. C'mon down to my office. We need to call security."

When Natalie didn't move, Marie tugged on her arm, guided her down the hall toward her office.

Natalie stood near the door while Marie called the campus police. She could hear Marie's voice, but nothing seemed to be registering. Visions of her trashed office fogged her brain. Who would have done such a thing? And why?

She stared down at the box in her arms and smiled weakly. Brian's roses. The only good thing about the morning. She set the box on Marie's desk and lifted the lid.

Instead of fresh red roses, the flowers were faded black, dry, and brittle.

Natalie jumped, shoving the box off the desk as if it were a poisonous snake, coiled, and ready to strike.

"Please hurry," Marie said, staring in horrified disbelief at the dead roses strewn across the floor.

Marie grabbed Natalie's wrist and steered her to the chair. She reached for a tissue and handed it to Natalie. "This morning appears to be going from bad to worse." She squatted beside Natalie. "Are you okay?"

Natalie saw Marie's concerned expression. "I really don't know." She leaned toward the desk, rested her elbows on the top and her face in her hands. "So much has been happening. Yesterday, and now this."

"What happened yesterday?"

"I was trapped in the stairwell on the west wing."

"Trapped? What do you mean trapped?"

"I had to pull some reference books for Heather Stansbury and when I was coming back to my office, someone had locked the door to the basement halls. Then the lights went out and I swear I could hear someone coming toward me. In the dark. Every time I turned the lights on, someone would turn them off. Then some students came in the second-floor door. I heard another door shut just as they turned the lights back on. I asked them to call security to come unlock the door.

"We still don't know how the door got locked." Both girls jumped, saw two security officers at the door. "Jeremy Scott and Ray Butler." Jeremy pointed a thumb at his chest as he provided introductions, indicating he was Officer Scott. We were on duty when you called yesterday.

Natalie and Marie led the men to her office but remained in the hall while they searched the room.

"Did you touch anything?" one of the officers asked.

"Only the door." Natalie answered. "It was closed. I usually keep it open but this morning, it was closed."

"Do you think this is related to the incident in the stairwell?" Marie asked.

"We're not sure but someone is not happy with you, Ms. Stover. Do you have another office you can use? We'd like to call in the investigators."

Before Natalie could answer, Thomas Salt, the head of personnel stopped in the hall by the open door. "I heard on the scanner we had an incident." He saw the mess, and cast a concerned look at Natalie. "You don't look too good. And neither does your office. Do you have any idea who might have done this?"

Natalie shook her head.

"Tomorrow is the Fourth." Mr. Salt said. "Why don't you take a long weekend?" He nodded to the security. "We'll have this mess cleaned up and maybe a few clues by the time you get back next Monday."

Natalie started to protest, but Marie interrupted her.

"I think that's an excellent idea. You know you'll never get anything done in all this mess. Let the men check it over and then the janitor can clean it. By Monday, you'll be more relaxed and ready to work." She reached for Natalie's pocketbook. "In fact, I'll walk you to the car." She pulled Natalie out of the office and down the hall.

"Why didn't you say something yesterday?" Marie scolded as they started up the steps.

"I was so shocked by it all," Natalie responded. "And since nothing really happened, I didn't want to blow it out of proportion."

"Well," Marie opened the door to the main lobby. "After what just happened, I'd say you made somebody mad. And I'm not so sure I'd be willing to come back next Monday."

Humid air smacked them as soon as they stepped outside, but Natalie shivered.

"You don't have to walk me to the car," she fussed when Marie remained by her side.

"I know, but I needed to get out of there. Are you sure you're up to driving home?"

"Yes. Yes, I'm fine. A little shaky, but I'm okay."

"I'd feel better if we knew who was behind this. You don't have any idea who it might be?"

Natalie shook her head.

They stopped at the intersection and looked both ways before crossing toward the parking lot. The sudden screeching of tires made them look around when they were partway across the street.

Marie shouted as she realized a yellow Volkswagen was heading straight for them.

"Look out! Hurry!" She grabbed Natalie's arm and pulled her friend out of the street.

Natalie felt the air brush the hem of her dress as the vehicle came within inches of her foot. She smelled the burned rubber, tasted the fear, and was nearly sick all in one instant.

"Can you believe that?" Marie exclaimed.

They both watched the car roar away. Marie looked at Natalie. "Are you sure you haven't made any enemies these past few months?"

"If I have, I don't know who it could be or why," Natalie whispered.

Her nerves shot, she tried to put on a strong front. Otherwise she knew Marie would threaten to camp out in her townhouse.

"I'm sure it was some crazy student in a hurry or upset about an assignment." Natalie unlocked the door. Ten more minutes, she thought. All she needed was to be strong for ten more minutes and then she could cry her eyes out. She knew Marie was watching her like a hawk and would follow her at the slightest sign of weakness. As much as she appreciated her friend's concern, Natalie wanted to be alone. She needed some downtime to process everything.

She tossed her purse inside the car, turned back to give Marie a hug. "Thanks for your concern, but I'll be okay."

"Are you sure?"

"Yes."

"Okay, but I want you to call me the minute you get home."

During the drive home, Natalie clutched the steering wheel tightly and tried to control the shudders that convulsed her body as soon as she pulled out of the parking lot. She silently cursed the person who had made her life so miserable these past few weeks.

The anguish and frustration accelerated when she had problems unlocking the townhouse door when she got home. As soon as she walked inside, she dropped her purse. She kicked it and the contents aside, grabbed books, magazines, anything non-breakable she could get her hands on, and threw them across the room.

When she ran out of objects, she paced non-stop between the kitchen and living room until she had exhausted her anger.

Bolting upstairs, she threw herself across her bed. She rolled over, reached for the box of tissues and let the tears come.

What was happening to her? What had she done to deserve this? Who was so determined to make her life a living hell these past weeks? As she sobbed herself to sleep, her last thoughts were the roar of the car engine as it raced past her.

She finally drifted off and slept until late in the afternoon. Exhaustion from a restless night, the scare this morning, and the tension of all the incidents these past weeks finally caught up with her.

Later that evening, she tried to put everything in perspective and made a list of everything that had happened. She noted the slashed tires, telephone calls, odd requests at work, moved items in her office and then the ransacked office. Too many scary incidents had happened. And they seemed to be getting scarier. She recalled the incident in the stairwell and the yellow car that came close enough to brush the hem of her sun dress.

She felt the baby move and rested her hand on her stomach to comfort it. Her jaw tightened, and she squeezed her fingers to her palm as fury raced through her. *If that car had hit her, she could have lost the baby.*

What was she going to do? She had obviously upset someone. Or was she being stalked? If so, she wasn't going to let whoever it was win.

Maybe she needed to alert the police. But did she have enough concerns for them to really believe her? She recalled visiting the stalking website. Reading how law enforcement tended to be slow reacting to stalking incidents. Reading the horror stories of those who had been murdered by their stalker. Did she have enough evidence? Was she really being staked?

All she knew was she needed her job. She couldn't afford to quit. Not yet anyway. Life might be a little easier now that she was published, but she still wasn't making enough to quit. And with a baby on the way, she'd have to stick it out a little while longer; hope whoever had taken a disliking to her would back off.

The heat and humidity made the Fourth of July almost unbearable. Natalie decided to stay in the cool, safe confines of her townhouse and do what she loved best: Write.

She did the same on Friday, but by nightfall, she'd had her fill of writing. She'd attained her goal for the week of words on the page and decided to take the weekend off. Decided she'd drive up to Baltimore for some sightseeing and much needed shopping.

The National Aquarium and Inner Harbor had always fascinated her and she needed to shop for some maternity clothes as well. Baltimore would be far enough away for her to shop without running into familiar faces. People who might question her need for a different wardrobe. She still hadn't mentioned the baby to anyone, not even Marie.

She called Marie, told her of her plans for the weekend, and promised to call as soon as she returned home Sunday evening.

Early Saturday morning, Natalie dressed in a purple plaid sundress, tossed her overnight bag in the car, and headed North.

She spent the morning walking through the Aquarium, studying the different species and laughing with a group of kids as they watched a diver feed the fish. After grabbing a quick lunch in one of the shops along the Harbor, she headed for the malls.

She was walking toward a maternity shop when she noticed a book store across the way and realized she'd forgotten to pack her Kindle. This might be a good time to stock up on the pregnancy and child care books she needed.

She paid no attention to the large crowd off one side of the entrance until she saw a display of Brian's newest release. The one he had autographed and mailed to her.

She stopped in her tracks when she saw the "autographing today" banner above the display. She realized the crowd was a group of Brian's fans.

As her gaze traveled across the store, she found herself staring into Brian's beautiful eyes.

CHAPTER 11

BRIAN BLINKED, EXPECTING THE IMAGE of Natalie to disappear as quickly as she had appeared. But when he looked again, she was still there. Natalie stood beside the display of his books, looking as surprised as he was.

His eyes feasted on her, his gaze travelling down her body from the slim straps of her purple plaid sundress to the sandals on her feet. She was radiant.

She was close enough he could see the flush of surprise on her cheeks.

It had been so long. His heart raced, his stomach clenched, and his hands ached to hold her. He ran a finger along the collar of his shirt and loosened the tie that suddenly confined his neck.

He wished it was the end of his signing not the beginning. He desperately wanted to be with her. Take her somewhere private. To kiss her. Love her.

A woman stepping up to the table blocked his view as she handed him a book. Brian smiled and quickly autographed it, worried that Natalie might leave before he could speak to her. He breathed a sigh of relief when she was still standing there when his fan stepped aside. It appeared she was frozen in place. She hadn't even moved.

Brian grabbed a bookmark and scribbled two words on it His heart almost stopped when he looked up and didn't see her. Was she an apparition after all? Had he missed her so much that he'd imagined her?

He frantically scanned the room and found her further down the aisle, peeking around another display. She continued to watch him, but seemed hesitant, almost shy, to approach.

Brian called to the store manager. "Would you give this to the young lady in the romance section? I believe she's wearing purple."

Brian watched the manager hand the bookmark to Natalie. She read the note and then looked back at him. He worried she was going to ignore it. Then her features softened and she nodded her head before wandering further down the aisle.

Brian tried to keep her in sight, hoped she would stay until the end of his signing, but she quickly disappeared.

Unease struck suddenly. His stomach burned and sweat trickled down his spine. He stared into the crowd. Sara was here. He could feel it. Sensed it. She was out there watching him.

With a sinking feeling, he worried that Sara had witnessed the manager give Natalie the note. After all this time, being so careful, he didn't want to risk endangering Natalie.

He was glad he'd told Natalie to call him, not meet him at the hotel. This way, they could arrange to meet somewhere else and avoid Sara altogether. It also helped that Natalie didn't know where he was staying; there was no way she'd show up unexpectedly and put herself in danger.

Despite the burning sensation, Brian smiled. For once, he was two steps ahead of Sara.

Natalie couldn't get out of the book store fast enough. She collapsed onto a bench at the far end of the mall, tried to fan her suddenly hot body.

Her heart still pounded from the thrill of seeing Brian in the flesh, and then worrying that he might have noticed her pregnancy. Although the sundress discreetly hid her condition, the evidence was there if you looked close enough.

She stared at the note the manager had given her with a simple, "Mr. Cato asked that I give this to you." Brian had scribbled a telephone number and *call me*, underlined.

Natalie didn't know what to do.

Obviously, Brian wanted to see her. Why else would he want her to call? But did she want to see him? Could she risk it? She knew that if he touched her or even gave her a closer look, he would immediately notice the changes in her body.

She sighed. He had looked so handsome in the chino pants, teal and purple stripped shirt, and teal tie. She felt her cheeks flush, imagined being in his arms again. His hands moving across her body, exciting her, driving her to distraction as only he could do.

It had been so long, but it felt like it could have been yesterday.

The baby fluttered, a tangible memento of their lovemaking. Reminding her why she'd come to the mall—maternity clothes and nursery things.

She spotted a Motherhood Maternity shop across the way and decided to start there.

If the hot weather kept up, she'd be able to wear the loose dresses a little longer before having to tell anyone. She paused to stare at her reflection in the window.

What would people say when she told them she was pregnant?

How would she explain it? She'd been divorced for almost two years, so they certainly wouldn't think it was Sam's baby. That's what made it so embarrassing. The fact that there had been no one for so long and she had become pregnant so quickly after meeting Brian.

Although her coworkers hadn't met him, Brian had already made an impression with his crazy, outlandish gifts. Many thought it was sweet, but she wondered what they would think when they realized she had conceived on their first real date.

Marie would understand. She had been one of the few friends to read her books. Marie had also been her strongest supporter during and after her bitter divorce from Sam.

Natalie browsed the racks. She needed dresses for work and slacks and tops for writing. She carried them into the dressing room and started changing.

She stood in front of the mirror and stared at her full breasts. She'd need all new underwear before long.

If she were to meet Brian tonight, would he be able to tell? Her eyes moved down to her slightly rounded stomach. Yes, he would. He'd known her as intimately as any man could know a woman and he'd know.

She wondered if he was still thinking about having a son, or if he had decided to give up. Regardless, what would he think about her condition? Would he welcome it or demand parental rights?

She continued to stare at her reflection. Would he really do that to her? They were friends. Would he attempt to take something so dear from her because of his own selfish wishes?

Sam had been like that when he wanted the divorce. No amount of counseling or discussions would sway him from ending their marriage. It was as if his feelings for her turned off like a burned out light bulb.

Would Brian do the same? Their relationship was a long-distance one, but he was always concerned, and friendly, whenever he called. She wanted to think that he wouldn't try to take her baby away from her.

But he was so driven to have a son. She recalled how he had planned everything out. Remembered his disappointment and frustration when things fell through with the surrogate.

Did he value their friendship enough to share his baby? Or would he try to nudge her aside? Snuff her out of his life as Sam had done.

Natalie quickly dressed, grabbed the clothes. She needed to get away as quickly as possible. She didn't know how long his book signing would be, but it had already been a couple hours.

She noticed the teddy bears displayed near the check-out counter, and realized she'd been so busy, she hadn't bought anything for the baby. She smiled, reached for the soft toy. Her first gift for her baby.

Her baby, she reminded herself.

She realized now that she couldn't risk meeting Brian tonight. Couldn't even call him. She paid for the dresses and left the store.

She glanced nervously at her watch, hoping that Brian would be busy for another hour. She didn't want to risk running into him and headed in the opposite direction of the bookstore.

Glancing over the railing to the shops below, Natalie knew she was near where she had parked her car. She might get out in time after all.

She reached for the hand rail to go down the steps, heard a scuffling noise, and felt a hard push from behind. Even as she lost her balance and fell forward, she recognized that it was most definitely a hand at the small of her back.

Almost in slow motion, Natalie tumbled down the long marble staircase. She had time to scream and then her world turned black.

Natalie awoke to a circle of worried faces. She raised a hand to her head and groaned while trying to sit up.

She hurt all over. Her knees, her back, and her arms. Everywhere.

"Hold on," she heard a man speak then felt a hand on her shoulder. "Just wait for the paramedics."

Natalie stared at the black security guard kneeling beside her. "What happened?" she asked.

"You fell. Don't you remember?"

"I remember being jostled from behind. Felt a hand at my back. But then everything went black when I started falling."

"You took a bad fall. If it weren't for your bags, it might've been more serious. They helped soften the blow."

"My baby," Natalie whispered, placed her hand on her stomach.

The guard frowned. "You're pregnant?"

Natalie nodded.

"Step aside," Natalie heard another man's voice. She almost panicked because it sounded so much like Brian and she worried that he had heard her scream and come running. When the crowd parted, Natalie recognized the medic uniform and breathed a sigh of relief. There were two of them, a tall, lanky man and a short woman with curly red hair.

They rolled a gurney between them.

Natalie saw the woman exchange looks with the guard before kneeling beside her. "Took a fall, did you?"

Natalie nodded.

Her expression was professionally reassuring. "My name is Megan and my partner here is Adam. We're going to give you a ride to the hospital." Natalie felt Megan's finger at her pulse.

"She's also pregnant," the security guard added.

Megan's smile brightened. "How far along?"

"Four months," Natalie answered.

"Do you feel any cramps or lower back or abdominal pains?"

"No. I don't think so."

"We still need to get you to the hospital, just to be safe."

Megan nudged the bags aside, prepared to check Natalie's blood pressure. "Are all these bags yours?"

Natalie nodded.

"It's a good thing. They might have protected your baby."

After checking for broken bones, Megan and Adam strapped a brace around her neck and with the help of the security guard, carefully lifted Natalie onto the gurney. The overhead lights flashed by as they raced out of the mall.

Natalie heard them toss her bags inside before lifting the gurney into the vehicle. Megan stayed with her while Adam drove them to the hospital.

Natalie tried to remain calm. With the collar, her vision was restricted to the roof of the ambulance or out of the corner of her eyes.

The constant swaying motion of the vehicle jarred her aching body from time to time, but she only prayed that her baby was okay.

She listened to Megan relaying her vital signs to the hospital. Suddenly she felt something warm and moist between her legs and realized her worst fears might be happening.

"Please hurry," she said out loud. "I think something's wrong."

Megan glanced up. "Why?"

"I think I'm spotting."

Megan rapped on the window. "Let's move it," she said to her partner.

Natalie felt the sudden surge of the vehicle and heard sirens.

"Looks like you're spending the night in the hospital. I know the doctor who's on call and he's good. Cautious, but good."

Natalie was relieved to be going to the hospital. It certainly wasn't how she planned to spend her weekend, but she wanted to be sure her baby was okay. Hopefully it would just be overnight.

Another thought occurred to her. "What about my car. What about my things?"

"Do you have family nearby?"

"No, I'm from out of town."

Megan smiled. "Don't worry, I'll take care of you. Do you remember where you parked your car? I'll call Joe, the security guard, and tell him to alert the others. Keys in your purse? Adam and I will move your car to the hospital valet parking area when we get off shift."

Minutes later, the ambulance stopped, and the doors flew open. Once again, she watched the ceiling lights flash as they wheeled her down a hall and into a small examining room.

Natalie began shaking as the trauma of her fall settled in. She was exhausted. Drained. Worried about her baby. She tried to keep calm while Megan discussed her vital signs with the doctor on duty.

"Do you have anyone with you?" a nurse asked.

Natalie tried to shake her head. "No."

"Let's get you settled. Ready?" The nurse looked at Adam before they transferred her from the gurney to the hospital bed. "We can do the paperwork after the doctor checks you out."

Natalie stared at the pale lavender walls and then the white ceiling, tried not to think about the pain and worry about her baby.

Adam returned with her purse. "I left the packages in the vehicle but thought you might need this."

Natalie asked Megan to look in her wallet for her insurance card which brought an instant smile to the nurse's face.

"I'll be right back," she said, "and the doctor will be with you as soon as he can."

Natalie sighed, felt Megan take her hand.

"Everything's going to be okay," she said, smiling. "Dr. Carlton will check you out and make things right. The nurse on duty is a friend of mine; she'll take good care of you."

"Thank you. For everything." She handed Megan her car keys.

"I'll bring them back to you when we get the car moved. We'll put your bags in the trunk." She squeezed Natalie's hand. "Don't worry."

Natalie listened to the people walk, race, or stagger past her open door. She heard moans, crying babies, even laughter at the nurses' station. How much longer before the doctor got here?

Moments later, a tall, slender man with salt and pepper hair strolled in. He was reading her chart, then set it on the counter and stared at her over his bifocals.

"How are you feeling?" His hands moved softly up her arms and legs. "Any cramps?"

"No. But I think I might be bleeding."

He checked her eyes. "Before I do an internal examination, I want to schedule an ultrasound. After we receive the results of that, I'll be better prepared to talk."

Natalie jumped when flashbacks of the fall awakened her. She must have dozed off. She stared at the clock. It had been six hours and so far, there had been no pain. Only the spotting. The ultrasound technicians had been encouraging, but close-mouthed.

Dr. Carlton came in, her chart in his hands. He stopped at the foot of her bed. "It looks like everything is okay." He smiled. "You were very lucky."

"What about the bleeding?"

"The placenta may have been jostled during the fall, but the ultrasound shows that the baby is okay. I want you to have a more thorough examination with your own doctor as soon as you get home. Have you felt any movement?"

"A little."

"Good. Did you listen to his heartbeat when they did the ultrasound?"

Natalie smiled. "Yes, it was so loud. Does that mean the baby is going to be okay?"

"For now, I'd say yes, but if you have any more spotting, your doctor will probably put you on bed rest. But I'm pretty certain that your baby boy will be fine."

"Boy?"

The doctor looked over the rim of his glasses "You didn't know?"

Natalie shook her head.

"I thought the nurse told you it was a boy."

Natalie laughed. "No, and I didn't think to ask, I was so concerned."

"Well," he grinned, "I'd say you're carrying a strong healthy baby and five months from now you should be holding a seven-pound boy in your arms."

Natalie's eyes filled with tears of relief. A boy, she thought. The son Brian so desperately wanted.

Now, more than ever, she needed to stay away from him.

The aroma of her perfume surrounded him as he saw her at the door. She just stood there, watching him, her eyes full of passion. Out of nowhere, a breeze blew her hair away from her face, making her red gown shimmer against her sleek body, caressing her full breasts and slim hips.

He was speechless, his body pulsed with his tremendous need for her. He was supposed to be resting, but the sight of her chased away any thoughts of sleep.

She stepped toward him, raised the hem of her gown, and crawled from the end of the bed. His heart raced when she straddled him, making him want her even more.

She leaned forward her hands moved up his chest, nudged the robe aside and kissed his chest, shoulders, and neck. He was breathless, unable to touch her because his arms were trapped under the robe.

His heart pounded when she took him inside her, her hot flesh hugging his. He watched her eyes darken as she threw her head back and rode him. Each stroke took him deeper inside. He wanted to shout, exclaim his love for her, but was silenced by the intimacy.

A loud noise shattered the scene.

Brian's eyes snapped open and he stared at the ceiling. His heart still pounded. That had been one hot steamy fantasy. He grabbed for the ringing telephone.

"Hello," he growled into the receiver. "Who's there?" He demanded but was answered with a click and silence.

"Where the hell is she?" Brian barked when Max joined him thirty minutes later. "We were this close." He pinched his two fingers almost together. "I've called her cell, but it always goes to voice mail."

Brian thrust his arms up in frustration, stared at his friend. "Does she ever leave her phone on? Why hasn't she called?"

Max sat at the table and let him vent. He'd never seen his friend so worked up about a woman before. Brian had called him after Natalie failed to contact him. Since he was a few hours away, he'd decided to drive to Baltimore and help with the search. Fitz wasn't quite ready for a search and rescue challenge, so he'd left him with Bo for the day.

"I can check it out. Make some calls. Try the hospitals."

Brian stopped pacing, realized that Max had caught the brunt of his anger. He was upset, but that didn't mean he had to take it out on Max.

He just couldn't understand why Natalie hadn't called. Had something happened? Had that fantasy been like an omen?

He threaded his hands through his hair in frustration. "I'm sorry. It's just," he collapsed in the other chair. "When I saw her, she insinuated that she would call. Now I don't know whether she changed her mind or if something happened."

"I hate to add more fuel to the fire, but I saw Sara downstairs when I came in."

"I knew it," Brian muttered. "I could feel it at the bookstore, but hoped it wasn't true." He paced to the window, stared at the parking lot below. "She was probably the hang up I just had. God forbid that she should find out about Natalie. I can't risk trying to find her and then having Sara stalk Natalie too."

"I can look for Natalie." Max said. "After you leave."

"No. I think Sara has reached the point that she'd even watch you." Brian collapsed in the chair again.

"She can't watch us both at the same time. Not if we go in opposite directions."

"I realize that, but I don't want to risk putting Natalie in any danger. My tour is almost over. Let's wait. Think about it. Put together a plan. One way or another, I need to visit Natalie. Make amends for these strained months."

Deadly green eyes watched the people go about their business in the hotel lobby. She was tired of sitting, but it had all been worth it.

She smiled as she recalled watching the woman fall down the stairs. It had infuriated her when she saw the bookstore guy give her Brian's note. Then she couldn't believe her luck when the woman raced past her in the mall. She was so close, she could have tripped her then.

Sara knew the woman was spending the night in the hospital. She had followed the ambulance, then hung around in the waiting room. When the woman didn't come out, she'd pretended to be a concerned friend and thanked them when they allowed her back to the examining rooms.

When she couldn't find her in any of the cubicles, she wandered back to the front desk and learned that she had been checked into a room on the third floor.

Now, she was camped out in the lobby of Brian's hotel. She even saw Max come in a while ago. She'd have to move on soon. Management had been giving her some suspicious looks.

She smiled and headed for the women's restroom.

It was a matter of time now. Brian was almost finished with his tour and would return to her once more.

CHAPTER 12

NATALIE DROPPED HER OVERNIGHT BAG by the door as soon as she stepped inside her townhouse. Dr. Carlton had released her late that afternoon with stern instructions to see Dr. Smith as soon as possible.

She still couldn't believe she was carrying the baby boy Brian so desperately wanted. She felt guilty that she was keeping the news from him.

She wondered what he did when she failed to call him. Not that she could have. It was late when she finally located her cellphone in her purse and saw that it needed to be charged. And of course, she didn't have her charger with her.

She saw the flashing lights on her recorder and winced when she saw there were fifteen messages. He had probably called her townhouse instead. The phone rang just as she was listening to the last one.

"Where the hell have you been?" Brian demanded as soon as she picked up the receiver.

"I just got home."

"Why so late? And why didn't you call me last night?"

She had her lie all ready. "I'm sorry, Brian, but right after I left the bookstore, I ran into an old college friend who had settled in the Baltimore area. We got to talking and shopped some and time just slipped away. I'm sorry, I should have called you."

She reached for the phone and plugged it into her charger. "I hope you weren't too upset."

"Of course, I was upset. I didn't know whether something had happened to you, or if you'd just decided not to show."

"Brian, I'm sorry. I really am. But I couldn't help it. When I went to call you, I saw that my cellphone needed to be charged. And of course, I didn't have my charger. And there were so many hotels in Baltimore, I didn't know where to start." That sounded good, she thought. "And being the celebrity you are, I doubted anyone would tell me if you were registered there." That sounded even better, she congratulated herself.

"I hadn't thought of that. I was registered under an alias anyway."

There was a loud knock at her door. "Hold on, someone's at my door," Natalie lay the receiver on the dinette table.

She looked through the peephole and saw Marie standing on her doorstep. "What are you doing here?"

"I was worried when you didn't answer your phone."

"So was Brian. Come on in, he's still on the telephone."

Natalie returned to her conversation with Brian with an excuse to end it.

"Natalie, is there something you need to tell me? Is it my imagination, or are you pregnant?"

Natalie glanced at her friend, saw she was staring at her stomach. While talking to Brian she had placed a hand over the baby, stroked her belly as if to shield him from Brian.

Tonight was turning out to be a big one for lies, she thought. Or maybe confession would be better. She was tired of having to keep it to herself and since Marie already suspected something, now would be a good time to share the whole truth.

"Let's sit on the sofa. I think you'll need to by the time I'm finished with my story."

"Sounds like a winner," Marie joked.

"Do you remember that writers' conference I went to in Philadelphia?"

Marie nodded.

"That's where it all started. That's where I met Brian Cato."

Marie's jaw dropped. "The Brian Cato" Natalie watched as Marie seemed to put two and two together. "So Brian Cato sent you the book?" Her eyes grew wide. "The real Brian Cato? We all thought you had a secret admirer," she exclaimed. "That a friend had had it autographed for you. Not the real Brian Cato."

Natalie smiled. "He was the keynote speaker and we met in the elevator and then he literally swept me off my feet. I slept with him the second time we were together," she rambled, embarrassed to have been so loose with her affections. Her body.

Marie reached for her hand and chuckled. "Honey, with a man as good looking as Brian Cato, I can fully understand."

"I'm not normally like that. You know that. But he's so charming, funny, sweet, engaging, seductive..." Natalie sighed, and Marie chuckled a second time.

"I get the picture."

Natalie smiled sheepishly. "To make a long story short, we used no protection and I'm pregnant."

"Does Brian know?"

"No. And I can't tell him." She sighed when Marie shook her head in confusion. "You see, Brian wants a son. Really wants a son, but through a surrogate. When I met him, he was negotiating with a woman, but it apparently fell through. I almost told him once but worried he might manipulate things and try to take the baby away from me. I mean, he's rich and could provide so much more for a child."

"Really?" Marie asked. "Is he that callous that he would try to take your baby away from you?"

"It's not so much callous but the fact that he desperately wants a son. And I'm carrying that son."

"Wow."

"More than that," Natalie continued, "Things have been happening since I met Brian. Remember the reason I was off from work? My ransacked office? And the time you and I were almost run over by that crazy driver?"

Marie reached for Natalie's hand.

"I've also been getting hang ups both at home and at work, my phone line has been cut. And my tires have even been slashed."

Natalie stood and walked to the window. "My life was so ho hum until I met Brian Cato." She turned to look at Marie. "I know there are lots of women who are having children by themselves but I'm not like that. What will people say?"

Marie stared at her. "You're not the first woman this has happened to, you know," she finally said.

"I know but still, I worry about what people will think."

"Forget about what people will think. I wish I'd been as strong as you when it happened to me." Marie leaned back on the sofa.

"You?" Natalie returned to the sofa. "You got pregnant?"

"Yes. My junior year in college, I was dating this guy pretty regularly. We took precautions, but I still got pregnant. He was going to medical school and had bigger plans for his future. Dropped me like a hot potato. I knew my parents would be really upset and I had no way to support myself if I quit school. So," she shrugged her shoulders, "I sponged some money from some friends and had an abortion." Marie reached for Natalie's hand. "To this day, I've often wondered whether it was a boy or a girl, and what he or she would have been like." Her eyes filled with tears. "And every May fifteenth, I get this sick feeling in my stomach and cry for hours on end."

"You had no choice, Marie. You were so young."

"I'm so sorry. I wish I'd been stronger. Like you." She squeezed Natalie's hand. "Don't worry about what everybody says."

It was August, and everyone was getting ready for the fall semester. Soon the students would be back, research papers would be assigned, and it would be a race to see who would buckle first—the students or the library staff.

In addition to her regular cataloging responsibilities, Natalie helped track down resources, even worked the front desk while pages were being trained. Every Fall they also inventoried the library science classrooms which meant long days and tired backs.

Word was out that she was pregnant and despite her worries, everyone had been very congenial and supportive. Students and faculty were excited for her and Natalie often wondered if Marie had something to do with it.

She was headed out her office door when her cell phone rang.

"What are you wearing?" A male voice asked.

Natalie stared at the phone. She recognized the voice but was surprised by the words. "What would you like me to be wearing?" She whispered, playing along.

"Something seductive. I miss you," Brian said.

Natalie shut the door and returned to her desk. "Well, it's long. Red. Sheer. And flowing."

"Yeah?" Brian croaked.

Natalie smiled. "And I'm having some sparkling wine with my lunch. Too bad you're not here to enjoy it with me."

Brian laughed. "I'm sorry too. Did I mention that I miss you?"

"I miss you too. In fact, if you were here, I'd probably end up spilling the wine across your chest." Natalie listened to the silence and grinned. "Then I'd have to unbutton your shirt to lick it off. You know how I hate to waste wine?"

The silence continued.

"Brian? Are you there? Would you like me to tell you what I had in mind for dessert?"

Brian cleared his throat. "Ah, I can vividly imagine what you've got in mind. Does your office have a closet?"

Natalie laughed. "No, but I'm sure we could find one somewhere in this big library."

"You know, I'm between flights and thought I'd give you a call while I wait. Now, I need a medic. I'm sweating, my heart's racing and my collar's too tight. You've aroused me, I'm not fit to be seen in public."

"You're the one that started this conversation."

"I miss you. But it won't be for much longer. This tour is almost over. I'm looking forward to getting home and back to writing. Did I tell you I saw Matt Avery the other day?"

"The Matt Avery? The actor? Wow" she exclaimed. Matt Avery was one of those actors that had been around a long time and aged well. She didn't know too many women that hadn't been in love with him at some time in their life.

"Yeah. I mentored him a few years ago when he did his first Nick Armstrong movie. You like him?"

"What woman doesn't? Is he as awesome in person as he is in the movies?"

"He's one of a kind. Powerful and intense but friendly and generous too. Told me he'll be needing me again in a few months for another movie."

Brian ended their call because his flight was announced, and Natalie remained seated at her desk. If Brian was near the end of his tour, that meant she might be seeing him soon. What would he say when he saw how pregnant she was? He hadn't mentioned a surrogate for weeks. Had he given up? Would he pressure her for shared custody of their baby?

Should she start distancing herself? Maybe if she wasn't available when he returned home, and their calls became infrequent, their relationship might change to long distance friends.

If that were to happen, she would miss his deep voice that always offered opinions, jokes, or murmurs of desire. He always made her feel good whenever they ended a call.

Natalie stretched, rubbed her lower back. She'd have to give that some thought. Right now, she needed to finish working on a shipment of books, matching invoices and sorting the titles for processing.

Two days later, Natalie leaned against the wall, hoping to relieve some of the pressure on her back. She'd been busy with the inventorying and still had one classroom to do before calling it quits for the day.

She smiled and touched her swelling stomach when the baby moved. He moved again, and she almost laughed when she felt the brush of what could be a head, foot, or elbow.

It had been over a month since that disastrous weekend in Baltimore, but her baby was growing and appeared to have suffered no ill effects from her fall down the steps. She'd called Dr. Smith, who immediately ordered another ultrasound and confirmed that all was well with her baby and she was indeed having a boy.

The hang-ups continued. Marie had talked her into changing her cell number and promised never to divulge the number to anyone.

There were still frequent hang-ups at home and work, but the numbers were always different.

Dr. McAllister tapped on the door to her office. As with Heather's reference books, Dr. McAllister had denied asking her to pull the children's books. "How's it going?"

"Great," Natalie pushed away from the wall. "I have one more room and then we'll be caught up."

"I'm glad it's you and not me," she said jokingly. "Although I have my own work cut out for me." She patted the arm full of papers.

"Have fun," Natalie laughed. She reached for the computer-generated list and headed down the hall. In addition to their offices being on one hall, library science classes were held in many of the classrooms on the other halls. Reference resources were available in each of the classrooms and Natalie was on her last room. She worked her way through the desks toward the shelves at the back and prepared to get busy. The quicker she got started, the sooner she could get home and finish that chapter she'd plotted a couple days ago.

An hour later, Natalie had four more shelves to finish when she realized she had been subconsciously listening to someone close the doors along the hallway. She raised her head and listened, tracked the footsteps as they moved slowly up the corridor and stopped long enough to click another door shut.

She glanced at her watch. Five thirty. Too soon for the janitor. Besides, he would spend time in each room, sweeping it, straightening the desks, collecting the trash, not just closing the doors.

Memories of her nightmares in the stacks and on the stairs haunted her. She had a sudden urge to hurry and get this job finished. Maybe come in early in the morning and finish the last shelves. She had just leaned down to grab some books off the bottom shelf when the lights went out and the door was slammed shut.

Natalie remained where she was.

She was certain that someone was in the room with her. She sensed it. A cold chill crept up her back. Was this the same person who had locked her in the stairwell?

Except for Marie who was working in her office on the other hall, she was sure there was no one else on their basement floor.

What if something had happened to Marie?

Drawing a mental map of the darkened but generic classroom, she knew there were rows of desks between her and the intruder who was still at the front of the classroom. She remembered seeing a file cabinet in the far corner at the back of the room. Hopefully, there would be enough space between the cabinet and the wall for her to hide for protection. If she could get there, maybe she could wait out until the intruder gave up in frustration.

She held her breath and debated whether she could move without making any noise. You'll never know unless you try, she scolded herself.

Ever so carefully, Natalie stood and inched her way across the pitch-black room. The only light was a thin beam from the hall at the bottom of the door, which made the blackness more ominous.

Natalie held her breath, tried to focus on the other person in the room. She could hear the heavy breathing and feel the tension emanating from across the room. There was hatred in that tension. Someone wanted to hurt her.

She recalled the hand that had pushed her down the steps at the mall. And the car that had tried to run her down that day her office had been ransacked. Was this the same person?

She compared the slow steps in the hall with those on the stairwell. This had to be the same person.

Why? She almost groaned. Why was someone so determined to harm her? Was it because of Brian? All she did was go to work and then home to write. Not the life to be envied by anyone.

She could count on one hand her close friends. Certainly, not the social circle to be jealous of.

She stretched her hand out, felt the back of a desk. Recalled where she was before the lights went out. She calculated that there should be one more row of desks before the counter that lined the long wall leading to the file cabinet. She quietly took another step to the side, reached out, and felt the back of the next desk. She breathed a sigh of relief.

So far, so good, she thought as she took another cautious step past the desk, feeling for the counter beyond. Suddenly her hand brushed something tall that immediately tilted over. It might have been pencils or pens, but they sounded like fireworks—and alerted the intruder of her whereabouts.

Natalie held her breath, waiting to hear if her intruder would move.

First, she heard a snicker, then an evil laugh that almost had her knees buckling beneath her. Her stomach stiffened, as if the baby himself sensed danger.

Her intruder was playing her own cat and mouse game. Natalie realized the laugh seemed to be coming from near the door. It became louder as the breathing became heavier.

Did this lunatic intend to hurt her or just want to scare her? Whatever, Natalie decided she wasn't going to make it easy. Since the intruder was between her and the door, she needed to get closer to the protection of the file cabinet. She silently inched her way toward the far corner and the intruder became silent, as if listening for her; tracking her movements.

Natalie reached out and touched metal, felt the handle to a drawer and realized that she was standing in front of it.

As a blind person would read someone's face, she traced the outline of the cabinet. Cautiously checked to be sure nothing had been stored in the corner. Found a long rod and realized it must be a broom. She smiled with grim determination. At least she had a weapon. Nobody was going to hurt her baby. She backed into the corner, holding the broom in front of her, ready for attack. Two could play this game, she thought, as she waited for her intruder to make the next move.

Minutes seemed like hours as Natalie leaned against the wall, poised for action. The muscles in her legs and neck became tight, screaming with the tension that continued to build. If it hadn't been for the laugh, she would have thought she might have imagined it.

Suddenly she heard a noise from across the room. Whoever it was must have bumped into one of the desks. Ran into another—and then another. Natalie could hear the breathing become angrier, more uneven.

Her intruder was becoming frustrated. Natalie prepared to defend herself, raised the broom a little higher.

"I'm warning you to leave him alone," a female voice spoke from across the room. "You didn't seem to heed any of my other warnings, but I promise you, next time will be the last."

Natalie wondered if she had heard that voice before.

"He's mine," the voice shouted. "You can't have him."

Natalie's mouth fell open at the force behind the crazed voice. Who was 'he'? Was she talking about Brian?

She wondered if maybe it was a student playing some sort of sick joke. Until the voice spoke once more.

"You might be carrying his child, but there is no way he will love you. He loves me! Do you hear?"

Brian? She almost said it out loud. This woman was talking about Brian.

One more confirmation of her fears that everything had started after she met Brian in Philadelphia. The phone calls, the cut telephone line, the incident in the stairwell, the mixed up messages, her ransacked office. The dead roses.

The pranks were becoming more dangerous. Natalie recalled the hand that pushed her down the steps at the mall and became angry. She started to speak out. That fall could have hurt her baby. No one had the right to endanger a child.

Suddenly the lights were switched on and the door thrown open. Blinded by the sudden brightness and shocked at the sound of the door hitting the wall, Natalie missed seeing the person leave. She couldn't move, just remaining huddled in the corner, allowing the sounds of silence to surround her.

After a minute, Natalie stepped out of her hiding place and moved cautiously toward the front of the room. She stood at the door, listened. She thought she could hear footsteps further along the hall and dashed out of the room down the long corridor in the opposite direction.

The sound of a door opening around the corner ahead of her brought her to a stop. She leaned her back against the wall while her heart pounded. Footsteps moved slowly, steadily. Was the intruder returning?

Natalie panicked. There was no place to quickly hide in the open hallway because the doors had been shut. Even if she got to a door and opened it, whoever was around the corner would hear.

Was her intruder playing another game? Was this why she had shut the doors before? Had it been her way of getting Natalie to come out of the classroom?

Natalie realized she still carried the broom and raised it, ready to strike whoever rounded the corner. She listened as the steps became louder, came closer and closer.

There was maybe ten feet between her and her assailant when she came around the corner. More than enough room to launch an attack. Natalie held her breath when she saw a man's shoe? It was a very expensive looking shoe that complimented an equally expensive pair of pants.

Natalie followed the leg up to the chest and face as the figure appeared around the corner. Before she could raise the broom any higher, she gasped and fainted.

CHAPTER 13

NATALIE FELT LIKE SHE WAS floating in water. Her head bobbed against a hard object. She moaned only to be shushed by a too-familiar male voice.

She stiffened, realized she wasn't floating, but was being carried in strong arms that held her close. Her head bobbed again as she tried to remember why someone would be carrying her. Her heart rate tripled when the previous minutes flashed before her. She remembered being threatened in the classroom, sneaking up the hall and then seeing Brian come around the corner.

Brian.

Her eyes flew open and she lifted her head to see him. In the flesh.

Expressionless, Brian stared straight ahead as he carried her down the hall, turned into her office and gently set her in her chair. He took a second to swing the door shut, then returned to her side.

He knelt, reached for her hand. "Any particular reason why you would come after me with a broom?"

"I was scared."

"Of what? Me?"

"No. Someone—"

"Natalie?" Marie called out from down the hall. Natalie could hear her running toward them. Marie pounded on her door. "Natalie, are you in there? Are you okay?"

"Brian, please let Marie in. She's my friend and I know she's worried."

Natalie heard Marie's gasp when he opened the door, watched her lean against the jam, one hand pressed to the back of her head. Her complexion was alabaster, and she looked like she had a full-blown headache.

"Maybe I should ask the same of you?" Natalie said. "Are you okay? What happened?"

"I don't know," Marie moaned. "One minute I was working at my computer and the next I was seeing stars." She nodded her head from shoulder to shoulder. "When I woke up, my head was splitting, and I thought I heard someone run past my office."

"Did you see her? Did you see who it was?" Natalie exclaimed.

"No," she groaned. "Only stars. But I heard a door slam behind her." Marie winced. "What happened?"

Natalie looked at Brian, debated what to say. Whoever had trapped her in the classroom never mentioned him by name, but there was no doubting he was the object of this woman's affections. She wondered if he was aware that someone was in love with him.

Or could he be involved?

Everything had started happening right after that weekend in Philadelphia. Could he be responsible? Why? She couldn't imagine him doing all those things just to plot a story. Was he secretly married?

"Someone tried to scare me while I inventoried a classroom."

"I'd say they succeeded," Brian spoke. "You were as white as a sheet when I saw you."

"Again!" Marie exclaimed. "Someone did it again? That's it, I'm going to call security," she said over her shoulder as she headed to the office. Natalie sighed. Marie could have used her phone.

Brian stared at her. "What did she mean by that? Has this happened before?"

"Yes. A few weeks ago, I was locked in the stairwell."

"Why didn't you tell me?"

"Why should I? And at the time it didn't seem so important until—" she recalled her office being ransacked the next day.

"Until what?" He sounded agitated.

"Until my office was ransacked."

Brian jumped up, brushed a hand through his hair, began pacing the room. "My God, where's the security around here?"

"I'm sure it's just some kids," she said with no real enthusiasm.

Suddenly, events were becoming too coincidental. She needed to think things through before saying too much more.

Brian turned to stare at Natalie, saw the circles under her wide eyes, tight lips and tense shoulders. There was more to this than she was letting on.

His attention focused on her belly. Had she put on a little weight? he wondered or—

Watery eyes stared across at him.

He knelt beside her once more, shyly lifted a large hand to rest it on her swollen belly.

Natalie watched his eyes grow soft and then round as she felt the baby move against his hand. A tear fell down her cheek.

"Is there something else I should know?"

Natalie gripped his hand, held it tightly. "I'm pregnant," was all she could manage.

He smiled, his thumb lightly brushed the tear aside. "I gathered that. When did-?"

"They should be here in a few minutes," Marie rushed into the office. She skidded to a halt, her eyes widening as she registered that Brian was still kneeling beside Natalie, his hand on her stomach. "You must be Brian."

He looked up at her, then stood, extending his right hand. "Yes. I'm Brian Cato, a—" he paused and turned back to Natalie. "A close friend of Natalie's."

"Considering Natalie's condition, I'd say you were very close," Marie blurted out, then covered her mouth. "I'm so sorry," she looked apologetically at Natalie. "It just came out."

Brian smiled as he turned back to Natalie who stared at him with more tears streaming down her face. It was obvious she was still affected by the events of the evening, but now he saw fear, concern, and a little embarrassment in her eyes.

He turned back to Marie. "Could you give us a few minutes before security gets here?

"Oh. Yes. Sure. Of course," Marie jumped into action and backed out of the room. "I'll...I'll tell them what happened to me first." She closed the door behind her.

Brian reached for Natalie's hand, pulling her out of the chair into his arms.

"I've missed you," he murmured into her ear, holding her tight. "You don't know how my heart stopped when I saw you collapse like that. I didn't think I was going to catch you before you hit the floor."

"I'm sorry," she whispered into his shirt as tears flowed down her cheeks. "I was so scared. When you came around that corner, I don't know whether I was relieved or surprised."

"I'd be willing to bet it was surprise." He kissed her forehead, hugged her closer. "We can talk about the baby later. When we have a little more privacy. All I want to know right now is whether you're okay?"

"I'm fine" She rested her cheek against his chest. "Now."

Marie knocked at the door. She opened it slowly before entering with two officers in tow. Natalie recognized Jeremy Scott and Ray Butler.

"I know I promised you some time, but my story didn't take too long," Marie apologized, turning back to the officers who had been on duty when Natalie's office was ransacked.

"Ms. Stover." Jeremy Scott looked around at her office. "Your office looks better than the last time we were here. I'm sorry to be here again though. Are you okay? Can you tell us what happened?"

"I was taking inventory in Dr. McAllister's classroom. I thought I heard the doors to other classrooms being closed. Then suddenly the lights went out. The door was slammed shut and I was in the dark."

"Could you tell whether anyone was in the room?" Jeremy asked.

"At first, I wasn't sure but then I heard some heavy breathing. I was familiar with the room and knew I was near a file cabinet. I managed to get in the corner. I found a broom beside the cabinet and just waited."

"How long did you wait?"

"It felt like hours but I'm sure it was only a few minutes. First, she laughed,"

"She?" Jeremy and Brian said at the same time.

"Yes. It was a woman. At first, she laughed and then she must have tried to move, I heard her bumping into the desks. Then she got mad. Hollered at me."

"What did she say?" Jeremy asked.

Natalie peeked up at Brian. "She said, 'He's mine. You can't have him.'"

Natalie watched color drain from Brian's face. She reached for his hand. "I wasn't sure who this man was and thought maybe it was a student trying to scare another student.

Suddenly, the lights came on, the door slammed against the wall and I heard footsteps running up the hall. I waited a minute, then I ran in the opposite direction. That's when I ran into Mr. Cato."

"Can you show us Dr. McAllister's room?" Jeremy Scott asked.

Natalie led them to the room, where they found the pens and pencils splayed across the floor and several of the desks out of place.

"Did she say or do anything else?" Jeremy asked.

Natalie glanced at Brian who paced the back of the room between where she had worked and the file cabinet. She shook her head and decided not to mention that the intruder may have known him. Until she knew more about how Brian might be involved, she would keep it to herself.

Ray Butler had been making notes in his pad. "I'll go check with the main desk to see if they noticed anyone suspicious."

"I hope you understand we might not be able to apprehend this woman. Unless it's someone who has been giving you problems. If you have a name, we can certainly check her whereabouts. See if she has an alibi."

Natalie wondered if Brian should be the one answering this question. "I'm sure it was someone playing a sick joke," she finally said.

"Real sick." Marie rubbed the back of her head. She followed the security officers as they left, turning to head toward her office.

Natalie watched her friend walk away and realized that someone approaching Marie from the back might confuse Marie for her. They both had the same length hair that was close to the same color. She wondered if the intruder struck Marie by mistake and when she realized she had struck the wrong person, came looking for her.

Or did she hit Marie on purpose? So no one would be able to come to her defense?

Natalie stared at Brian. Before the evening was out, she intended to get a full list of his colleagues.

Natalie watched the two security guys head for the stairs to the main level. Worried about Marie, she turned to Brian. "I really need to be sure Marie is okay." And followed Marie down the hall. "Would you like to come home with me, Marie? You're welcome to stay in my spare bedroom tonight."

"No, I'm fine." She lifted a hand to Natalie's arm when she started to protest. "Really. I'm fine. I think I'll just stop by the Health Clinic though, see if one of the doctors can give me a mild sedative." She smiled at Brian. "You have company, anyway."

"At least let us follow you home," Brian said.

An hour later, Brian pulled up in front of Natalie's townhouse. They had left her car in the college parking lot, waited as Marie stopped at the Clinic, then followed Natalie's friend to her apartment. He made Natalie wait in the locked car while he checked Marie's apartment.

Brian turned the car off, went around to open the passenger side door and help Natalie out. After tonight, he was determined Natalie would never be out of his sight again.

Was it Sara that had frightened Natalie? Obviously, not just once but several times. Despite all his precautions, had Sara found out about Natalie? Was that why she had been absent lately? She had shifted her attention to Natalie?

He doubted he would ever forget that feeling of utter helplessness watching Natalie collapse in the hall. Her terror-filled eyes would haunt him forever.

She still had a scared look when he helped her out of the car. Was she up to facing all they needed to discuss?

He followed her to the front door. Too much had happened while he'd been on his tour. He'd give her fifteen minutes to compose herself before he started the questions—and explanations.

Natalie dropped her purse by the door and headed toward the kitchen. It was after eight and she was famished. She also had her baby to consider.

If Brian weren't here, she'd probably just fix herself a sandwich and then go to bed. To cry. But she knew they had a lot to discuss and she wasn't sure she was up to it. She needed to eat not only for the health of the baby, but to fortify herself for the brewing confrontation.

She heard Brian behind her, felt his hands on her shoulders.

"Let's order something," he whispered near her ear. "You're exhausted. And we have a lot of catching up to do. What'll it be? Chinese? Pizza?"

An hour later, they were seated at the small table in her kitchen. Brian grabbed the last slice of pizza. "Can't say that pizza is the healthiest food for a pregnant mom, but at this hour, anything works.

Natalie had changed into her long fleece robe; Brian into his jeans and sweatshirt.

He had planned to get a room nearby, but considering what had happened, and the late-night conversation they had ahead of them, he suggested that he stay here.

Natalie sat back and watched him eat.

He'd called her a mom. Until now, she'd never thought of herself as a mother. It had always been the baby. Eating for the baby. Buying clothes for the baby. Protecting the baby.

"I'm sorry I didn't tell you, but I had my reasons."

Brian wiped his hands on a napkin. "I'd be interested in hearing some of those reasons."

"First, it was such a surprise. Sam and I tried to have a baby for several years but never succeeded."

"Maybe he wasn't the right candidate." Brian leaned back in his chair.

"Apparently so, in light of what happened. Anyway," she sighed, "for several days I was in a state of shock. I didn't know what to do, what to say, or how I'd handle it."

She stood, carried the empty box to the trash, and remained standing beside the sink. She needed some distance between them.

"Did you know when you met me in Richmond? At the Museum?"

"Yes. I'd just found out."

"Why didn't you tell me then?"

"Think about it, Brian. You were negotiating with that surrogate mother. All I could think about was what you'd said about wanting a son and no wife or mother. And having just met you, how was I to know that you wouldn't try to take the baby away from me?"

She returned to the table and sat back down. "I still don't know." Her eyes filled with tears. "Even now."

Brian reached for her hand, started to say something but she continued. "I was so confused. I almost said something, but when you told me that the negotiations with the surrogate had fallen through, I got scared." She sobbed. "The only thing I could think was that you'd come after my baby."

Brian was speechless. It was his turn to pace. He shoved his hands in his pockets in frustration and moved toward the living room. Everything she said was true. Considering how he had gone on about how much he wanted a son, he could understand her hesitancy.

But he wouldn't have taken her baby, their baby, away from her. He turned, saw her elbow on the table, head in her hand. He hated seeing her so upset and found himself kneeling in front of her.

"You are carrying our baby," he said silently. "Our baby," he repeated.

"Yes, but when you completely ignored me at the dinner that night, I didn't know what to think." A tear streaked down her cheek. "Brian, that really hurt."

Memories of the evening at the Virginia Museum flashed back. She had been hurt by his withdrawal and he had been worried about Sara. "I'm sorry. I didn't mean for that to happen."

Another tear escaped down her cheek. "Brian, I didn't know what to think. If you can turn your feelings off so easily, how could I know you wouldn't take my baby?"

"Considering how I acted, I don't blame you. But Natalie, I would never do that to you. This is our baby," he repeated. "Something we created together."

"But how do you know? Think about it. You were desperate. Determined to have a son. Can you honestly say you wouldn't have thought about taking my baby? At that time?"

"I admit I might have considered it," he conceded, "but I do not think for one minute I'd have done anything. Natalie," he squeezed her hand, "this baby is our creation, not some fetus from an egg fertilized in a test tube then implanted in a virtual stranger. Some woman whose primary interest was the money."

He lifted her chin, looked directly into her eyes. "Natalie, I'm not saying I wouldn't have wanted this baby, but I wouldn't have taken it away from you either. What you said about a mother's love was beginning to sink in."

Natalie gave him a watery smile.

"You got me thinking about it. A lot. I'd even reconsidered my original goals. Now that you're pregnant, I want us to get married and raise this baby together."

"No." She stared at him in surprise. She stood and paced toward the living room "I will not marry you."

Brian rested his forehead on the table. Somehow, he knew she was going to say that.

"You said you had no room for a woman in your life," Natalie continued from the living room. "And I won't use this baby to trap you into marriage. Right now, I don't want to do anything but have a healthy baby." She turned when he followed her into the living room. "This is all new to you. I've had five months to adjust to it. I don't want to do anything we might regret after the baby arrives."

Before Brian could speak, the telephone rang. Natalie grabbed for it but heard the disconnection before she could even say hello. She slammed the receiver down in anger, returning to their conversation.

"I'm sorry, Brian, but I will not marry you just because I'm pregnant with your baby. We hardly know each other, and I don't want to be accused of making your life miserable years down the road. I've survived one marriage and know how things can change."

"Natalie," he whispered, "I would never accuse you of that. Granted, the baby puts our relationship on a different level, but we're friends. We're Lovers. I've missed you. Desperately. I want you and this baby in my life."

Natalie rested her hand on the back of the chair at the desk. "You might feel that way now, but things have a way of changing. When I married Sam, I thought my world was complete. We'd been high school sweethearts, graduated from college together, and were going to take the world by storm. Little did I know that less than five years later he would meet someone more exciting. Or that he would become jealous of my writing." She threw her hands up in frustration. "I've been writing since I was twelve years old. It should have been no surprise to him."

"That's where your husband and I differ. You and I share that love of writing. I understand your passion to write as well as the need to be alone. I go through it too. I enjoy discussing your ideas." He held up a hand to prevent her from interrupting him. "Okay, I agree we need to—"

The telephone interrupted their heated discussion a second time. They stared at each other in silence. Natalie reached for it on the third ring, but again there was an immediate disconnection.

Brian squinted suspiciously at the phone. "That's the second hang-up in as many minutes. Does this happen very often?"

Natalie shrugged. "I guess we all get our share of hang-ups and wrong numbers." She reached for the whistle.

"But not in the same night. When we were in your office, you mentioned some other things. Someone locked you in the stairwell?"

"Yes. But nothing happened. Fortunately, some kids entered the stairwell two floors up a few minutes later and I asked them to tell the security that the basement door was locked."

"Why didn't you do it? Call security?"

"I had my hands full of books and thought someone had followed me. In fact, I heard a second door shut after they left."

Brian didn't say anything, stepped closer. "And what about your office?"

Brian grabbed the phone when it rang again.

"Who's there?" He demanded, then frowned when he heard the instantaneous click. "You're not telling me everything."

Natalie stared up at him in silence. Round two was about to begin.

They couldn't come to an agreement on the baby, but now she'd find out what he knew about her mysterious intruder. Somehow, he didn't seem a bit surprised about all that had been happening.

The phone rang again but they continued to stare at one another.

"Your turn," Brian offered. He nodded toward the whistle and moved out of her way.

Natalie picked up the receiver, was prepared to blow her whistle but this time, the caller had something to say.

"You didn't heed my warning, did you?"

CHAPTER 14

BRIAN WATCHED NATALIE'S FACE TURN a chalky white. Angry that his worst fears had apparently come true, he grabbed the receiver in one hand and yanked the phone from the desk with the other. The long cord flew in the air as he threw everything in the trash can.

He turned back to Natalie. "What did she say?"

"That I didn't heed her warning." Natalie flew into his arms and wrapped her arms around his middle. Held on tight. "Brian," she whispered into his shirt. "She sounded so malicious. Do you know this woman?"

Natalie felt the restrained violence in his hands as he wrapped them around her, held her close. "Unfortunately, I believe I do," he grumbled. Things were slipping out of control, he brooded as he glared toward the patio doors.

What if he hadn't been here? Hadn't shown up when he did at the college? Would Sara have done something? Harmed Natalie?

No doubt, she was watching them both now. Planning. Fuming. Getting more and more dangerous.

Natalie shivered, and he hugged her that much tighter. He terrified something would happen to her. And the baby. Something had to be done before someone was hurt.

Brian nudged Natalie away, leaned down to kiss her forehead then her lips. He steered her toward the sofa. "You might as well get comfortable. I have a long story to tell. A long, sick story. But I need to do something first."

He closed the blinds and pulled the drapes on the patio doors, then left the room to check the rest of the windows. He made sure they were locked and the blinds closed. When he returned downstairs, he double checked that the front and kitchen doors were locked, chains in place. He left the kitchen light on and turned on the second lamp in the living room. There were enough shadows lurking outside; they didn't need any inside.

Brian joined Natalie on the sofa, pulling her into his arms, and wondered how she was going to react to what he was about to tell her. It was time she learned about the dark side of his life. A dark side that had apparently broadened to include her as well.

"Who is she?" Natalie asked. She rested her head on his shoulder.

"Her name is Sara, and for the past two years, she has made my life a living hell."

"But how? She said you loved her."

Brian stiffened. "When? When did she say that?"

"Today. In the classroom."

He squeezed her hand. "I tried so hard not to draw her attention to you. I should have just stayed away but I was sure I could get around her. Despite all my precautions she's come after you anyway."

"Oh, Brian, if you only knew. Since meeting you-" the telephone rang once more.

"I thought I took care of that damn nuisance." Brian stared at the telephone in the trash can.

"It's my extension in the bedroom." She started to get up, but Brian stopped her.

"I'll go." He dashed up the stairs, pulled the line from the jack then put it in the closet. "That should give us some peace and quiet for a while," he said as he sat beside her once more. "Now," he reached for her hand again, "tell me what has been happening to you and then I'll tell you about my hell."

"She has been calling me at the library and here for weeks. She shivered, "She ransacked my office. Today is the first time I've heard her voice. In the classroom and just now. She disguised herself as one of our teachers and left a long list of books for me to pull for her class. Then she typed a note supposedly from the student I'm tutoring. Made it look like Heather asked me to pull some reference books for her paper. When I talked to both, they didn't know what I was talking about and denied making the requests. I'm convinced that she pushed me down the steps at the mall."

"Pushed you down the steps?" Brian felt his pulse race, a pain in his chest while his heartbeats thrashed in his ears. He sat up straight. "I thought you said she locked you in the stairwell at the bottom of the steps."

"She did. But she also pushed me down the steps at the mall. After I saw you in the book store."

"But you told me you ran into a college friend and lost my note."

"I lied," she murmured. "When I was so surprised to see you at that signing, I wasn't sure I wanted to see you. Because of the baby. And then after I decided not to meet you and was leaving, she somehow got behind me and pushed me down the stairs. Someone called nine-one-one and before I knew it, I was in the hospital."

"Are you sure you were pushed?"

"Positive. I distinctly remember feeling a hand on my back before I fell and blacked out."

Brian stared at her, alarmed that Sara had been able to get so close to her. He jumped up, and, rammed his hands in the pockets of his jeans as he made a quick circuit across the room. "Why didn't you call me? I could have taken care of you. Me or Max."

"Max?"

"A good friend of mine," Brian answered. He prowled between the patio windows and the front door. "He's helped me through this whole ordeal," he rambled. "In fact, you've seen him. Just didn't know it."

Natalie frowned.

"When we were in Richmond, he spoke to you in the hall and then he followed you to your hotel. On my orders. The alarms had gone off and I was worried that Sara was there. Turns out she was the one that set off the alarms."

Natalie tried to recall the events of that evening but it seemed so long ago. All she could remember was the hurt she had felt when Brian ignored her. So much had happened since then, it seemed like years instead of months.

Brian stopped mid-stride in his tirade. "Why didn't you mention the hospital when I called you the next night?"

"Because I was worried you would come here."

"Wild horses wouldn't have kept me away," he roared.

Natalie was shocked at his outburst. "Brian, who is this woman? What's wrong with her? Why has she latched on to you? How can she upset you so?"

Brian heard the concern in her voice and saw the worry in her eyes. This whole ordeal was scaring her and he realized his rash, moody behavior wasn't helping.

But his stomach was burning, his heart raced, and his head pounded. He needed to calm down. If not for her peace of mind, for their safety. For all he knew, Sara could be outside right now, watching them, planning her next move. He needed to be alert and calm.

Giving himself a mental shake, he sat beside her and continued his story.

"Like I said, her name is Sara and she claims to be in love with me. But if you ask me, she's crazy. Off her rocker. About to go off the deep end. For over two years she has called me, written me, followed me...stalked me. That's why I built my home up in the mountains. She doesn't bother me as much there but still I know she's around. She likes to leave little hints that she is always watching. Whenever I leave the house for errands or book signings, I find myself looking over my shoulder with every step I take."

"Has she threatened you?"

"No. Not like she has you. At first, I thought she was just a love-sick fan. Figured she'd grow tired of it if I didn't respond, but when the letters and emails continued, and she began ringing my doorbell at all hours of the day and night, I knew something had to be done.

"I had another friend managing a Facebook page for me but when she hacked that, I had to shut it down."

He rested his head against the back of the sofa. Then turned to look at her. "Once, she crashed a party I was attending. Claimed we were engaged. Can you believe it?" He brushed his hand through his hair. "She actually sent the engagement notice to the newspaper."

Natalie's mouth fell open. She couldn't believe anyone would be so brazen.

"Fortunately, the editor of that particular paper is a friend of mine. He called me to either check it out or congratulate me. Anyway, I straightened it out and had a protective order issued against her. She was forbidden from coming near me or my house or making any phone calls or other public proclamations."

"Did it help?"

"For a while. Then she started sending me flowers and other gifts and before long, the calls had started all over again. I guess she thought she could court me, or win me over. Frankly, it made me sick to my stomach." He rubbed his chest. "That's how I know she is nearby. I get an uneasy feeling and when I look up, she's there. That's what happened at that book signing. After the manager gave you the note, I had the uneasy feeling then turned around and saw her standing there."

"No wonder you don't want any women in your life," Natalie murmured. "I'm sure it has been difficult."

"Damn right it has. At one point, I couldn't write. Hell, I couldn't even concentrate much less meet a deadline. That's when Max moved in. He'd just retired from the Secret Service and became my bodyguard of sorts. Began answering my calls, checking the mail, scheduling appointments, cooking—you name it, he does it."

"At least you had Max." Natalie whispered, thought about Marie. She realized she should have confided in Marie, instead of becoming paranoid and withdrawn, thinking she might have imagined everything.

"And then I met you," Brian smiled, reached for her hand. "I'll never forget when I set eyes on you in that elevator. Something clicked, and I couldn't believe how we meshed. Until that weekend, my appearance at that writers' conference in Philadelphia had been top secret. The morning after we made love, there was a hang-up. I realized too late that I shouldn't have answered it. I knew it was Sara. That's why I left so suddenly."

He pulled her close to his side. "I didn't want any harm to come to you. And now, it appears that despite all my efforts, she has latched on to you anyway. That worries me It sounds like she is becoming more vicious. Considers you a threat."

Natalie rested her head on his shoulder. "Fortunately, nothing serious has happened."

"It could have been serious when she pushed you down those stairs. Those are grounds for assault."

"But I can't prove it was her."

"You know it and I know it. I saw her outside the book store. But you're right, we have no proof that she's the one who pushed you." Brian looked down at her. "Does she know you're pregnant?"

"Oh, yes," she sighed. "She mentioned it in the classroom tonight."

He hugged her. "You might not want to marry me, but from now on, you're stuck with me. There is no way I'm going to let you out of my sight. Not while you're pregnant with my baby and most definitely not until Sara's been put away for good."

"But Brian, I live and work here. In Virginia. You live in Pennsylvania."

"You can quit your job," he suggested.

"Quit my job?" She croaked. "I can't afford to quit my job. I need to work. Especially now that I'm pregnant. In fact, I need to work harder at getting my book published so I'll have some reserve to support this baby I'm carrying."

"If I support you, you can quit. Think about it," he suggested, when she started to argue. "If you won't marry me, this is the only other option."

He glanced at his watch. "It's late and I need to call Max. Now that Sara has found you, we need him here to help distract her. And I'm staying here with you." He smiled when she didn't object. "I'll sleep in the guest bedroom if I have to."

"That won't be necessary." She tried to smile as cold shivers ran down her spine. "Considering what has happened today, I think I'll sleep a lot better with you beside me."

Brian called Max on his cell phone while Natalie took a shower.

"I guess that explains why our lives have been so quiet. Is Natalie okay?"

"A little shaken, but she's tough. Now that we've had our talk she's put everything in perspective. She'll be more cautious. I shudder to think how closely Sara came to harming her."

"Sounds like the bitch is getting more aggressive."

"Definitely, which is why I need you here. Oh, and you can expect a little surprise when you get here, old buddy." He grinned, imagining Max's reaction to Natalie's pregnancy.

"Do you have that perfect woman waiting for me, like you're always promising?"

"Well," Brian thought about Marie. His friend was approaching forty. Time to settle down. What little he knew of Marie; she could give him a run for his money. "Maybe that too. Listen, I want Natalie to come back with me and I'm having a hard time convincing her."

"Maybe she's smarter than you give her credit. You're not the easiest person to live with, you know."

"Ha. Just get your ass down here. Fast."

Natalie stepped out of the bathroom just as Brian finished his conversation with Max. He'd been sitting at the end of the bed where he could hear any noise downstairs and see anyone coming up the steps. He didn't put anything past Sara. Her behavior had become more reckless and vicious.

He was worried for Natalie's safety

He tossed his cell phone onto the chair, focused on her. Appreciated her natural beauty. She didn't need make-up or any of the other frills women used to make themselves more attractive.

Or maybe it was motherhood that enhanced her beauty.

His eyes travelled down her body noting how pregnancy agreed with her. Her breasts were fuller, straining against the lacy top of her gown. Any weight she had gained was in her middle. Her legs were still as shapely and beautiful as before.

He shivered, recalled the erotic fantasy he'd experienced in the hotel room. Noted that her gown wasn't sheer but red all the same. And she might be pregnant, but she was still one sexy lady.

Ever since she had fainted in his arms earlier that evening, he'd wanted to touch her. Hold her. Protect her. It was like his body was addicted to her. Craved the fix only she could give him. Tightened his loins that yearned for the passion only she could provide.

He'd missed her. Wanted to make love to her. But he didn't want to hurt the baby.

A baby, he thought as his heart swelled with pride.

All these years he had contemplated raising a son on his own and had just about given up on the idea. Now it seemed his dream might come true after all. He no longer cared whether it was a boy or a girl. All he wanted was a healthy baby. And Natalie there beside him.

She hadn't moved from the door. Just like when they met in the elevator, she had been watching him just as he had been watching her. He stood, stepped toward her. Her eyes sparkled with desire as they slowly travelled up and down his body.

"You're very beautiful." He wrapped his arms around her, hooked his hands at the small of her back.

"I've heard that line before," she smiled up at him. Her hands moved slowly up his arms, linked behind his neck.

Brian stared down at the exposed cleavage. "And it got you in a spot of trouble," he chuckled, kissed her lips.

Natalie leaned back, her eyes round with concern. "You're not upset, are you? About the baby?"

"Upset? Ecstatic is more like it." He lifted her in his arms. "You've fulfilled a dream I was beginning to think would never come true."

"An impossible dream," Natalie smiled, patting her swollen stomach as he lay her on the bed.

"My impossible reality." He knelt beside the bed. Reached for the hem of her gown then looked at her as if to ask permission. When she smiled, he lifted her gown and stared at her bare belly. His eyes widened when he saw a movement. He placed his hand there and felt something brush his palm. Was it an arm? Leg? It amazed him that there was a baby growing inside her.

His baby, he thought as he looked at her through watery eyes, leaned forward to kiss her bare stomach. "You've made me the happiest man alive. Don't you ever forget it."

Natalie brushed her hands through his dark hair, stared deeply into his eyes. She was desperate to believe him but still had her doubts. Knew anything could happen. For now, he seemed sincere. But once Sara was out of the picture, he might see things differently.

She could feel the heat from the bedside lamp. Another warmth was building when his hand moved from her stomach toward her breasts. Her nipples tingled and hardened as she registered the desire that was so obvious in his eyes.

"He's mine," drummed through her thoughts as she recalled Sara's words earlier that evening. Sara was probably outside her town-house this very moment.

But seeing Brian's desire, Natalie realized she didn't care about Sara, the uncertain future, or whether Brian might try to take the ba-by away from her.

If Sara was as crazy as Brian said she was, there may be no tomor-row. Her emotions reminded her of the ticking pressures of time and rather than stifle them, worry about what could be, Natalie wanted to free them. Allow them to breathe the freedom of love and passion she craved.

Brian leaned forward, touched his lips to hers. She hugged him closer, returned his kisses.

"I've missed you," he murmured, his lips moving down her neck, nudged the thin straps of her gown aside. "Terribly," he continued as his mouth whispered soft kisses across her breasts now heavy with de-sire.

He inhaled the lavender of her soap and heard her gasp as his mouth took her breast, his tongue brushing the hardened nipple. He felt his own body harden, yearn for her warm softness.

"I've wanted you for so long," he whispered, pulled the material down and moved to the other breast.

Natalie arched, her head pressed against the pillow while her hips swayed to a language of their own. She threaded her fingers through his hair and reached for him, but his hand caressed her long smooth legs while his lips moved toward the center of her desire. She gasped when his lips possessed her. Drove her over the cliff of passion.

Natalie reached for him but instead, he covered her with a blan-ket.

"I don't want to hurt the baby." He smiled as he backed toward the bathroom. "I also need a cold shower."

Natalie tried to stifle the groans of arousal that still screamed throughout her body. She wanted him, needed him. She sighed when she heard the shower.

Despite her condition, she knew there was no danger of their lovemaking hurting the baby. She decided she'd just have to heat him up all over again.

Brian opened the bathroom door and almost dropped the towel he'd draped around him. He stared at the candles that glowed from the bedroom. She wasn't making it easy for him.

She lay in the bed; it appeared she had fallen asleep. He couldn't blame her. Not after all that had happened today.

He himself had felt drained until he'd found the burning candles.

He made his way to the opposite side of the bed, dropped the towel, and slipped between the covers. Natalie was facing away from him, but as soon as he'd settled, she rubbed a cold foot along his leg.

"God, your feet are cold," he gasped, turned to spoon behind her. He leaned in closer to warm her and realized she was completely naked. His hand rested against one of her breasts that had so enticed him earlier. He cupped it and kissed her ear.

"I thought you were asleep."

"After what you just did? No way," she giggled, snuggling even closer.

"Honey, I don't want to hurt the baby."

"You won't. The doctor said the last six weeks are the critical time."

"Last six weeks, huh?" He kissed her neck and shoulder. "The way I feel though, I'd worry about being too rough. It's been so long."

Natalie rolled over and faced him. "We'll just have to take it easy, then," she said, rubbing her breasts against him as she pushed him onto his back.

Brian groaned, "Natalie, I'm serious. We need to be careful."

Natalie smiled then kissed him while her hand slid down his body, pleased when she found him hard. Her lips followed the path as she proceeded to show him the passion he had shown her earlier.

Before he lost total control, Brian reached for her, pulled her up his body to kiss her once more. They both gasped when Natalie straddled him, took him within her. It had been so long. She paused and shivered in pleasure, then moved sensually, fanning the fire that had been simmering for months.

Brian watched her and realized she might not be wearing the long red gown of his fantasy. She was bewitching all the same. Intoxicating. Ravishing. He'd take reality over fantasy any time.

Just as in his fantasy, her eyes never left his as she took him along the path to love.

Moments later, Natalie collapsed beside him. They both stared up at the ceiling, breathed heavily. She reached for his hand and squeezed it.

"It's a boy." She whispered.

The room was pregnant with silence, but when he rolled over and stared down at her, he was smiling.

"Just when I was hoping it might be a girl." He kissed her. "We'll just have to try harder next time."

Laser green eyes flared with anger as she stalked around the sleek Ferrari parked outside the woman's apartment. He wasn't supposed to be here, she fumed.

How could he do this to her? All he had to do was wait a little longer. She was so close to getting the woman out of their lives. If he'd only waited a few more days. She'd planned to return to him as soon as the job was done.

She was still angry about the botched job in the classroom. All she'd wanted was to give the woman a good scare, but instead, the woman had hidden. Like a coward. She didn't want to turn the light on for fear of being recognized. Instead, she'd left, planned to finish up here at the townhouse, and then get back to Pennsylvania. To Brian.

Now, all she wanted to do was get rid of the woman for good.

She'd almost ruined things when she saw Brian across the lobby of the library. He had been headed toward the other door to the basement offices.

"Hey," she heard a voice from across the parking lot. Her heart almost stopped when she saw that a man was hollering at her. "What're you doing around that car?"

She remained still, knowing the hood of her sweatshirt hid her identity, hoped he would ignore her. But the man started walking toward her.

"I said, what are you doing here? If you don't leave, I'll call the police."

That one word—police—jumpstarted her adrenalin. She couldn't have the police involved; Brian would know she knew about the woman. That she knew he was being unfaithful.

The judge had warned her that the next time she went near Brian, she would be put in jail. It wouldn't be the first time. She didn't want to jeopardize things when she was so close to making them happy.

She heard a low, vicious growl and saw a very large dog standing beside the man. They were obviously taking a midnight stroll, but he looked like he might release the dog on her instead.

She shouted obscenities at him and bolted away from the dog. Away from the car. Away from Brian.

Toward the attic room she had rented two blocks away.

She'd be back, she vowed.
She'd get even.

CHAPTER 15

NATALIE AWOKE TO THE FEEL of a warm hand on her stomach. Brian lay beside her, his concentration on the baby's movement across her stomach. There was a look of awe in his expression. He glanced at her and smiled.

"It amazes me that a little body is actually in there, stretching and moving just as we do. Waking up to a new day."

She chuckled. "I sometimes think he's playing football." They watched what could be the heel of a foot move across her stomach. "And I feel like a football player, with the weight I've gained."

"A beautiful football player," he leaned down to kiss her.

"With natural padding." She hadn't really gained a lot of weight but like all women, she hoped she'd regain her trim figure once the baby was born.

"I'm not complaining," he whispered, nuzzled her chin and then her neck.

Natalie smiled, then saw the digital clock next to the bed. It glowed a bright nine thirty.

"Oh, my gosh!" she started to sit up, "I should have been at work over an hour ago."

"Why don't you call in sick? I'm sure everyone is aware of what happened yesterday. Brian murmured, restraining her. "You had a scare I'm sure they'll understand."

"But Brian, I have to go to work."

"Not today. Not after what happened yesterday. I'm sure your supervisor will understand. In fact, I think I'll call right now. What's the number?"

Natalie gave him the number before dashing into the bathroom. When she returned, he smiled. "She said to take as long as you need."

Natalie was taken aback. Mabel Smithers wasn't the most agreeable boss. "What did you do, promise to dedicate your next book to her?"

"Not exactly." Brian smiled. "She hesitated a moment, but I just explained that you and Marie had both had a bad scare while on the job last night and it wouldn't be good for the college's reputation if it was leaked to the press. Especially since a similar incident occurred last month."

"I'm sure she had a good comeback for that," Natalie chuckled. "She doesn't take kindly to threats."

"There wasn't much she could say. I did smooth it over by promising to do a reading for the college next spring."

Natalie stared at him, then smiled. "In that case," she jumped into the bed, slid a hand around his neck and pulled his mouth toward hers.

"Pregnancy seems to agree with you," Brian chuckled when he came up for air. "Makes you more aggressive."

"Are you complaining?" She shoved him onto his back and straddled him.

"Me?" He sucked in a deep breath when her fingers whispered across his stomach, inching their way toward the dark nipples hidden in the hair on his chest. "Have you been in my dreams?" he croaked as her hips moved against him.

"Dreams?" She purred, "Or fantasies?"

"Whichever." He cupped her breasts, mirrored her own movements. "The only thing missing is the long red gown, but I'm not complaining."

Natalie laughed, proceeded to act out what she thought would be any man's wildest fantasy.

"**Y**ou're becoming as obsessed with me and the baby as Sara is with you!"

They had been arguing for over an hour. Natalie was being as stubborn about staying in her townhouse as he was about her going to live with him in Pennsylvania.

But now, Brian felt as if he'd been rammed in the stomach when the truth of her words hit him. She was right. She was always in his thoughts. And those gifts? The tickets to the Museum. The soup, paper, and birthday gifts he had showered her with? She was right. But he had done it in fun and as a joke. What one friend would do for another.

Not some sick person that intruded in her life.

With Sara in the picture, he couldn't help worrying for her safety.

Brian turned to Max, who leaned against the kitchen counter. He had arrived while Natalie was preparing breakfast.

"Talk to her, damn it." Brian grumbled as he stormed out of the kitchen. A moment later, the front door slammed.

Natalie stared from the kitchen table. Her shoulders fell, tears welled in her eyes. Was this what it would feel like when he left her for good?

It amazed her that in the span of twenty-four hours, she had become so dependent on Brian. Needed his warm body in the night, loving eyes during the day, and soft words of comfort every hour.

She looked at Max. He was dressed in black jeans and black tee, his hands in his pockets and his eyes stared at the floor. After his initial surprise at her pregnancy, it seemed he had decided to stay out of their confrontation.

"He'll be back. He's upset right now. He wants to protect you and isn't used to someone arguing with him, standing up for herself. Someone not following his directions, not listening to him.

"But he doesn't understand," she whispered, reached for a napkin to wipe her eyes. "I can't just quit my job. I need it to survive." She wiped her cheeks, blew her nose. "And I can't just take a sabbatical. I don't think they'd even allow such a thing. Not for people in my position, and certainly not until after the baby is born."

Max sat across the table and reached for her hand. "He understands. Believe me, he understands. More than you know." He gave her a little squeeze. "He's concerned. He knows what Sara is capable of and doesn't want anything to happen to you." He squeezed her hand a second time. "Or the baby."

He stood, pulled her toward the living room. "Come. Let me tell you a little story." They sat on the sofa.

"This sofa has heard a lot of strange stories lately," Natalie tried to smile.

Max leaned against the cushions, stretched, and crossed his legs at the ankles.

"I'm sure you know how successful Brian is as a writer."

Natalie smiled. "Yes, of course. I've read and cataloged all of his books for the college."

"Up until two, two-and-a-half years ago, he was living the good life. Enjoying his passion, success, and investing his royalties. He wasn't one to party all the time, but he did have a few friends, including me, who he palled around with.

"He even had some lady friends. And acquaintances. One of those acquaintances was Sara Goldman. She latched onto him at a writers' conference and was always asking him to critique her stories.

"Being the nice guy that he is, he would meet her from time to time but quickly realized that she wasn't really interested in writing. She was more interested in him and began showering him with unwanted and sometimes inappropriate gifts.

At first, he thought it was funny but when the gifts kept coming, he asked her to stop. Then he noticed that she would always turn up wherever he was. He tried changing his routine, but she would always eventually manage to find him. I don't know how she could afford it, but she even started following him when he was on his promotional tours.

"He complained to the authorities, but it was always hard to prove. She just happened to be wherever he was. And it's not like she was doing anything to him. But then she started crashing his parties and making outlandish statements."

"Brian mentioned Sara's fictitious engagement announcement."

"And when he finally confronted her and told her to stay away from him, she became angry. She started calling him and hanging up, ringing his doorbell and disappearing, even going through his garbage. But when she keyed his car, he went to the authorities again and got a protective order."

"Did it help?" Natalie asked.

"For a while but by then she had disrupted his life and driven away the few friends he had. He became a recluse. Withdrew more and more. The whole experience had even begun to affect his writing. His stories became darker and darker.

"I had just retired from the Secret Service and when he told me all she had done, I offered to move in with him. I assumed the day-to-day responsibilities so he could concentrate on his writing. I also monitored Sara's movements and for a while she left him alone."

Natalie frowned. "That's just so unfair. I can understand how Sara might have fallen in love with Brian, but didn't she realize her obsessive behavior was driving him away? Didn't she realize what she was doing to him?"

"Sara's crazy. Crazy in love with him, crazy in her desire to pursue him, crazy to possess him. She left him alone for a time, but then last year, it started up again. That's why he's so concerned for you. He's worried that her jealousy will drive her to harm you and he'd never forgive himself if anything happened to you."

"But-" she started to downplay everything, but Max interrupted her as if reading her mind.

"Haven't you been getting phone calls? Unwanted requests?" He stared at her. "And didn't you say you felt someone push you down the steps? What about last night? In the classroom? She was so close anything could have happened. Maybe she was spooked, I don't know, but you've got to realize that this woman is mentally unstable. Believe me, I've followed her and watched her for the last eighteen months." He reached for her hand. "She's obviously feeling threatened by your relationship with Brian and the very fact that you're carrying his baby."

"Why can't she just accept that he doesn't love her? Why can't she just leave us alone?"

"That's how unbalanced she is." Max decided to deal his trump card. "If you won't think of yourself, think of the baby. Would you want her to harm your baby?"

Natalie paced. Where was he? Now that she had accepted that some changes needed to be made, she wanted to discuss them with Brian. But he'd been gone for almost three hours and she was worried that something might have happened.

There was a knock at the door.

Max reached the door first and motioned Natalie to be silent.

"Do you know this woman?" He moved so she could look through the peephole.

Natalie immediately recognized her co-worker. "That's Marie," she reached for the door knob.

"Are you okay?" Marie dashed in as soon as the door was opened.

"I'm fine," Natalie squeezed Marie's hand. "A bit frayed around the edges, but I'm okay. How's your head?"

"Still a dull ache, but I'll survive. I used it as an excuse not to go in, though," she laughed, but stopped when her gaze fell on the dark headed hunk with brown eyes standing beside Natalie. "And who is this?" Her heart melted and she wished she'd worn something better than her frayed jeans and tank top.

"Marie, meet Max; Max, Marie," Natalie introduced the two. "Max is a friend of Brian's," she explained as the two stared at one another.

Max turned toward the kitchen. "I'll leave the two of you to talk."

Natalie frowned, watched him saunter away. She wondered if her friend might have had some effect on him. Come to think of it, he'd sounded slightly winded.

Max paused at the kitchen door. "Maybe I'll see about starting some dinner."

"A chef too," Marie smiled, watched him leave. "Some people have all the luck."

Natalie grinned as they walked toward the living room, sat on the sofa. "Seriously, how are you?"

"I still have a headache, but you know me, I can't stand to be away from the excitement. A little headache isn't going to stop me from checking up on you."

"I'm sorry it happened. Brian and Max have been trying to convince me to move in with them until this either blows over or the police actually catch Sara."

"Sara? Who's Sara?"

"The woman who attacked us last night. It seems she's been stalking Brian for over two years."

"My God," Marie exclaimed. "And now she's coming after you?"

"Looks like it."

"Well, they wouldn't have to do much to convince me to move in with them. If I had two good-looking men concerned for my safety, I'd do anything they asked," she joked.

"How about taking this pill for me?" Max asked.

Both women jumped. They hadn't heard him enter the room. He stood beside Marie with an oval tablet in one hand and glass of water in the other.

Marie gaped up at him, embarrassed that he had obviously over-heard her. "What is it?"

Max raised an eyebrow, stared down at her. "What happened to that trust you were proclaiming seconds ago?"

Marie blushed and he winked at Natalie.

"I heard you mention the headache and thought this might help."

"But what is it?" Marie persisted, staring at the pill.

Max tossed her a bottle of Advil. "Give it a few minutes and you should be feeling better."

He smiled when Marie swallowed the pill then turned to Natalie. "You don't have too much in your pantry. Or the refrigerator. So, if Marie would like to stay with you, I'll run out for some supplies and prepare the four of us a gourmet meal this evening."

"I don't need a baby-sitter," Natalie started to complain.

"Be my guest," Marie interrupted. "I don't know about you," she turned to Natalie, "but it's not often I receive an invitation to a home-cooked gourmet meal." She stood and followed Max to the door. "I'll even give you the directions to the best store to shop at."

Max pulled her outside before she could close the door. He caught a whiff of her perfume as he leaned in to shut the door behind her. He felt as if he'd been hit between the eyes by a three-hundred-pound bouncer. All thoughts of control went AWOL as he stared down into her sky-blue eyes.

"I want you to lock the door and don't let anyone in," he spoke sternly. "Only Brian. Or me. No special deliveries, no salesmen, no concerned neighbors," he listed possible guises. "Nobody. Got that?"

"Yes, sir," Marie saluted when he turned to leave.

"Oh," he stopped half-way down the sidewalk, gave her a wink and smile. "If your headache doesn't go away, I'll give you a massage later."

"I can't wait," Marie smiled. She watched him sprint toward the car and was awful glad she'd decided to call in sick this morning.

Marie locked the door behind her. Natalie was still seated on the sofa staring into space. She rubbed her stomach as if calming the baby.

"Don't worry, everything's going to be okay," Marie started gabbing. "You just have to be patient. Now," she sat beside her friend, "tell me about this hunk."

"Which one?" Natalie joked but proceeded to tell her friend all she knew about Max.

Although she met him only this morning, she knew he was a black ops trained Marine and had just retired from the Secret Service when Brian's problems with Sara began.

The phone rang unexpectedly. Max must have fixed it while she and Brian argued earlier this morning. It rang a second time but she continued to stare at it, debating whether to answer.

Was it Sara? Had she seen Brian and then Max leave? Did she know that Marie was here?

But what if it was Brian? She checked her cell phone and saw there were no missed calls. What if he needed her? Or had run into Sara?

She raced to answer it only to hear the click of the disconnection. She didn't know whether Sara or the telephone would drive her crazy first.

Almost immediately, the phone rang again and Natalie grabbed it on the first ring.

"Hello," she whispered, but there was silence. "Hello," she repeated, "who is this?"

Again, there was silence.

Natalie slammed the receiver down, then jumped when it rang again. This time she ignored it. She and Marie stared at one another when it rang ten times. Finally, she answered it. Still there was nothing on the other end. She decided to leave it off the hook, dared her tormentor to say something.

Twenty minutes later, she and Marie were still trying to ignore it when a loud knock sounded at the front door.

Marie had to restrain Natalie from opening the door before checking the peephole. No one was there. Suddenly, there was a louder knock at the back door.

"You stay here," Marie ordered, remembering Max's instructions. She went through the kitchen to check the other door.

No one was there. As Marie turned to head back to the living room, a loud crash sounded. Glass exploded everywhere as a large rock flew through the window above the sink and bounced off the wall behind the kitchen table.

Marie dashed out of the kitchen and grabbed Natalie who had remained near the front door. They leaned against the wall separating the living room and the kitchen, and tried to reassure each other as they stared at the shattered glass all around them.

They both jumped when a loud knock sounded at the front door again.

"Go away!" Marie shouted. "We've called the police."

There was another, more impatient knock. The door vibrated from its force.

"Natalie?" Brian hollered from outside. "Are you there? Open the damn door!"

Natalie dashed over to pull the door open and flew into Brian's arms.

"What happened?" When Natalie couldn't speak, he turned to Marie for answers.

"We've had hang-ups all afternoon and when she tired of that, she started knocking at the doors. She just threw a rock into the back window."

"That's it," Brian barked, kicking the door shut, "you're definitely coming with me. When will it be? Tonight? Or tomorrow?"

"I don't care," Natalie whispered into his shirt. All she wanted to do was snuggle closer to the security of his warm body and rest her head against his solid chest.

"Now don't give me any arguments. I've already talked to the head of personnel, even the college president and they've agreed to give you—" He suddenly stopped talking, held her away so that he could see her face. "What did you say?"

"I said, I don't care." Natalie sobbed.

Brian cast her a dumbfounded stare and then looked at Marie. "Let's go sit down," he finally groaned. "Where's Max?"

"How did you manage to convince them to grant me a sabbatical?" Natalie asked several minutes later as they sat in the living room.

"I briefly explained my problem with Sara and how she is now harassing you. Then advised him that in the interest of your safety and the school's reputation, it would be best if you were away from the school until Sara was apprehended."

"A very wise decision," Marie said. "In fact, I'm not so sure I'll be able to go back into my own office after all that's happened."

Natalie stared at her friend. Remembered thinking how Marie resembled her from the back. "I don't want to alarm you, Marie, but I'm wondering if Sara might have thought you were me when she struck you."

"What do you mean?" Brian asked.

"Last night, while we were waiting for the security guards, it suddenly occurred to me that from the back, Marie and I look alike."

Brian stared at both women. "That's a possibility."

Marie leaned back against the cushions in her chair. "Do you suppose she'll try again? To attack me?"

"Not if Natalie leaves with me, she won't." Brian answered. "She's only interested in me. And now, Natalie."

CHAPTER 16

NATALIE'S JAW LITERALLY DROPPED WHEN Brian finally reached the end of the long drive and pulled up outside his house. She had caught glimpses of it during their long winding road up the mountain.

"Designed it myself and then had it built on the side of a mountain."

"It's beautiful."

The two-story cedar sided chalet sprawled across the open space. A porch stretched across the front. Floor-to-ceiling windows looked out on the circular drive. Built on the side of a mountain, the only access to the house was the front drive. She appreciated that visitors would be immediately seen.

She heard garage doors open then watched Max drive his car inside the attached garage.

Almost as soon as Brian got out of the car and walked around to her side, the front door opened and a tall, stocky man stepped outside. He was followed by what Natalie thought was a German shepherd dog. Just taller, lankier and with a longer snout.

"Stay still for a moment," Brian cautioned her, "let him check you out."

The dog pranced over to greet Brian and then looked at Natalie. He circled her, sniffed her shoes, sat beside her.

"Natalie, meet Fitz." He turned to the man. "And Bo. Bo, meet Natalie."

Natalie smiled at the dog whose head was almost level with her hip. She slowly raised her hand to pet his head and then laughed when he licked it.

While Max and Bo talked, Brian took her on a quick tour of the house. The front door opened into a large foyer with the living room on the right and dining room on the left, with a den and office across the back of the house. Stairs led to a landing upstairs that looked down on the foyer.

The kitchen fascinated her. It had an Italian look. Cream cabinets with rust edging, multi-faceted marble counter and floor tile. A large island with a bar sink and wine-refrigerator with a wine cabinet on each end was situated in the middle of the room. What a great work-space for cooking and gathering place for parties, she thought.

The floor-to-ceiling windows offered a view of the front lawn and drive from the eat in kitchen area. Again, she appreciated that, despite so many windows, no one could drive up the driveway without being seen. Brian explained that the windows themselves were tinted, allowing for privacy from the outdoors.

The open kitchen spread into the long den with a fireplace at the other end. Brian's office was the other side of the fireplace.

The tour ended on one of the multi-level decks that spread across the back of the house. Brian explained that the higher level at the far end was his bedroom view.

"You designed all this yourself?" She asked admiring a spectacular glimpse of the mountain across the way and the valley below.

"Remember that dark period I mentioned? Since I couldn't focus on writing, I bought this property and designed my escape. Figured with a mountain all around me, Sara wouldn't be able to haunt me. Unfortunately, that didn't happen."

"She's been here? But where does she live? In the woods?"

"Don't know for sure. She's managed to get inside a couple times when I was away. Moved a few things around. Guess it was her way of telling me she's still in the picture. It's also why I got Fitz. Hoping he will scare her enough to keep her distance."

I could get used to this, Natalie thought as she relaxed in the front porch swing. She watched Brian work with Fitz. Brian threw the tennis ball, Fitz sat and waited for the command to retrieve it. The dog had so much energy. Always wanted to play but was very alert for strange sounds too. She often laughed at the way Fitz's head would jerk up whenever she, Brian, or Max entered the room or looked his way.

She had been at Brian's for two weeks now and it was almost as if she belonged here. He had furnished the chalet with his parents' antiques as well as a few investments of his own. Every day she awoke to wonder what new piece of furniture she would discover, cooking skill she would learn from Max, or vital tidbit of information Brian might offer as he critiqued her manuscript.

Brian had offered one of the four guest bedrooms for her writing convenience. Although she used her laptop for most of her writing, she'd also brought her desktop which was set up beside the window. Her small library of resources were scattered about the bed and dresser.

She was used to clutter while she wrote and was more than a little proud of the quality writing she had done in the last week Her manuscript was coming along and should be completed before the baby came.

She, Brian and Max had settled into a routine. Max did the cooking while she and Brian wrote. She didn't mind that they never went out. Instead, they played cards, watched movies, listened to music, or read books.

Once the three of them had simply talked, 'til two in the morning. The men learned that in addition to gemstones, she enjoyed listening to Neil Diamond for inspiration and Yanni for relaxation. She learned that Max enjoyed history and was very fluent on the Civil War and two World Wars. Cooking helped him to relax. He was creative with food where Brian was creative with words.

Natalie also learned that in addition to writing Brian enjoyed antiques and interior design. He was an early riser and she usually found him in his office already at work.

Just the other night, the three of them relaxed in the den with their books. She chuckled when she recalled Max's eyes open wide in disbelief when he happened to see the baby roll over and move the book that had been resting on her stomach.

Some nights Max retired to his bedroom with a book. She and Brian used this time to talk about their manuscripts or escape to Brian's bedroom for lovemaking. Like last night. In the Jacuzzi.

She loved his master bedroom. It was large and roomy, took up the entire end of the house above the living room and his office. The fake fireplace with gas logs and loveseat offered her a cozy setting for afternoon naps. Huge windows led to a deck that overlooked the valley. She and Brian often cuddled in the hammock, enjoying spectacular sunsets.

Brian continued his Italian theme in the large open master bath with ceramic tile walls and floors and an open shower with no door. The centerpiece of the room was columns on either side of two ceramic steps that led to a Jacuzzi in front of the large window. It could be bright and sunny by day or warm and cozy in the glow of the candles at night. Her favorite feature though, was the heated tiles.

She recalled his laughing at her worries about the window the first time they used the Jacuzzi. "Don't worry, nobody can see you. We're on the side of a mountain, remember?"

"There's such a thing as binoculars, you know."

"Don't be ridiculous. And if someone went to the trouble, you're worth the view."

"Oh sure," she complained when she allowed him to help her step into the tub. "Fat belly and all."

"Don't you know the miracle you're carrying?" Brian said as he settled beside her. "My miracle." He leaned forward to start the jets.

"Who cares what anyone else thinks," he whispered, leaned down to kiss her, "I think you're beautiful."

Natalie frowned as she recalled the tension she had momentarily felt when Brian referred to the baby as his miracle. His baby. She still couldn't let go of the feeling that one day he might tire of her and want only the baby.

Although he had been a wonderful host, friend, and lover, he'd never told her he loved her. She dreaded that one day he might meet someone else. Things had been good between her and Sam until he decided he wanted to spend his time with Victoria. For all she knew, Brian could meet another aspiring writer who challenged him more.

And then there was Sara. Would they ever be free of her? And if they did, would he once again become consumed with his writing and lose interest in her?

Anything could happen, she thought as her hands moved up and down her swollen stomach. A child would be involved, and she knew she would never leave her baby behind. Brian was stuck with her for life, or they were doomed to a battle of wills should anything happen. Certainly no life of happiness for a child.

They hadn't discussed marriage since she had refused his proposal in her townhouse. She figured he was biding his time. Still, she worried that the novelty of the situation would wear off and they would become bickering significant others like some of her friends.

She was still worrying as she watched Fitz race across the yard, search the bush and then return with his tail wagging. He never tired of running after the ball, she wished she had some of his energy.

Fitz had also adjusted to their routine. He slept in his bed beside the fireplace, but would look up whenever any of them got up to leave the room. He always enjoyed a romp around the property.

"I think he likes the ladies," Brian teased her one night when Fitz followed her into the kitchen.

Natalie understood Brian's need for privacy and the quiet life. She herself had craved it all her life. But Sara had forced them to withdraw further than either had envisioned.

Sara. She was never far from their thoughts. Natalie couldn't decide whether Sara thought they were still in Fredericksburg, or if she was laying low for a while.

She watched as Fitz dashed toward the garage where Max was changing the oil in Brian's Ferrari. Before retrieving the ball, something apparently caught his attention. He tracked the air and then moved off down the drive, his nose to the pavement. Every ten or fifteen seconds, he would turn to look back at Brian.

"Max," Brian alerted his friend. "Do you think he's picked up something?"

Max looked up from the car and glanced toward the dog that seemed to be waiting for them to follow.

"Maybe. Wouldn't hurt to check it out."

"Wait." Brain said as he headed over to the porch.

He reached for Natalie's hand and pulled her toward the front door. He nudged her inside, handed her the baseball bat that leaned against the corner.

"Lock the door, set the alarm, and stay inside. Keep the bat by your side and use it if you have too." He kissed her and then turned to leave.

Natalie peeked from one of the long panes that bordered the door and watched Brian dash toward Max who was already heading to where Fitz waited. The three of them—humans and canine—jogged up the drive.

Cat-green eyes watched the men and the dog jog away from the house. She'd been watching from a patch of woods at the far end of the house. Behind where the woman sat in the porch swing.

That annoying dog made it more difficult to get close to the house. If they weren't exercising him, the mutt constantly patrolled the area.

She bristled, remembered how they had tricked her in Fredericksburg. But not for long. She had watched the townhouse hoping for a glimpse of Brian, but all she ever saw was Max. Fixing the window she had shattered and then spending time with the woman's friend.

It wasn't until she saw Max packing a large suitcase in Brian's car, that she realized Brian and the woman were no longer there. She had been so focused on looking for Brian she had never missed the woman's car.

When she realized her mistake, she'd raced back to her attic apartment and trashed it. The landlady caught her before she could leave, and she'd had to pay another week's rent just to shut her up. Money she couldn't afford to waste. Her inheritance was beginning to dwindle, and she needed to get the woman out of Brian's life. She and Brian needed to start planning their wedding.

She snarled at the front door. Now might be her opportunity to scare the woman off for good.

Natalie tried to write, but the enthusiasm just wasn't there. She worried what Brian and Max might find. Would Fitz lead them to Sara's hideout? If so, would she be there?

She felt silly carrying the bat with her but knew Brian was serious when he told her to keep it with her. This was the first time she had been alone since the attack at her townhouse and she found herself listening for any out of the ordinary noises. At least the alarm system was on. If Sara tried to break in, she would have enough warning to defend herself.

She sat on the sofa and stared at the mountain's quilt of colors across the way. Maybe she'd relax with a book but first she needed a sweater. She started toward the stairs but froze when she saw a movement on the deck. Were the guys back? Surely, they would have let her know.

She jumped when she recognized a familiar black-hooded sweatshirt and dark jeans. Noted the pale complexion and harsh stern mouth in her profile. Was this Sara? Had she managed to get past Brian and Max? Or harmed them?

Her heart raced, and her stomach tightened as she watched Sara's tall, thin figure creep slowly across the deck.

Natalie quickly ducked further into the shadows when Sara stopped and looked in her direction. Could Sara see her? When the woman moved on, Natalie stepped closer to the sliding doors to get a better look.

Her heart jumped to her throat as she watched Sara jimmy the lock and open the door. Natalie heard the beeping of the alarm system and waited for it to go off. Instead, she heard four short beeps and then the long beep that indicated the alarm had been turned off.

How had Sara learned the code for the alarm system? What good was it to have the system if she could bypass it? What was she going to do now that she knew Sara was in the house? She grabbed for her cell phone but saw that she had no service. Had Sara somehow managed to jam things?

She and Brian had never really discussed any emergency procedures. The alarm system was supposed to prevent situations such as this. He had given her the panic code that would alert the police, but she had to get to an alarm box to punch it in. Then it would be another twenty minutes before the deputies would get to the house. At least they would be on the way, she mentally scolded herself.

There was a box in Brian's bedroom. She'd key in the panic code, then find a place to hide.

She could hear Sara in the kitchen, opening drawers. Was she searching for a knife? Did Sara even know she was in the house? Brian said she used to break in when they weren't there. Did she think Brian and Max were hiking with Fitz?

Natalie heard the swish of the refrigerator door, then the pop of a canned drink being opened. Suddenly, she was angry. It galled her that Sara thought she could just enter the house and help herself to anything she wanted. Her jaw tightened, lips flattened, and hands formed fists. This woman needed to be stopped.

Just as she had when she was trapped in the classroom, Natalie tried to stay calm, worked her way to a safe place. She pressed her back to the wall and inched her way toward the stairs.

Quietly and quickly, her eyes focused on the other end of the dining room, Natalie moved around the banister and then dashed up the steps. Raced into Brian's bedroom and punched in the panic code.

Brian said it was a silent alarm and only the police at the other end would know the alarm had been reset. She prayed Brian was right and breathed a sigh of relief when there were no beeping sounds.

Her next challenge would be to find a good place to hide until the deputies arrived.

Natalie was sure Brian's bedroom would be the first-place Sara would look. Max's room would probably be next. Her computer and things were in another bedroom so that was out. She dashed to the smaller bedroom. Opened the door to the closet and saw winter coats and boots. She could hide behind them.

Grateful she wore dark slacks, she backed into the closet. Arranged the boots in front of her, the coat around her, held the bat in front of her. Waited. She hoped she blended with the darkened corner but if Sara should find her, the bitch would be greeted with a blow from the bat.

She'd left the door ajar hoping to hear Sara's movement throughout the house. Then jumped when she heard Sara scream from downstairs.

"I know you're in here." Natalie heard the door to Brian's office slam shut. "Your time in this house is up. I am the one who will make Brian happy."

Natalie clenched her jaw to prevent her teeth from chattering. The sound of breaking glass startled her. Was that the vase of flowers in the foyer? The vase that Brian's grandmother had given to his parents on their wedding day? The flowers she had arranged just that morning? She tried to control the silent sobs that escaped her. She was sure the baby could sense her tension as her stomach tightened and he moved.

She listened as Sara opened doors, shoved furniture aside. Natalie was so attuned to Sara's movements it was almost like she was in the same room. She tightened her grip on the bat, ready to strike.

"You know I'm going to find you," Sara shrieked. "They'll never get back here in time to save you."

Natalie jumped when she heard another loud crash and tried to place the noise. Was Sara trashing the den? Was the noise the TV? Or one of the lamps?

"I'm getting tired of you interfering in Brian's and my life. It's time for you to go."

Natalie's heart fluttered and knees trembled as she strained to hear. The noises stopped. Had Sara left? Given up? Then she heard Sara coming up the steps. With each step, there was a loud bumping noise. Like Sara was dragging something up the steps behind her.

"Come out, come out wherever you are," Sara said and then laughed loudly. "You're up here somewhere and it's only a matter of time before I find you."

Natalie guessed Sara headed for Brian's bedroom. She heard the closet door bang against the wall. "We'll have to do something about all these extra clothes in Brian's closet."

Natalie could hear the hangers moving then material being ripped. Sara's rage was escalating. Her own anger was growing as she listened to Sara destroying her new outfits.

But she had to stay calm, quiet, and hidden.

There was more shattering glass, then the fragrance of her perfume drifted through the walls. She was sure Sara had just cleared the top of Brian's dresser.

Natalie worried that she would trash the beautiful bathroom but instead she seemed to leave Brian's room, and another door opened instead. Was that Max's room? When she felt the thud behind her, she realized Sara was in the middle bedroom. The room she used for her office. The muffled sounds of her reference books being thrown against the wall behind her almost unnerved her. Those were her prized possessions. Sara had no right to just destroy them.

The door to the small bedroom creaked and she imagined Sara nudging it open. Her heart pounded so rapidly and loudly in her head, she was sure Sara could hear it as well. Sweat trickled down the small of her back.

Where were the police? she fumed silently. They should be here by now. It felt like she had been in the closet for hours. Would Sara trash this room? Empty the closet as she had done in Brian's bedroom? Natalie tightened her grip on the bat, prepared to swing when necessary.

It was so quiet. Almost as if Sara knew she was in the room. Natalie held her breath as her hideaway became brighter. Sara was inches away from her.

Just as Sara yanked the door to the closet open, angry barking erupted from downstairs.

Natalie wanted to cry out but knew that she was still in danger. She braced herself, prepared to swing the bat as hard as she could.

"Natalie!" she heard Brian call out. "Where are you?"

Sara gave a shocked gasp. Natalie peeked over the coat as Sara turned toward the windows and saw her stumble over the suitcase that had been left at the foot of the bed. The woman grunted loudly as she heaved open the bedroom window.

Fitz's barking got louder. Sirens signaled the arrival of the police.

Sara screamed as she threw herself out the second-floor window. Natalie could only imagine the crazy woman had tried to jump for the trees next to the bedroom window. It was a long way down and the screams continued as Sara fell through the branches to the ground below.

Natalie dashed out of the closet and reached the window in time to see Sara limp along the edge of the woods.

Fitz dashed into the room and raced for the window. It was all Natalie could do to grab his collar before he jumped out of the window after his prey.

"Heel," she shouted to the dog. He whined but followed her command.

"Natalie!" Brian raced into the room and caught her as she collapsed onto the floor.

"That's the second time in as many weeks she has frightened Natalie and it's got to stop."

The police arrived in time to see Brian help Natalie down the stairs. They noted the damage Sara had done and listened to Natalie's recount of the terror she felt as she waited in the closet.

They were seated in the den, the disarray of Sara's anger littered around them. While Brian remained at her side, Max and Fitz went outside with one of the deputies to see if they could track Sara.

The search party was forced to return with no clues when it started raining. Max hung his jacket on the hook beside the door while Fitz gave himself a good shake. He followed the dog into the den and watched Fitz sit beside Natalie. The dog whined before resting his big head in her lap.

Max smiled when Natalie cast a surprised look at him, then petted the dog's head. Fitz had finally accepted his new family.

"I want to know how she found out the code to the system," Brian demanded when a deputy followed Max into the room.

"Ms. Stover, did you call the security company last Wednesday?"

Natalie frowned at the deputy. "No, I've never called them."

"You didn't call saying you had forgotten the code and needed to get inside?"

"Until today I haven't been alone much less need the code to get inside. So no, I did not call them."

Brian glared at the deputy. "What are you implying?"

"The security company said a woman named Natalie called them last Wednesday saying she had forgotten the code. Said she had just moved here and you usually took care of the alarms. You had just left and she needed to get inside for something."

"Well, that's a lie. Ms. Stover knows the code and like she said, until this afternoon she hasn't been alone since we got here two weeks ago."

The deputy made a note in his report. "They asked that you give them a call to change the code. They also suggested that you list only yourself as the primary contact regarding your house. That will authorize them to talk to no one else. Not Ms. Stover, Mr. Donovan, or the Goldman lady."

"Fair enough." Brian reached for Natalie's hand.

"Did you tell them what we found?" Max asked.

"Haven't had the chance. You do it."

The deputies looked at Max. "We weren't here because Fitz picked up a scent and we went to investigate. About half-way down the drive, he veered off into the woods and we must have followed him a good two, three hundred yards. Came upon a cave that was obviously inhabited."

"In addition to breaking and entering, she has been trespassing. Living in the woods outside my house, making my life a living hell." Brian said.

CHAPTER 17

THIS WAS BECOMING HER FAVORITE time of the day, Natalie thought as she lay back in the lounge chair on the deck.

Life was gradually getting back to normal after Sara's break-in last week. Thankfully, it was a matter of cleaning up. Sara had indeed shattered Brian's grandmother's vase in the foyer and a lamp in the den. The lamp could be replaced but she knew Brian was heartbroken about the vase. The deputies set up a camera outside the cave but after a week, Sara had not returned. Either she had found another hideaway or moved on.

Natalie found that she wrote best in the early morning and late afternoon, taking some time after lunch to snooze on the deck or just lay back and appreciate the view. After plotting two chapters this morning she decided to take advantage of the warm autumn day and soak up a little sun.

She glanced down and saw deer grazing near the entrance of Brian's "Therapy Trail." He had built it when Sara started stalking him and he couldn't concentrate on his writing. It led to a cliff that offered a spectacular view of the valley below. When the trail was finished he channeled his energy into constructing a gazebo which they had already enjoyed a few times.

"You have no idea how violated I felt," he had said. "It was as if my life wasn't my own anymore. Day after day I came out here and bullied my way through the woods. As if each sapling and tree I pushed aside was getting her further out of my life. Every day I cut down trees and forged ahead. It was like I knew this cliff was here and I was struggling to get here so I could end it all. Took me months but when I finally finished and looked down on the splendor of nature, all I could do was collapse and enjoy the view. That's why I want to put a gazebo here."

Natalie recalled hugging him as she reassured him. "Your emotions and frustrations were struggling for an outlet. I'm glad you channeled those frustrations in a positive manner. I wouldn't have you now if you hadn't."

"Well, it worked. When I finished, it was like I had exorcised her and I was ready to get on with my life. Max was living with me by then and we cut and stacked the wood to make the path what it is today. I guess it's still my Therapy Trail. I often come down here when I need to think."

The bright yellow trees across the way caught her attention and Natalie appreciated how brilliant the leaves were. She rubbed her stomach. The trees were shedding their dying leaves and she would soon be giving birth to a new life. A tiny helpless baby who would need her to love and care for him.

Unlike the vivid colors that signified the end of a year on the mountain, she would nurture and prepare her son for life. A wonderful life. A life filled with the love of two parents who loved him.

"When did this come?" Brian's angry voice carried through the screens from the den.

Natalie straightened, listened for the rest of the conversation.

"Sometime today," Max answered. "I found it on the wood bin outside the laundry room. She must have known I'd be restocking it today."

Natalie stood, moved closer to the door. They probably thought she had gone upstairs to take her nap.

"I don't want Natalie seeing this. She's finally calmed down from last week and I don't want to scare her again."

Natalie frowned, squinted her eyes. Her nerves bristled at the fact that they felt they had to protect her. Granted, she had been frightened, but she didn't need to be coddled every minute of the day.

Obviously, Sara was up to her tricks once again, and she had as much right to know about it as he did. Sara had become her problem as well as his.

Natalie reached for the latch and opened the door. Both men turned. She realized she might have been hasty when she saw their reactions. Brian was surprised but if she didn't know better, Max appeared to be ready to tackle her. Even Fitz stood at attention.

"You don't want me to see what?" she closed the screen behind her. "After last week, what else could possibly scare me away?"

"It's not important," Brian grumbled. She watched him tuck a piece of paper in his jeans pocket. He stared at her so hard she looked down to be sure her blouse wasn't out of place. Even Max stared but had a smile on his face.

She marched up to Brian and reached inside his pocket for the paper. "Anything that concerns you is important to me."

Brian sucked in a breath, almost groaned out loud when her hand came too close to what seemed to be in a constant state of arousal these days. He heard Max chuckle.

"I think I'll go check on my roast."

Natalie ignored both men and turned to read the note.

Darling, It's so wonderful to have you back home, but don't you think your houseguest has been here long enough? She's only distracting you. You need to concentrate on your book. She's also very pregnant. What are you going to do with a baby in your life? How do you know it's your baby? And if it is your baby, I bet I can name the date she conceived. I was there, remember? All my love, Sara.

"This is disgusting," Natalie ripped the letter in two then tossed it into the fire. "You don't believe her, do you?" She frowned at Brian.

"About the baby? Of course not." He walked toward her. Wrapped his arms around her. "I've never doubted for a minute that this was my baby. My only regret is that we can't seem to relax and just enjoy being together without worrying about when she'll make her next appearance."

Natalie wrapped her arms around his middle, looked up at him. "Was she really there? That night in Philadelphia?"

"Yes, unfortunately." He leaned his forehead against hers. "Maybe not in the room, but she'd might as well have been. She called early that morning, remember?"

Natalie nodded, rested her cheek on his chest "You told me that was why you left the room."

"I was angry. And frustrated, when I realized she'd somehow managed to track me to the hotel. Especially when it had been so top secret. Then to have caught me in your room, it's like I don't have a life of my own. I'm accountable to her yet she has no place in it."

"You don't have a life of your own," Natalie stated. "Neither of us do. Not now. While she can disrupt our lives, and create havoc with our nerves, she has control. We need to break that control."

"I'm working on it," Brian whispered.

"How?" She looked up at him. "What are you doing?"

"It's time for me to start the legal process all over again, and that note you so quickly burned could have helped me start the proceedings."

Natalie stared up at him. "I'm sorry. I shouldn't have done it, but she makes me so angry."

Brian smiled, kissed the tip of her nose. "I know. I've had two years of it remember?" His hands held her closer as his mouth covered hers. "You know you took my breath away a few minutes ago. You know, anger becomes you. Your eyes get dark, cheeks flush and lips almost beg to be kissed."

Natalie laughed. "I won't forget the look of agony you had on your face when I reached into your pocket. No wonder Max left the room."

"What do you say we go upstairs and relieve some of these erotic urges you so carelessly stirred up. Besides, you haven't had your afternoon nap yet, have you?"

"No, and I doubt that I will. Now."

"Come let me show you, my love," he murmured as he led her toward the stairs.

Natalie awoke a couple hours later feeling blissfully refreshed. She stretched her arms above her head and noticed that Brian had turned the gas logs on.

Brian's house was all about space and he obviously wanted a large, spacious bedroom as it took up the end of the house above the living room and his office. The gas logs took the chill off the coolness of the hardwood floors and wall of windows across the back. She stared at the love seat in front of the fireplace and recalled the afternoon reads in front of the fire.

She glanced at the mantle clock and saw that if she rushed, she could shower and try on the new dress she had bought yesterday in time for dinner.

Yesterday had been her first visit with the new doctor recommended by Dr. Smith. Dr. Burnside assured them that all was okay, promised them that they would have a healthy seven-pound boy in a couple months. Brian had been full of questions about the delivery and what to expect. He worried about the distance to the hospital and how much time should before he risked delivering the baby himself.

She and Brian had celebrated by taking a driving tour of the city, ate lunch in a secluded deli owned by one of Brian's friends, and then shopping for a few maternity outfits for her and furniture for the nursery. The new clothes were hanging in the closet she shared with Brian, but the furniture wouldn't be delivered for several more weeks.

She grabbed her robe and headed into the master bathroom to start the shower. Waiting for the water to warm, she wandered back into the bedroom to stare out the windows. She hoped she and Brian found a way to stay together because she doubted she'd ever be able to leave the majestic view of the mountains behind.

A brief sparkle from across the way caught her attention and she moved closer to the window. Obviously, the sun's rays found a piece of glass or half-buried crystal. Suddenly, she felt the hair lifting on her nape and arms. Her heartbeat raced, nearly exploded as she pressed her hand against the pane of glass and searched closer. Surely Sara couldn't be out there watching them. Not on the side of a steep mountain.

Green eyes cold with fury glared at the pregnant woman made even larger by the lenses of the binoculars. Apparently, Brian hadn't heeded her advice. The woman was still there.

Maybe he wasn't so smart after all. Maybe he was like all other men and let his testosterone influence him. Maybe he needed to be taught a lesson.

She shivered. The nights were getting colder. After her failed attempt last week, she knew she'd have to do something soon. The snow would be starting.

The leaves were already beginning to fall which made her treks around the house more dangerous. Either making too much noise when she moved or tracking her footsteps along the path. She now had to cover her tracks whenever she returned to the new cave.

Max had almost caught her last night when he'd stepped outside to see about the noise she'd made when she'd accidentally knocked over the axe.

She'd been so angry having to watch the three of them laugh, have a good time as they ate dinner on the deck. She should have been up there, not the woman.

Enough was enough she thought as the anger festered. It was time for more action.

She smiled. Things were already in the works. All she needed was to be patient just a little longer. Then Brian would be hers.

Natalie noticed the light in Brian's office as she descended the stairs. She debated telling him about seeing the brilliant sparkle before taking her shower. But she didn't want thoughts of Sara interfering with their evening.

She hoped he'd experienced a sudden surge of creativity. Many times, she would grab her journal which she kept within reach and jot down notes and ideas which might be useful for future stories.

She found him standing at the window with his hands in his pockets, staring off into space. He was either plotting a scene or stewing about Sara.

She glanced around his office. It was neat. And tidy. So different from her make-shift office. The file cabinet drawers were closed, books neatly arranged on the wall book case, even the papers around his computer were precisely stacked.

There were two monitors. One on his desk for writing and another on a side table. The security company had installed cameras at various stations around the house and the split screen displayed black and white views from each camera.

Framed covers of his sixteen books hung on one long wall.

"Brian?" she whispered. "Are you okay?"

He turned with a smile and extended a hand, welcoming her into his office. "No, not really."

She rushed to his side. "What's the matter?"

"Just received an email from my agent. Seems he and my editor want me to come to New York to discuss my new proposal."

"But that's good, isn't it?" She brushed the hair along his forehead.

"Not if I have to leave you here."

Natalie shrugged a shoulder. "Oh. Yeah. No more extensive travelling for me. Sorry."

"I'll be worried the whole time I'm gone."

"It won't be for so long. Besides, Max will be here."

"I'll still worry."

"Brian, I understand your concern, but we can't worry about Sara. We're going to get past this. Everything will work out."

He held her close. "I still have this awful feeling that something will happen."

She hugged him. "When do you have to go?"

"Day after tomorrow. Fortunately, the meeting is scheduled for ten o'clock, so if I leave here early, I should be able to get back that evening."

Natalie smiled. "See. Nothing to worry about. You won't even have to spend the night away."

Brian cocked an eyebrow at her. "Scared someone else might tempt me?" He teased.

"Not really. You had more than your fair share of chances while on your tour and nothing happened. I guess I can chance leaving you on your own for twelve hours," she joked.

"You keep looking like this and I'll never leave."

"What? Fat and pregnant?"

"No." He kissed her forehead. "Sexy and seductive," he murmured. He nudged her away to admire the emerald green silk dress. She had discreetly left the top button unbuttoned to expose some cleavage. "One of your new dresses?" His nose brushed her neck, inhaling her perfume.

"You don't know how often I found myself following women who wore perfume like yours. None smelled as good as you though. You're unique. I plan to keep you well stocked in it."

"I'll remind you the next time we go shopping. C'mon, I'm sure Max is ready to eat yet too discreet to come looking for us."

"He knows better," Brian laughed.

Brian left before dawn the day of his meeting in New York. He wouldn't allow Natalie to come outside, preferring to check the locks of the house as he exited. He hoped Sara wouldn't miss him till he was back.

Natalie knew he was worried not only about Sara, but the baby as well. She had done everything she could to assure him that everything would be okay and that she and Max would be waiting for him later that evening.

She tried to do some writing but dozed instead.

Max found her asleep on the sofa in the den. Her papers were scattered across the floor having fallen from her lap. He appreciated her stillness and was happy that his friend had found his soulmate. Brian was finally happy again and all they needed to do was get Sara out of their lives for good.

He smiled when Natalie stirred, stared sheepishly at him.

"How does a big pot of soup and homemade bread sound? Vegetable soup is one of Brian's favorites. Healthy for you too." He knew she would worry about Brian until he came back home. Since she couldn't concentrate on writing, he'd give her something else to occupy her time.

They spent the morning cutting up vegetables and mixing the dough. Soon, the house was filled with the aroma of soup and rising yeast bread.

Natalie tried once more to do some writing, but knew until Brian was back home, she wasn't going to get any constructive writing done.

She reached for the newest Nora Roberts book she'd picked up on their shopping spree and decided to spend a couple hours on the deck. Nora always inspired her.

Natalie could never just come out and sit down on the deck without appreciating the view first. Located on the end of the house, outside the den, it offered a panoramic view. She smiled. The mountainside across the way was one big rainbow of colors. She looked down and saw six deer grazing in the patch of grass Brian had planted near the entrance of Therapy Trail. Like humans, animals were creatures of habit and she could always count on seeing them this time of the day. Hunting season would be starting soon, and she hoped they would remain safe in Brian's sanctuary.

She turned toward the lounge chair and saw a shopping bag next to the pot of mums beside the door. *That's strange*. She and Brian hadn't been out here for several days. And they certainly wouldn't have left any trash behind.

She looked over the edge at the ground below. The deck was too high for the wind to have blown anything up here.

She reached for the bag, intending to toss it in the trash bin next to the door, but frowned when she saw *"For Natalie,"* scribbled in red on the bag.

Natalie froze. Was this from Sara? She wondered. She looked over the bannister again. Surely Sara couldn't have climbed the timbers or scaled the railing. She glanced behind her, fearful that Sara would suddenly appear. She recalled Brian's comments about preserving evidence so he could use it when he went to court. The bag had her name on it but she knew it was intended for Brian. She took a deep breath and peeked inside, saw emerald colored material. Green was her favorite color, but she was sure Sara didn't know that. She hesitantly pulled the emerald material out of the bag and held it out in front of her. It was one of her new dresses. The one she wore for the first time the other night.

She looked closer and noticed that it had been ripped from top to bottom. Sara had somehow gotten inside the house, stolen her dress, destroyed it, and then left it for her to find.

Natalie dropped the bag, and raced for the door.

Oh God, Brian was right. Sara had been waiting for him to leave.

CHAPTER 18

IN HER HASTE TO GET inside, Natalie jammed the screen door and couldn't open it. Her heart pounded as she looked behind her, worried that Sara might appear out of nowhere. She turned back to the door and yanked again.

Fitz barked loudly from the other side of the screen.

"Natalie!" She heard Max yell from within the house. "Where are you?"

"Max," she sobbed, "I'm outside the den. Quick, please help me with the door."

Within seconds Max opened the door and pulled her inside. Fitz dashed past them, sniffed the perimeter of the deck.

Max pulled her into his arms. He hugged her tightly while she shivered uncontrollably. "What happened?" he whispered. "Was it Sara? Did she hurt you?"

Natalie felt his racing heart next to her cheek. When the shaking stopped, she pointed to the deck behind her. "It's out there. The bag. I dropped the bag on the deck."

Max settled her on the sofa, then stepped outside to retrieve the bag.

"Fitz," he commanded the dog, "Inside." He closed and locked the doors then knelt in front of Natalie who had her elbows on her knees, her face in her hands.

"You okay?"

Natalie swallowed, then nodded. "Did you see it? Did you see what was in the bag?"

Max held the remnants of the dress up.

"That's my new dress. Remember? The one I wore the other night. How did she get inside without our knowing about it?"

"It's not your dress. See?" he pointed to the tag that hung from the side. "She must have seen you shopping. Saw you wearing it the

213

other night. She has done this to Brian a couple times and I'm sorry to say, you've become her victim as well. I'm so sorry. I should have had Fitz check things before you went out." He put the dress in the bag and tossed it on the hearth.

Natalie reached for his hand. "It's not your fault. You can't be everywhere at the same time. Second guessing her."

"We need to show this to the deputies. I'll take it in tomorrow after Brian gets back. And you will no longer be left alone." He shook his head. "I just can't believe she's back so soon. Usually she waits a couple weeks between visits. And after almost getting caught last week," he paused, glanced at the bag again, "she's getting more brazen. We'll have to be extra careful today."

"But what about Brian? Should we call him? What about his car? Could she have sabotaged his car like she slashed my tires? If Sara could leave that bag on the deck, she could also get inside the garage and tamper with his car. Why didn't the alarms go off?"

Max shook his head. "We keep the garage doors locked at all times. Plus, I checked the car last night. Everything was okay."

"Should we call him though? Warn him?"

"No. I don't think Sara means to hurt Brian. I think she's focused on you now. She's jealous and wants to get you and the baby out of his life."

Natalie fell back against the cushions and hugged her swollen stomach. Now was not a good time to have to be on alert and ready for action. The baby was growing, and she couldn't get around as quickly. "I can't believe she wants to hurt my baby."

"At this point, anything is possible. She's getting more dangerous and has obviously been watching the house. Knows your routine. That's why she left the bag on the deck. She knew you'd go out there sometime today."

"Max, that deck is so high," she exclaimed. "It's not even accessible from the other deck How did she get up there?"

"It's hard to believe she could leap that far but she could have used a rope. She's obviously had some training."

Natalie bristled at the confirmation that Sara could barge her way into their lives any time she wanted. It galled her that she was monitoring their every move. "Then we'll have to start changing our habits."

Max smiled, pleased with her rapid recovery. Her eyes were brighter, cheeks flushed and her grip on his hand had tightened. He chuckled. "We're stuck in this house. Unless we change our eating and sleeping habits, there's very little we can do to change our routines."

"Well, we'll just have to make it harder for her to keep track of us."

"I guess if we stay in different areas of the house, that's possible. The house is big enough."

"And I guess we'd wear ourselves out if we constantly went from room to room turning the lights on and off," she laughed.

Max grinned. He stood and helped her up. "C'mon, let's go check on the soup."

After lunch, Max challenged her to a game of cards. Hard as he tried to distract her, he knew Sara hovered in the back of their minds. They kept their eyes and ears open for any unusual sounds.

It wasn't until Max noticed the gray clouds that he remembered he needed to restock the wood bin.

"It'll be okay," he said, when Natalie's eyes grew wide. "I'll be just outside the back door. If the storm wasn't brewing, I'd say forget it, but we'll need the dry wood."

"Can I help?"

"When hell freezes over." Max chuckled. "Brian would have my head if he found out. Here," he handed her a key. "This is for the deadbolt in the laundry room. Lock the door behind me and don't let anyone in. I have my own key. Just stay here with Fitz. I should only be ten minutes. Fifteen at the most."

"Please be careful. I'll watch from the kitchen window."

Natalie paced between the bar and the window, checking on Max. Pacing and worrying seemed to be all she did these days.

Fitz prowled alongside her. She knew he was anxious to get outside with Max and debated letting him out when the front doorbell chimed.

Natalie stopped in her tracks, stared down at the dog who stared toward the door. "Who could possibly be here so late in the afternoon?" She wondered out loud. No one had ventured up that two-mile drive the entire time she'd been here."

She backed toward the kitchen window to check on Max. Could he see whoever was at the front door? Had he heard anyone drive up? Or maybe it was Max. She watched him reach for another load of wood.

The bell chimed once more. Might as well see who it was, she decided. At least she could peek around the long window panes before opening the door.

She appreciated that true to his training, Fitz was alert but hadn't barked. If silence greeted the visitor, maybe they would leave. When she headed for the door he was ahead of her, then broke into a run. When he stopped at the foyer and looked back, Natalie signaled for him to be quiet and then sit. He whined but sat.

Natalie was thankful for the tinted windows as she slowly wobbled across the dining room. She bumped into the chair beside the antique washstand in the foyer and stopped. Could the person at the door have heard her?

She looked at the window, but saw no shadows. When she moved closer, peeked through the pane beside the door, she saw no one there. Maybe they decided to leave. She looked toward the drive but saw no car. Or tail lights.

Was it Sara? She knew she hadn't imagined it? Fitz wouldn't be sitting beside her. He had heard the doorbell as well. But who could it have been? Her heart jumped to her throat. Sara. It had to be Sara.

She swiftly turned to rush back to the kitchen but noticed something laying on the mat outside the door. Thankful for the long glass pane, she crouched on her hands and knees to get a better look. Gasped when she saw what appeared to be a head from a doll. When she leaned forward, she saw that the doll had been stripped and mangled, its body parts in a small heap.

Natalie collapsed against the wall, covered her mouth with her hand to stifle the scream that almost erupted from within her. Sara was here. Again. Only a very sick person would mangle a doll, then leave it on the door step.

"Max." She whispered out loud. Fitz broke into a run the back door.

Natalie grabbed the door knob to pull herself to her knees, reached for the chair beside her to stand. On her feet, she turned and tried to move as fast as she could and stumbled against one of the chairs.

Max was still outside. She needed to warn him. As she made her way past the long mahogany table, she noticed the shadows were getting longer. She glanced toward the windows and saw that the anticipated storm was about to break. The skies were almost black, and the wind blew leaves and pine tags across the yard, against the windows.

She needed to get Max inside. Quickly.

When Natalie reached the kitchen, she could see Sara's dark figure sneaking up behind Max as he stacked split logs in his arms. The woman's arm was held high, her hand clutching a long, thick stick. Natalie hollered as loudly a she could. "Max!"

Max heard her, turned toward the house but Sara immediately brought her club down on the back of his head.

Natalie gripped the edge of the sink and watched, hoping he was only stunned. When he dropped the load of wood and turned to fight her off, Sara struck once more, and he fell to the ground.

Natalie prayed that Max would get up again, but he remained still. She whimpered silently when Sara turned and stared in her direction. Although it was dark inside, Natalie was sure Sara had heard her scream and knew she was in the kitchen.

What now? She couldn't leave Max outside. But how would she get him inside? And keep Sara outside? She reached in the pocket of her sweater and felt for the key to the dead bolt to the laundry room door. She saw his unconscious body next to the woodpile. Should she risk going out there to get Max?

Where was Sara? She was no longer there. *Where had she gone?*

She raced over to the alarm box and punched in the emergency code. There was an ear-splitting crash at the back door. Natalie whirled to see Sara standing five feet away on the other side of the door. They stared at one another.

Finally, Natalie was face to face with her tormentor. There was a moment of recognition as Natalie remembered this woman in the library. The same woman who had brushed past her in the parking lot outside her townhouse. She remembered noticing the mole above her lip.

How could someone so evil and disturbed, have been so close and she not know it? Not pick up the vibes?

"You don't belong here!" Sara screamed over Fitz's barking. The hood of her sweatshirt had fallen back and Natalie saw the matted hair and wild eyes that almost glowed in the darkness.

Natalie's heart did a flip-flop when Sara shattered one of the panes in the door, then pushed a hand inside to reach for the door knob.

Fitz leaped, snapping, for Sara's wrist, but she was too quick and snatched her arm back. The dog frantically scratched at the door, anxious to get to his target.

Sara seemed possessed and snarled as she beat at the next pane up.

She's going for the dead bolt! Fortunately, there was no knob on the deadbolt to turn. You needed a key. The key which was in Natalie's pocket.

Sara ignored Fitz's barks, she was so focused on getting inside the house. To her.

Natalie remembered the mangled doll on the front porch and thought about her baby. She was not going to let anything happen to her baby. She needed to act. Now. Max was lying unconscious on the ground outside, Fitz was trying to protect her, and Sara was determined to get inside. She needed to keep her baby safe from this mad woman.

She spied Max's rolling pin in the drainer and sprang into action. By now, Sara had shattered the second pane and would soon realize she couldn't get inside without the key. *That will really piss her off. Make her even crazier.*

Natalie needed to be prepared.

Just as Sara reached through the second pane for the dead bolt, Natalie grabbed the rolling pin and lunged toward the door. She struck Sara's arm as hard as she could. Fitz's barks and pure adrenalin drove Natalie to steadily hammered at Sara's arm. Sara screamed with each blow but continued to scrabble at the dead bolt.

Fitz started to bite at her arm, but Natalie ordered the dog to heel. She didn't want to risk hitting him and should Sara get inside, she wanted him ready to pounce. Sara's arm was already bleeding from the jagged shards of glass that ripped her skin.

Sara paid no mind to the dog or the broken glass. She seemed to be possessed; in a trance with one goal in mind: Get inside.

Natalie pounded at Sara's bleeding arm with all her might.

The shattering of the bone was audible and Sara's concentration broke. The woman screamed once more. Pain finally registered and she backed away from the door, tripped over the piece of wood she had used to assault Max, and fell to the ground.

Sara jumped up, clutched her arm to her side, and ran off into the woods.

A bolt of lightning slammed into the ground near the well. The storm had finally arrived and Sara was nowhere to be seen. She'd disappeared into the safety of the trees.

Fitz barked, reminding her that she still had to get Max inside. She pulled the key from her pocket and dashed toward the door. Blood was everywhere. On the broken panes, down the door, and puddled on the floor.

She unlocked the deadbolt while Fitz quivered anxiously at her side. As soon as she pulled the door open, the dog made a mad dash for the woods.

Max was turning over as she reached his side. He stared up at her blankly when she called out his name. She watched his eyes grow wide when he looked down and saw that she was covered in blood. On her face and down the front of her sweater. He tried to sit up, to help her, but collapsed. "What happened?" he groaned.

"She was here," Natalie exclaimed, her voice shaking with anger. "Fitz took off after her, but we've got to get you inside. Before she comes back."

Max whistled for Fitz and then tried to stand, leaned heavily on Natalie as she helped him stumble inside. Fitz quickly followed, and Max turned to lock the door. When he was sure it wasn't Natalie's blood splattered all over her, he keyed in the code to quiet the alarm. He was sure the phone would start ringing any minute. More than likely, the police were already on their way.

He collapsed into a chair at the dinette table. "I feel like a bull-dozer hit me."

"She was pumped up, all right." Natalie paced between the table and the bar. "I've never seen anything like it. I thought I was scared n the stairwell at the library. That was nothing compared to just now. You have no idea how hard it was to watch her hit you from behind and not be able to help you. Then she tried to come in the back door. I'm so glad you had me lock the deadbolt when you left. She kept trying to break in and I kept whacking at her arm. I'm sure I broke it. I heard the snap. And Fitz," she stroked the dog's head. "He stuck by my side the whole time. Didn't you boy?"

Fitz whined, and Max tried to smile.

"She probably won't be back for a while," Natalie continued. "Not after what I did."

Max could only shake his head. "Brian might be in for a rude awakening when he gets back."

"Why?"

"You're not as helpless as he'd like to think you are."

"I never claimed to be helpless. It's just that I've never felt so threatened before."

Max reached for her hand and gave it a squeeze. "We survived, this time. And it looks like we might finally have enough evidence to file formal charges. Put her away for a while." He frowned, rubbed the back of his head.

Natalie leaned forward to examine his head. In their haste to get inside, she'd forgotten about his wound. She found a two-inch cut that was still bleeding some.

She reached for a dish towel, wet it at the sink, and returned to his side to clean the wound. "What did you mean? About putting her away for a while?"

"There are stalking laws, but they're sometimes difficult to interpret. In many cases, you must show that the stalker means bodily

harm before they can take official action. We got their attention
when she broke in last week. But this latest incident obviously shows
that Sara wanted to hurt you. That should be enough evidence to take
her to court."

"But for how long?"

"Probably not long enough," he sighed, "but maybe she'll be
forced to get help."

They both jumped at the sound of the front door slamming shut.

Max reached for the bat, Fitz barked, and Natalie grabbed for the
rolling pin even as police sirens came to a blaring halt outside.

"Natalie! Max! Where are you?" Brian shouted from the foyer.

"Kitchen," Max shouted, then collapsed into the chair. He held
the towel to his head.

"Are you okay? What's happened? I pulled up the drive and saw
the place was dark. Why are all of the lights turned off?" Brian rattled off as he turned the kitchen lights on.

"And why are the police here?" He turned to look at the deputies
that were coming in the front door. "What's she done now?"

Natalie and Max squinted at the brightness. In all the excitement,
they'd forgotten to turn on the lights.

When Brian turned around, he saw Max leaned over the table,
holding a towel to his head. Then his heart stopped when he saw Natalie. She was white as a sheet and had blood-splattered all over her.

"What the hell's going on around here? And what's that doll doing out on the porch?"

Natalie gasped. She'd completely forgotten about the mangled
doll.

"Sara was here," Max said, winced as he moved to stand.

"What do you mean?" the deputies said.

Brian took another look at Natalie, then collapsed into a chair.

"She hit Max from behind, knocked him unconscious and then
tried to get inside." Natalie explained to everyone. She pointed to the

back door. "Fortunately, the door was locked but she tried to break the panes. I managed to stop her, and she ran into the woods. I think I broke her arm."

The deputies walked over to the door.

Max stared at his friend and smiled. "Natalie fought a good battle. And it looks like we might have enough to put Sara away for good."

"Oh, we definitely have enough evidence. But she's gone too far this time. My meeting in New York was a set-up." He looked up at the deputies. "If you don't catch her soon, I intend to get rid of her once and for all."

CHAPTER 19

NATALIE GAVE UP. SHE'D BEEN doing so well with her writing until Sara tried to break into the house again.

Brian and Max had replaced the back door, then spent endless hours on the telephone or sequestered with the rep from the security alarm company.

Not only was her writing taking a hit, but she had also taken on more of the household chores since Brian and Max were always in conference.

With the baby growing, her movements and energy level were almost nil. She didn't say anything. Brian and Max were focused on their safety and catching Sara. She could certainly do her part and take care of the cooking and cleaning.

But when she began feeling her stomach tighten up for seconds, even minutes at a time she worried that Sara's attack might have triggered something with the baby. She breathed a sigh of relief when she had called her doctor and he'd said it was normal. The baby was simply moving into position.

But she didn't want a premature birth either. Living on the side of a mountain, miles from civilization, she could just see Brian and Max having to deliver the baby. She began reading up on the delivery process and decided she wanted to take Lamaze classes. She realized it was a little late in the pregnancy to be doing this but the hospital was willing to work her into one of their classes.

"Lamaze classes?" Brian nervously paced the kitchen. He and Max had been carefully reading over the final changes for the alarm system when Natalie dropped her little bombshell. He watched her take the salad ingredients from the refrigerator and set them on the counter. Just when he'd been so proud of the way she had stepped up. He knew her condition made it more difficult but he appreciated her helping so they could focus on Sara.

"Natalie, here I am in the middle of upgrading the alarm system—again—and you want to go to Lamaze classes?"

"Not right now, silly." She chopped the romaine leaves. "They start in a few days. At the hospital. By then, you two should be wrapped up with the alarm system."

"But I'm trying to keep us safe and you want to leave the house."

"Brian, we can't stay locked inside for the rest of our lives. Soon, my appointments will be every week. Or were you planning to have the doctor come here to deliver the baby?"

"Of course not. I just don't want to take any more risks than necessary. At least until I can get Sara off our backs."

"But the baby isn't going to wait." Natalie paused in her salad preparation to look up at him. "And neither will the classes. They start day after tomorrow and run right up to the week before the baby is due. It's now or never.

"But Lamaze classes?" Brian muttered. He leaned against the counter, crossed his arms across his chest. "Isn't that where you do it naturally?"

Natalie nodded, reached for a carrot.

"Why put yourself through so much pain? I don't want to see you suffer any more than necessary."

"Lamaze will help me to deal with the pain. As the pain gets harder, you change your breathing pattern to accommodate it. Besides, I want to know what's going to be happening to my body. I'm not going to just let them sedate me and deliver the baby."

"Even I know they don't do that anymore."

"Still, Lamaze is the easiest, safest way for the baby." She stopped chopping the carrot and stared up at him.

Brian felt himself weakening. He'd always been a sucker for her pleading eyes.

"Brian, I want our son's birth to be special. I want to experience it all. See him take his first breath." She returned to chopping the carrot.

"This is also a way for you to be involved. You'd be my coach. Help me along."

"What? Now I have to help with the delivery too? Why the hell do we need with the doctor then? Natalie, you know I'll be there but-"

Brian cast a desperate look toward Max who was seated at the dinette table. He knew Max was only pretending to be engrossed in the security literature spread across the table. The smile gave him away.

"It'll be so risky," Brian finally said. "Going out will give Sara another opportunity to get to us."

Natalie reached for a cucumber and smiled. "After the other day, I doubt that she'll be back for a while."

"Don't count on it," both men spoke at once.

Natalie frowned, looked first at Brian and then Max.

"Okay, maybe not," she conceded, "but do you intend to let her rule our lives? Dictate what we can and can't do? Must we just sit back and wait for her next attack?"

Neither man spoke. And Natalie refused to give up.

"When she knocked Max unconscious and then tried to break into the kitchen, I realized that I had to accept some responsibility for protecting our baby. I wasn't going to let her get inside and harm us. Just as I refuse to let her tie me to this house. We need to move on, Brian. Be ready. For her and the baby."

"May I say something?" Max leaned his chair back. "I've tried not to interfere in any of your arguments, but you each have a point." He turned to Natalie. "Natalie, you're right. You shouldn't have to give in to Sara's dominance, but Brian's had two years of it and only wants to protect you."

Natalie cast Brian a frustrated look.

"We've all been under a lot of pressure these past few days," Max continued, "with Natalie doing more so we could concentrate on the alarm system. And I know neither of you have done any writing since Sara's last attack, right?"

Natalie sighed, Brian shifted and crossed his arms again.

Max stood. "Maybe we all need a break." He looked at Natalie. "The Lamaze classes start day after tomorrow, right?"

Natalie nodded. Max turned to Brian. "That's the same day the security system is being upgraded. Why don't the two of you plan to spend the day in the library and then go to the classes? I'll be here to oversee the installation."

Natalie smiled, but Brian remained skeptical.

"How can we be sure Sara won't try anything?" Brian asked.

"She won't," Max said. "If anything, she'll be watching. There will only be two or three men inside the house and if I can't keep an eye on them, I'm in the wrong line of work."

"Please, Brian," Natalie touched his arm, cast her pleading eyes up at him. "We need to get out. Even you have to admit it's time to show her she can't contain us."

"All right," Brian faked a heavy sigh. "But for that, you're going to have to name the baby Percival."

Natalie smiled, leaned toward him to give him a kiss on his cheek. "We'll see."

They both winked at Max who shook his head and laughed.

Tired green eyes watched the van pull up to the house two days later. Because of the darkness, she couldn't read the logo, but she smiled. They had probably come to repair the door she had broken.

She wondered why they hadn't done it sooner. And why they'd start so early in the morning.

She winced at the pain in her arm. Between the deep cuts from the glass and then the bitch breaking her arm, she hadn't been able to sleep the past few nights. She'd convinced the doctor that she had fallen through a window.

While he cleaned and set her arm she had gone over the scene at the house again and again. Her annoyance with the slut had flared to grudging hatred for not just the physical pain, but for somehow enticing Brian away for her. Her love for Brian, which she had always considered unshakable was morphing into an alienated bitterness because he was so engrossed in the woman.

That wasn't right. It wasn't *fair*. Brian was supposed to be hers. Now, after all the effort she had gone to, he had proven himself unworthy. He didn't deserve her. And that woman didn't deserve him. They didn't deserve to have *anything*.

During the sleepless hours that had followed, she'd plotted her next moves.

The woman and the kid had to go first. She wanted to watch Brian suffer the agony of losing them. Dreamed of his begging her forgiveness. But she didn't care anymore. Her love for Brian had evaporated when he continued to house that woman after what she'd done to her. If he didn't want her, so be it. But the woman wasn't going to have him either.

She perked up when she saw Brian's Ferrari back out of the garage. *That's strange. Where was he going? Why so early?* She debated following him. Would this be her chance to get the woman?

Brian drove slowly down the long drive, searched for any signs of Sara. He was still worried that she would somehow sabotage the crew that was already busy inside the house.

The four men had arrived at the crack of dawn and immediately started to work. Because of the complexity of the system, it would take several days, but they promised to get as much done as quickly as possible.

He glanced over at Natalie and grinned as she tried to fit her briefcase between her swollen stomach and the dash.

Their baby was taking up more and more of her lap. Pregnancy certainly agreed with her. She looked radiant. The early morning sun's rays glinted off her coal-black hair. She'd pulled the mass of curls into a bun.

"Here," he handed her a small black box.

"What's this?" She gave up on the briefcase and set it behind his seat. She opened the box and found a marcasite pin inside. "Oh Brian, it's beautiful." She took it out and examined it while Brian concentrated on passing a car.

"I'm glad you like it. In addition to being a pin, it's like a wiretap. You have the pin and Max and I have the earbuds. You go about life as usual and we're able to hear everything you say and do. Same goes for Max and me. I can hear him, and you and he can hear you and me."

"But how do they work?"

"They're wireless. Whenever we're in the house, it recognizes the wireless internet. Outside the house, it channels over the cell phones. All you do is press that little button on the back and I can hear anything you say. We got it mainly for when we are in large crowds or working in separate areas. I don't want a repeat of last week like when she left that dress on the deck. I want you to keep it with you all the time. If you don't want to wear it, keep it on you. In case you should go into labor, or if you should just need me, all you'll have to do press that little button and talk to me."

"Interesting. I can talk to you but I can't hear you. I suppose you and Max can talk to one another and hear me too."

"We didn't think you'd want to wear the earbud. But if you want one, I can certainly get you one. We each have a frequency. Press once to talk to me, twice to talk to Max and three times to talk to us both."

"You're all I need," she smiled, leaned over to kiss his cheek.

"I'd better be," he threatened.

Brian glanced in the rear-view mirror and noticed a familiar yellow Volkswagen tailing them. He didn't know whether to be relieved or frustrated. At least if Sara was following them, she wouldn't be monitoring the installation of the security system.

He remembered the first time he'd noticed her following him and had wondered why she persisted in being so obvious. In the beginning, he had laughed and called her Tweety Bird, but as she continued to trail him over the months, and then years, he had changed her name to the Wild Banana.

He hated to admit it but Natalie was right. It was time to move on with his life. A life with Natalie and his son. Sara had come too close to hurting Natalie the other day, but he hoped to have that under control within the next few days. Between the ear bugs, enhanced alarm system, and a new court order, soon she'd be out of their lives.

His one fear was that Sara would somehow manage to outsmart the state-of-the-art security system as she'd done at the Virginia Museum in Richmond and the house. She always managed to do so.

He looked in the rear-view mirror again. So far, she was keeping her distance although she remained within sight. He was sure she was taunting him.

Brian glanced at Natalie, who so far was oblivious to their shadow. He checked the gas gauge, and realized he needed to refuel. He pulled off at a gas station and watched Sara continue down the road. While the gas pumped, he called Max on his cell phone.

"She's found us. We'll head for the Library as planned and I'll try to lose her before the class."

"Things are moving along here. They may finish up ahead of schedule," Max said.

"I gave Natalie the pin. We'll try it out at the library."

Minutes later, Brian and Natalie were on their way and within seconds, Sara was tailing them again.

"The Wild Banana is back," he finally said when Natalie noticed him watching the mirror.

"The what?"

"Sara," he nodded behind them. He reached over and flipped down her sun visor. "Do you see that yellow Volkswagen behind us?"

Natalie shifted in her seat to get a better view. "That's her? I remember seeing a yellow Volkswagen in the parking lot at work." She shivered, remembered the car that drove close enough to brush the hem of her dress. "What are we going to do? Suppose she follows us to the library?"

Brian smiled. "I've eluded her before."

Suddenly, there was a slight jolt to the car. During their conversation, Sara had closed the gap and bumped them from behind.

Brian cursed silently, angry that he'd been distracted by Natalie and failed to see Sara's approach. "You okay?" He gripped the steering wheel with one hand, reached for her hand with his other. "I'll never understand how she thinks her little Volkswagen can damage this Ferrari. Hold on, she's coming back for more."

Although he was expecting it, Brian almost lost control when she bumped them a second time. Harder.

He looked in the mirror and saw she was just inches away from his bumper. She was so close he swore he saw the hatred in her eyes.

When she continued to ride his bumper, he hit the accelerator and raced down the road. He didn't intend to give her another chance to run them off the road.

Brian looked over at Natalie. Her face was ashen, her eyes glazed over. She stared straight ahead while her hand tightly gripped the door handle. "Sorry. I guess I should have warned you."

"I'm fine. I just didn't realize how powerful this car is."

"The Wild Banana won't be able to do that again," he mumbled, checking the rear-view mirror once more. Sara was still back there and they were fast approaching the city. He pressed the accelerator to the floor, and her car became smaller and smaller as they were soon swallowed up by the city traffic. He tunneled along the narrow Philadelphia streets and made a roundabout path to the public library. He thought about stopping by the police station, but it would probably take more time than they had to report it. He'd just talk to the local authorities when they got back home.

The Arrington Public Library was housed in what used to be the State Legislature Building. Unlike the modern open libraries, the large stone building offered a quaintness with old world charm. It had the distinct smell of old books, reminded Natalie of her own library and how much she missed it.

She had visited their website and knew it was the headquarters for the system. The administrative offices were housed upstairs and the main level for public use. The Information Desk was situated in the center of the large lobby with a casual reading area near the entrance. Reference and genealogy rooms were to the left of the entrance and the reading rooms to the right.

Brian and Natalie immediately headed for the reading room. He wanted to blend with the patrons in case Sara should track them to the library. He had parked in the monstrous parking lot but knew his fancy car would stand out to anyone that was looking for it.

Natalie observed that the reading room was the only concession to modern times. A row of computer stations lined one side of the room with tables and a lounge area strategically arranged throughout the rest of the room.

Brian and Natalie decided to sit at opposite ends of the room but within sight of one another.

Familiar to the staff, Brian had greeted each of them by name. He opened his laptop and began reviewing his proposal while awaiting the books the desk clerk was gathering for him.

Natalie also worked at her laptop, but found herself more interested in the people in the room. She was still a little shaken from their run-in with Sara and couldn't help but be suspicious of those around her. She scolded herself about her paranoia and immediately set to work.

A giggling noise distracted her a short time later and when she looked up, Natalie noticed two young women poking one another as they pointed toward Brian. They obviously recognized him, and she felt a swell of pride to know that he was hers.

When she glanced over at Brian and saw him returning their smiles she felt a flash of irritation. And when they stood to leave, she was sure he was watching their sleek figures sashay across the room. Natalie became conscious of her own very pregnant body and was immediately envious of the slim women.

She looked at Brian once more and realized that while she had been musing about her pregnant body, he had been watching her. He smiled and winked before returning to his work.

"Jealousy makes you more beautiful," he texted her.

Minutes later a woman sat two tables away from her. Although she couldn't really see her face, her features were very much like Sara's. Natalie immediately tensed when the woman reached inside her purse but relaxed when she pulled out an MP3 player and headphones.

"You're really getting paranoid," she murmured to herself.

Deciding not to let these observations go unnoticed, she pulled out her journal and began jotting down descriptions, actions, and mannerisms of the different people in the room for future characters.

Three hours later, she smiled at all she had accomplished. Not only had she gathered some great character sketches, she managed to orchestrate an argument between Adam and Cecelia, the hero and heroine of her current manuscript as they tried to piece the puzzles of their murder investigation. She'd decided to trap them with the murderer and now had them trying to outwit the culprit.

Much like her situation when Sara broke into the house. Nothing like personal experiences to make the story more believable.

Natalie glanced over and noticed a woman settling at a table midway between her and Brian. She wore a beige raincoat and hat pulled down over her long straggly brown hair. She flipped through a magazine.

Natalie kept watching her and froze when she noticed the mole beside the woman's mouth. The woman had kept her raincoat on but when she tugged at the sleeve, Natalie saw the cast on her right arm.

Sara had somehow found them.

Her heart pounding, Natalie looked across the room and saw that Brian was thoroughly engrossed in his research and hadn't noticed Sara's entrance. How could she discreetly attract his attention?

What would he do once he saw Sara?

Better yet, what would Sara do when she realized she had been spotted?

She needed to get Brian's attention. Remembered the pin he had given her and was glad she'd put it in her pocket. She discreetly studied it, tried to remember Brian's instruction on how to work it.

Once for Brian, twice for Max, and three times for both. She knew Max wouldn't hear it because they were out of range. She found the little button on the side and pressed it one time. Then stared across the room to watch Brian.

Brian immediately looked her way, tapped his earbud, and nodded.

"The Wild Banana has found us," she whispered.

Brian stiffened, looked around, and immediately spotted Sara.

"Follow my lead," he texted her. She watched as he closed his laptop, stowing it and his papers in his briefcase.

Natalie began to gather her materials, anxious to know how he planned to slip past Sara.

When he was ready, Brian picked up the two books he'd been reading and headed for the main desk. She saw him stop at the front desk and speak to the desk clerk who then cast a nod in Sara's direction.

Brian turned, looked directly at Natalie and nodded his head toward the exit.

Natalie stood and quietly pushed her chair back under the table. A chill ran up her spine as she proceeded out of the room. She held her breath and tried to pace herself when she sensed Sara watching her every move. The hairs on her neck rose and she bit her bottom lip as she moved to put as much distance between her and Sara as possible.

She wondered how Brian had managed to live with this woman's stalking for over two years.

Avoiding eye contact, Natalie steadily made her way out of the reading room, almost running through the security gates. Suddenly, Brian was three steps behind her, his hand at the small of her back, hurrying her even more.

Natalie didn't need to see whether Sara had followed. Within seconds, she heard a commotion as the alarm system went off.

Brian held her elbow as they raced around the corner of the lobby and out of the building. He was chuckling as Sara's shrilling voice echoed behind them.

"What did you do?" Natalie asked when they raced toward the parking lot.

"Called in a favor. I asked the desk clerk to detain Sara and I guess she set the alarm off."

He glanced at his watch. "We have enough time for some lunch and even a little shopping before the classes. But I will admit that the sooner we get home, the better I'll feel."

CHAPTER 20

"THEY INSTALLED ANOTHER TELEPHONE LINE," Max said as they relaxed in the den later that night.

"Why?" Natalie asked.

"We discovered that the one we have is tapped."

"I'm not surprised," Brian said, noting Natalie's frown. "This isn't the first time that's happened."

"But how can she continue to get away with this?" Natalie demanded. "That's invasion of privacy. Harassment. Can't you have her arrested?"

"Believe me I've tried, but it never seems to do any good. They lock her up for a little while but once she's out, she's back to her old tricks. I've had so many unlisted numbers, even I couldn't keep them straight," Brian complained as he stood and paced the room. "I've even had to change my cell phone several times."

"But what about restraining orders?" Natalie asked.

"Until now, we've been unable to really prove that it's Sara," Max answered. "I decided to leave the other line as bait," he continued with his original topic. He glanced at Brian. "You ready to proceed with the other plans we discussed?"

Brian glanced at Max, then Natalie.

"What plans?" Natalie asked, looking from one man to the other. The way they stared at her, she was starting to wonder if they intended to use her as bait.

Brian gave her a guarded smile. "You and I are going to host an engagement party."

"A what?"

"What better way to draw Sara out than to announce our marriage plans?"

"But we don't have any marriage plans."

"Sara doesn't know that."

"Brian, you know how I feel."

"It will only be a small party with a few of our friends. After we catch Sara, we can call it off if you want."

Natalie remained silent.

"We'll make all of the arrangements on the original line," Max said, drawing Natalie's piercing eyes away from Brian. "Sara will hear everything we want her to hear."

"Are you sure she won't find the second line?" Natalie asked.

"Quite sure." Max smiled. He stood, stretched. Now that they had brought the engagement party out into the open, he decided Brian could handle the situation from here on out.

He knew Brian was worried about how Natalie would react. Whether she would even co-operate. Max shook his head. If she didn't say yes soon, he didn't know what his friend would do.

"Been a long day. I think I'll turn in." He signaled for Fitz to follow him and left the room.

Natalie refused to look at Brian; focused instead on the flickering flames that reached for the chimney. Why must there always be problems? Today had been so good. They had gone to the library, eaten lunch at his favorite deli, attended the class, even did a little shopping for the baby.

The Lamaze class had been great and made her more excited about their baby's birth. Now she had this fictitious engagement party. Just when she had settled into a comfortable routine, even considered a future beyond the birth of their baby. Beyond the publication of her book. Beyond getting rid of Sara.

Now she had to wonder if this engagement was a ploy to get the baby.

Brian stood near the fireplace. He watched her. She was so quiet, he wondered what she was thinking.

"Natalie, I know you said you didn't want to get married, but I hope you'll give this engagement party some thought."

When she remained silent, he continued. "I admit that originally I may have had the wrong attitude about marriage and having a son, but having you, and the baby in my life has changed me. Yes, I want the baby, but I also want you. You've become a part of my life and I don't want to lose you."

Still, she refused to look at him. Made him more nervous.

"I've enjoyed having you here and want you to stay after the baby comes."

He moved to sit beside her on the sofa, reached for her hand. "And even though Sara will soon be out of the picture, that doesn't mean I want you out of my life."

Natalie stared at the fire. She heard him but couldn't bring herself to look at him.

He sounded sincere, but she wondered if he really meant it. How would he feel once the baby was here? Would he still want her here? Or would he grow tired of her and come to love the baby more?

Agreeing to marry him might give her a permanent place in his life, but she also knew that another marriage without love would destroy her.

She finally looked at him, stared into his dark brown eyes. True, they shared an interest in writing and had learned to adjust to one another, but would it continue?

And what if they were never able to shake Sara? Would she want her son exposed to such a life?

She stood and carried their mugs into the kitchen.

Brian followed, watched her go through the motions of rinsing them and putting them in the dishwasher. He stuffed his hands in his pants pockets, leaned against the door.

Why didn't she say something? Didn't she know how much she meant to him? How his world would tilt on its axis should she decide to leave?

He studied her hair that streamed down her back. She'd combed it out as soon as they got back from the city. The long teal sweater might conceal her rounded stomach, but the black tights emphasized her long legs even more. Despite her pregnant condition, he knew that only she could arouse him.

It suddenly occurred to him that he desperately wanted to marry this woman. She brought completeness to his life. Her beauty sometimes took his breath away and warmth always filled his chest when she smiled at him. Her passion for writing reignited his. She was his shot of inspiration, cornucopia of ideas, and lifeline to sanity.

Not even Max could calm his frayed nerves the way Natalie could with a quiet look, serene smile, or soft stroke of her hands. The tables had been turned on him. He loved this woman with a passion and desperately needed her in his life.

By some strange quirk of fate, she was to him what he must be to Sara. He wanted to be near her all the time. Needed her affection, craved her touch and hungered for her happiness. He now understood how Sara must feel—though he could never see himself stalking Natalie as Sara had him.

He only hoped that Natalie would come to share his feelings in the end.

He could use the baby as an excuse, but he wanted Natalie to marry him because she loved him.

Brian stepped behind Natalie and wrapped his arms around her. He felt the baby move beneath his hands.

"You know I'm in love with you," he whispered into her ear. His lips grazed her neck. "I don't know what I'd do if you ever left me," he nuzzled her earlobe while a hand cuddled a plump breast.

Natalie rested her head against his shoulder. She lifted her hand, threaded her fingers through his hair.

Suddenly, she was a mixed bag of emotions. Excited that he admitted to loving her and confused about her own feelings. Happy that she might be able to have a life with Brian, but wound tight with Sara's intrusions.

She turned in his arms and stared up at him.

"Brian, I understand how you feel, and I share those feelings. But I'm also scared of making another mistake. I don't want to watch your love die, just as Sam's did."

"That was a different situation," he snapped. "Sam didn't appreciate what he had. He was threatened by your success and found someone else to dominate. I love you for your fierce independence and determination to succeed. I also want you for a lifetime," he whispered before his lips covered hers.

"A lifetime and a day," he murmured before he picked her up and carried her upstairs to their bedroom.

An hour later, they were both stretched out in the Jacuzzi, enjoying the feel of their touching bodies. She sat between his legs, her back to his chest.

Scented candles lined the window sill and counter top, their flames creating shadows that danced around the room. Outside, the full moon cast its bright beams across the mountainside.

Their life seemed so beautiful. And peaceful.

Brian had been so gentle just now. Unlike Sam, he had always been the considerate lover. She knew she loved him and wondered if she would ever be able to say goodbye to him.

It would be so easy to just let him take over, protect her. But did she really want to surrender to another man?

Or would she really be surrendering? She and Brian shared a life so different from her marriage to Sam. Brian understood her desire to write. Her need to create.

The marcasite pin glowed from the counter, reminding her of the reason their life was in such a turmoil. A sense of doom clouded her euphoria as she realized that little pin might one day be their lifeline.

She rested her head against his shoulder, enjoyed the feel of his fingers travelling up and down her arms.

"Brian, I hope we get Sara soon. Her behavior today was so irrational. I'm just glad you were able to control the car when she rammed into us this morning."

She snuggled closer to his chest. "And although it was comical in the end, I don't know that I could ever get used to her interfering with our life the way she did at the library. We might not always be so lucky."

"Now you should understand why I want you here with me. At least I can protect you if you're by my side. And although I balked at the Lamaze classes, I hope you understand why I hate having to leave the house. At least with the security system, we'll know when she's near us."

"But we can't remain locked inside forever."

"True, but we've got to make the best of the situation. Hopefully, this engagement party will turn things around. Get her out of our life once and for all."

"Would you like to practice some of those breathing exercises we learned at the hospital? Watching you do them kinda turned me on this afternoon."

Natalie smiled. "I noticed."

The afternoon Lamaze class had been a real eye-opener for Brian. He'd never realized how quickly their delivery might go. He smiled as he recalled doing the breathing and relaxation exercises. Several of the men, himself included, had relaxed so much that they had almost fallen asleep in the class.

And when she had focused on him while doing the panting exercises, he had been more than a little aroused. Of course, it was like a bucket of cold water had been dropped on him when they watched the movie of an actual childbirth. He was well aware of the delivery process but seeing the birth of a child had been a very humbling experience when he thought about it being his own son.

"Was it that obvious?" he asked.

"Only to me," she laughed. "I've become so accustomed to your insatiable desires."

"No offense," he shifted his legs, "but it's a good thing I had an oversized tub installed in here."

"Hmm, it is," Natalie agreed. She rubbed her back against his chest, smiled when she felt his arousal at the small of her back. She had him just where she wanted him.

"Long and wide," she teased as she snuggled even closer. "I've been working on this particular love scene for the end of my book. Adam and Cecelia have gone to the Poconos for their honeymoon and I understand everything there is heart-shaped. I was wondering about the Jacuzzi though. Have you ever made love in a Jacuzzi?"

She reached for the soap and proceeded to stroke his legs.

"Not this one," Brian croaked when she brushed the inside of his leg.

"Would you care to try it?" Natalie asked, turning around to face him.

"I'm always glad to do research. But are you sure it's okay for you to be doing this? Aren't we supposed to be cutting back on the love-making?"

"What do you think?" she asked, as she stroked him.

Infuriated green eyes stared icily at the wood support beam outside Brian's house. Her body shivered while her mind seethed with anger as she listened to the current conversation on Brian's line. They'd been on the phone all day.

"Finally did it?" Brian's editor asked.

"Yep, she finally accepted," Brian answered. "And you're invited to a small engagement party this Friday evening. I want to make it official before she has a chance to change her mind." Sara heard Brian laugh. "If I had my way, we'd be having the actual ceremony on Friday, but she's not quite ready for that step yet. I'd still like to make it official. Before the baby comes."

Her nostrils flared as she pounded her fists against her thigh. Brian had asked that woman to marry him.

She sneered. They could make all the plans they wanted, that didn't mean they would succeed. Not if she had anything to do with it.

Almost as soon as he finished that call, the woman was on the phone calling her agent.

"You're what?" Dixie exclaimed. "I can't believe it."

"Neither can I," Natalie chuckled. "Brian wants to have a small engagement party this Friday evening. Can you come?"

"I'd love too! I may be a little late, though. I have an afternoon appointment, but I'll drive down as soon as it's finished."

"Great," Natalie said. "I'll email you the directions. Otherwise you'd never find this place. Wait till you see it, you won't want to leave."

Then the woman had called her friend from work. Sara smiled. The one she had hit over the head.

"How's it going?" Natalie asked.

"It's been a little crazy here. I don't think everyone realized how much you did until you were gone!"

"You're just saying that," Natalie giggled.

"I wish I was, but seriously, we've been swamped here."

"Do you think you can get away to come up here for a little party this Friday evening? An engagement party?"

"You're engaged!" Marie squealed. "Wild horses won't keep me away. Is his good-looking sidekick still there?"

"Of course. I understand he has called you a couple times."

"Yeah," Marie laughed. "It'll be good to see him though."

Despite the nausea that built with each call, Sara continued to listen to the conversations. She already had a plan, but didn't want to miss anything important.

She was still angry that Brian had slipped away from her at the library yesterday. She'd ridden around the entire afternoon, but never found him.

Worse, when she'd returned to peek into the house late last night, she'd witnessed the little love scene in the kitchen. It made her sick to think that he would make love to that woman.

It was only a matter of time, now. Sooner than she'd planned. This engagement party just might be the link she needed to put her plan into action.

First the woman and then Brian. A thrill ran through her.

"First the woman and then Brian," she spoke out loud, then laughed as visions of her revenge played through her mind.

"First the woman and then Brian!" she shouted, laughing even louder.

"**W**hat was that?" Natalie started awake from her nap on the sofa. Her head throbbed and her heart pounded. It had seemed so real. Had she dreamed Sara's laugh? Or had she heard it?

It had been a busy day. The trap had been set. Now they waited to see if she took the bait.

The warm fire must have lulled her to sleep as she and Brian relaxed in the den.

"You okay?" Brian asked from his chair.

"Yes, but did you just hear something?"

Brian shook his head.

"I did," Max spoke as he walked into the room.

While Natalie and Brian spent the day on the telephone, Max spent the afternoon at the police station, planning the strategy for trapping Sara. He had just driven into the garage and heard the laugh as he was coming into the house. "I also noticed that the trash has been rearranged."

"The trash?" Natalie asked. "Do you mean she's actually been that close to the house and we didn't hear her?"

"Unfortunately. And a few of the important lists about the party are missing."

"Such as?" Brian asked.

"Such as the notes I made about the caterer. And the list you made of whom to invite. I believe she also got some of the notes you'd scribbled, Natalie."

"Do you normally go through our trash?" she joked.

"No," he smiled. "I set them out as bait."

"And she took it," Brian answered resignedly.

He watched Natalie's complexion grow pale. "It won't be for much longer. In fact, within forty-eight hours, this whole ordeal might be over."

CHAPTER 21

MARIE PARKED HER CAR ON the edge of the woods, eyed the rain, and pulled up the hood of her jacket. She grabbed her suitcase and started across the yard toward the front door.

A weight knocked into her from nowhere, tackling her to the ground. Her luggage flew across the grass.

"Oh, my God!" she shouted as a long, lean body covered hers. She was pinned on her back, helpless. Her assailant had grabbed her hands and forced them above her head.

"Max?" She gazed into the dark brown eyes that glared down at her and realized she recognized her attacker. "Max," she repeated. "What the hell are you doing? It's me, Marie."

Dumbfounded, Max stared down at Natalie's friend.

As good as she felt beneath him, he was embarrassed that he had mistaken her for Sara."

All he'd seen was a female form in a jacket with the hood over her head. As far as he was concerned, Sara was the only person he knew that dressed that way.

"Sorry," he quickly jumped up, offered her a hand. "I thought you were Sara."

"That's okay." Marie laughed as she brushed herself off. "Nice welcome, though."

Max shook his head, admiring her tight jeans when she moved to retrieve the suitcase. "Here, let me," he reached for the handle, then stepped aside to watch her sashay toward the front door. He managed to get there first and opened it for her and caught a whiff of her perfume as she walked past him. He set the bag beside the stairs.

"Marie," Natalie exclaimed as she hugged her friend. "I'm so glad you were able to get here early."

"Yeah, me too." She nodded her head toward Max and chuckled. "Nice welcoming committee you have too."

"I mistook her for Sara," Max explained when Natalie and Brian gave him puzzled looks.

"Yup, tackled me before I had taken two steps."

"You okay?" Brian asked.

"Oh sure."

All three of them cast amused looks at Max who stared down at Marie. He reached for her wrist. "Would you two excuse us for a moment?" he said as he pulled Marie down the hall.

The laundry room would be the closest place for privacy. He smiled. And confined quarters. He stepped inside, shut the door, and pulled Marie into his arms.

Before Marie could utter a word, his mouth covered hers. He had simply grabbed her in his arms, backed her against the door, and locked lips.

God, she felt good. Tasted good. Smelled good. He hadn't realized how much he had missed this woman. "Now that we have that out of the way, I can concentrate on getting Sara. The sex will have to wait til later."

Marie could only stare up at him at a loss for words. When he reached for the door knob behind her, she grabbed his face between her hands and pulled him down for another kiss.

"I've missed you too."

"**H**ow do you think she'll make her appearance?" Natalie asked as she slipped the post of her pearl earring into her ear lobe.

Their first guests would be arriving in thirty minutes and already several of the undercover police were busily laying the groundwork. Some were posing as the catering crew, some as friends attending the party to wish them well.

Max had called in reinforcements from his Secret Service buddies who weren't on assignment. They were set up in the caterer's van where they would be observing the party, studying the cameras on the security monitor, and staying in touch with Brian and Max.

Everyone knew Sara was aware of the engagement party and would be watching the house. Although alerted to her description, no one had spotted her yet.

Natalie hooked the marcasite pin to her dress and stood back to check its effect. Perfect, she thought as she glanced down at the blush-colored cocktail-length dress. Its full empire waist covered her stomach while the ivory lace collar emphasized her breasts. She'd put her hair up, but left a few strands to dangle along her neck.

She smiled at herself.

Felt very beautiful. Desirable. Mission accomplished, she thought as she noticed Brian watching from across the room.

"Who knows what Sara will do?" Brian answered as he buttoned his shirt.

He watched Natalie dab her perfume along her neck, wrist, and behind her ear. He'd always enjoyed searching for those spots whenever possible and planned to do so later this evening.

He wished he could contain the feelings of arousal which always surface whenever she was around. She looked ravishing this evening and he wondered how he'd keep his hands off her.

"What about the police?" Natalie slipped into her flat shoes. "Have they even been able to trace her whereabouts?"

"No. She's obviously living in the woods, but they haven't been able to pinpoint where," he finished buttoning his shirt. "At least not without alerting her. You'd be surprised at the number of caves there are along the mountainside. And no one seems to have noticed anything out of the ordinary around the house. Not since those pertinent pieces of information went missing from the trash the other night." He stepped into the pants of his tuxedo.

"Max talked to the caterer this morning, and she said no one has approached her about working this evening."

"Suppose she doesn't come?"

"She will. I can feel it." After zipping and buttoning the pants, he walked toward the window and stared into the moonlit mountainside. "She's out there. Somewhere. My stomach burns and my head aches. That's how I know."

Natalie stepped up behind him and hugged him from behind. She sighed, rested her cheek against his back. "I can't wait for this evening to be over. It seems like forever and I can't believe the end is so close."

"Let's hope all goes as planned," he whispered. He turned, stared down at her, his eyes taking in her glowing complexion, sparkling eyes, and too-easy smile. Except for the occasional tensing of her jaw, she presented the picture of ease.

"You look very beautiful tonight. Like a woman in love. Are you giving my proposal some serious thought?"

Natalie smiled her secret smile and shrugged a shoulder. She didn't want to give away all her secrets. Not yet anyway.

Brian grinned and kissed her forehead. "I see you have your pin on. Remember how to use it?"

"Yup. One for you, two for Max, and three for you both." She stepped away from him. "Does it look okay with the dress?"

"If anybody says anything, just tell them that I gave it to you tonight and you wanted to wear it." He reached for his jacket. "And if you want to practice contacting us during the evening, that's okay. The number of people attending the party seems to have grown slightly, and I can't promise to be by your side all evening. Even Max will have his hands full although I'm sure Marie will be more than glad to help him."

Natalie recalled Marie's arrival this afternoon. "Wonder what they were up to in the laundry room," she chuckled. "Marie was looking very pleased when she came out. Do you suppose we'll be announcing another engagement soon?"

"No telling. I've never seen Max so mesmerized by anyone before. It's been rather interesting to watch him fall so hard."

Natalie kissed him on the lips. "I'm sure he thought the same of you," she joked, then turned to leave. "I'm going to go on down and be sure everything is ready."

Brian waited until he was sure she was downstairs before reaching for the holster he had hidden in his drawer. He knew Natalie had an aversion for guns, but wasn't going to let that stop him from using it to protect her. He had the required license and was fully trained in using it.

Firearms had become another necessity with Sara's intrusion in his life. Not that he relished the idea of using it on her. On anyone for that matter. He had learned early in the stalking game that he needed to protect himself. And he planned to be prepared for whatever might happen tonight.

Calculating green eyes stared through the binoculars, watched the people arrive. The woods offered cover and although the tinted windows of the living room and dining room distorted the view she had no problem recognizing Brian, Max, or the woman and her friend. She could hear the music and smirked at the smiling faces as the people drank their drinks and laughed with their friends.

She'd almost been caught once, but managed to hide in the shadows as soon as she heard the man coming around the corner of the house.

Brian must be expecting her, she thought. Security was tight. There were people everywhere. Obviously, he didn't realize that half the fun of pursuing him was getting past the obstacles he constantly placed between them.

Tonight, would be no different. She fully intended to make an appearance, but it wasn't time. Not yet. There were still a few things she needed to do.

Brian looked across the room and watched Natalie chatting with Marie. The party was in full swing and he was already anxious for it to end.

Not that he wasn't enjoying himself. It had been interesting to watch everyone's reaction to Natalie's pregnancy. They had purposely neglected to tell anybody when they invited them to the party. After the initial shock, everyone was happy for him.

But the tension of waiting for the unexpected was beginning to grate on his nerves.

Sara had yet to make her appearance, and he was becoming impatient. He knew she'd be here. She'd never missed a chance before.

All those other times, she'd been able to surprise him, but this time would be different.

He mentally checked for the gun she'd felt beneath his coat. He was becoming desperate and hoped that after tonight, Sara would no longer be a nightmare in his life.

Her jealousy of Natalie was making her more dangerous. She might have been a nuisance before, but her latest tactics had been life-threatening.

Not only to Natalie, but to him as well.

In all his studies about stalking, he calculated they were approaching the final stages of the process. When the stalker falls out of love and decides if she can't have him, no one can.

He was sure Natalie's presence in his life brought about the change.

His eyes settled on Natalie's swollen stomach. His unborn child. Unless he managed to put her away, his son would be exposed to the constant harassment he'd experienced these past two years.

He'd had enough of Sara's terrorizing and interfering in his life. It was time to take care of the problem. Remove it, then start a new life with Natalie and his son.

A life without Sara.

Natalie watched Brian move about the room. She knew he was nervous about what Sara might do, and she wished there was something she could do to make him relax.

She herself was more worried about the holster she had realized he was wearing. Although surprised, she didn't say a word.

She voiced her concern with Max a short time later when they had found a few moments alone.

"It's okay," Max had said. "I trained him. He's more than capable of using it."

"I just worry that he might react too quickly. He's so wound up."

"Honey, we all are, but we know what we're doing." He smiled down at her. Then leaned down and kissed her cheek. "You need to relax a little, or we'll be making an unexpected trip to the hospital instead of trapping Sara."

Natalie watched Max as he strolled toward Brian. They exchanged some words before heading toward the bar.

"Isn't he gorgeous?" Marie interrupted Natalie's thoughts.

"Very," Natalie sighed, and then grinned when Marie looked surprised. "Oh! Were you talking about Max? I was thinking about Brian. But now that you mention it, they're both easy on the eyes. Of course, we might be a little prejudiced," she laughed. She felt like a school girl when Brian was around.

"Being in love definitely agrees with you," Marie chuckled as she complimented her friend. "Any news when the baby will arrive?"

"Six weeks," Natalie answered, sipping her soda water. "The furniture should be arriving next week, and hopefully setting up the nursery will make the time go faster."

"So you're definitely going to marry him? Max said this engagement party was a ruse, but that Brian hadn't given up."

"No, Brian will never give up. And yes, I think I'm ready to accept his proposal. We've been through so much and share so many interests; I think what we have is real. Certainly, better than what Sam and I had."

"I heard some scuttle-but on Sam the other day," Marie murmured, and then smiled. "He's going through another divorce. It seems wife number two caught him in bed with a student and kicked him out of the house."

Natalie laughed out loud, causing a few admiring faces to turn her way. Brian and Max included. "I guess it wasn't me all along."

"Oh, he's a regular snake," Marie chuckled. "And somehow, I don't think he'll fare too well with this divorce. I heard she's suing for everything."

"Good." Natalie said as she sipped her drink. "He deserves it."

She glanced at her watch. "I wonder what's taking Dixie so long. She said she'd be a little late, but I thought she'd be here by now."

"Relax Brian, everything's under control," Max said to his friend.

"You sure? It's already been two hours, and nothing has happened."

"When I last talked with the guys, they said all was fine. One mentioned that he thought he'd seen something earlier, but it turned out to be nothing. Don't worry," Max said rubbed Brian's tense back between his shoulders. "It'll all work out. With all we have looking for her, she won't get too close."

"I hope you're right," Brian turned to see Natalie leaving the room. "Where's she going?" He asked as Marie joined them.

"To the library. Dixie finally arrived but wanted to see her. Said something about some exciting news."

Brian debated following her. He didn't like the idea of Natalie being out of his sight. He looked at Max. "Any way we can monitor her whereabouts? Listen in on her conversation without her contacting us?"

Max shook his head. "I guess we should have told her to keep it on."

Brian knew she would use the pin if she had too, but he preferred to keep her nearby. Before he could follow her, his editor stepped up.

"Brian, you're finally taking the plunge."

"Yep," Brian tried to smile. "If not before the baby is born, shortly afterwards."

"I understand she's a writer too."

Brian nodded. "Her books so far aren't your genre, but you might be interested in her current project. It's a suspense. Maybe you could look at it once it's finished. I've been critiquing it. Its quality material."

"We will definitely give it a look-over. Let me know."

Natalie smiled at one of their guests as she moved along the hall off the kitchen toward the library.

She didn't know a lot of the people who were here and found herself examining everyone very closely. Looking for the identifying mole. And arm cast.

Sara had been known to wear wigs, but the mole and cast couldn't be covered so easily.

She was relieved that Dixie had finally arrived, but surprised when the waiter told her she wanted to meet in the library. She wondered what good news Dixie had to tell her that she couldn't do so in a room full of people.

She frowned, hesitating. Could it be Sara? Surely someone would have recognized her. They had enough of her pictures discreetly posted throughout the house. And the security team had been briefed.

As she started down the hall once more she remembered her pin. She could always signal to Brian if anything happened. He would hear her and be there within seconds.

The library door was slightly ajar and Natalie nudged it open before stepping inside.

The lights had been turned down and it took her eyes a moment to adjust, but she'd know that hot pink coat and hat anywhere. Her back was toward Natalie while she stood at the window. As if she were watching something outside.

Natalie gave a sigh of relief. "I'm so glad you finally made it," she said, as she started across the room. "I thought something might have happened-" she stopped mid-way when Dixie turned and Natalie realized her mistake.

That might be Dixie's coat and hat, but it was Sara who was wearing them. She also held a gun in her hand.

"Gotcha."

CHAPTER 22

NATALIE'S MOUTH FELL OPEN WHEN she stared at the woman who had terrorized her all these months. Saw the hatred in her eyes.

A hand flew to her chest when she realized that despite all their precautions, Sara had managed to get inside the house. She looked for the mole but saw that it was covered. Even the cast was concealed in the sleeve of the coat.

Anger and fear set in as she realized no one else knew that Sara had arrived. In Dixie's coat and hat.

And what had Sara done to her agent?

"Where's Dixie?" Natalie demanded.

"Never mind about that little bitch. She'll be asleep for a while. You and I have some unfinished business."

Natalie's shoulders slumped in relief to hear that Dixie wasn't dead. "You'll never get out of here. Everyone's looking for you, you know."

Sara chuckled. "Oh, I know they're looking for me, but I still managed to get in here, didn't I? They're so busy searching for the obvious they missed me when I just strolled right through the front door."

Natalie groaned to herself. She knew Brian, and Max, would be angry that despite all their precautions, Sara had still managed to get into the house. She hoped she would be able to warn them; survive the evening. She stared at the gun that was aimed at her and realized that Brian and Max were right. Sara was desperate and had reached the point of no return.

Since learning Brian was being stalked, Natalie had done a lot of research and uncovered horrifying stories of other stalkers.

They might start off loving their victims but in the end that love turned to hatred and far too often, the victims were killed by their stalkers.

That wasn't going to be the case with Brian Cato. Or Natalie Stover.

Natalie reached up slowly to turn on her pin.

"Not so fast," Sara sneered, noting Natalie's actions. "Keep your hands where I can see them."

Natalie quickly raised her hands. Much as she wanted to alert Brian and Max, she didn't want to risk the baby. "What do you want?"

"I want you, and that kid," she pointed the gun at Natalie's stomach. "Out of Brian's life. And once you're gone, I plan to take care of him as well."

"What do you mean, take care of him?"

"I mean that if I can't have Brian, nobody will."

"Sara... please... you need help. You're sick. You need someone to take care of you."

"I can take care of myself," Sara interrupted her. "After tonight, everything will be all straight again. Right now, I want you to turn around and head toward the garage. Move it," she demanded when Natalie remained where she was.

Natalie quickly turned to the door. She debated dashing in the direction of the party, but before she could make a move, Sara had stepped behind her and rammed the barrel of the gun against her back.

"In case you decide to make trouble, you'll get the first bullet. Now move," Sara snapped, and nudged her down the hall toward the garage.

Although she could hear the revelers behind her, Natalie prayed someone might see them leaving and report it to Brian.

She didn't want anything to happen to anyone at the party, but she also didn't want anything to happen to her or the baby.

Moving slowly, they approached the garage door.

The kitchen on the other side of the wall was abuzz with activity, but no one saw them as they approached the door at the end of the little hall. The door to what could be her doom.

"Open it and keep walking," Sara demanded.

"What are you planning to do?" Natalie asked as she carefully made her way down the garage steps and walked past Brian's Ferrari.

She was worried that Sara might have her yellow Volkswagen there and make her drive. Once they were away from Brian's house, anything could happen. She'd even be out of range to alert him with her wire-tap.

"Just shut up and keep walking. You'll find out soon enough."

A shiver ran through Natalie as they stepped out of the garage into the cold night air. The short sleeves of her dress were no protection from the brisk breeze that whispered across the mountainside.

Running her hands up and down her arms to create some heat, Natalie realized that Sara was concentrating on the trail up ahead and not her actions.

They were nearly at the edge of the woods. She needed a way to defend herself. She'd broken Sara's arm once before, and was sure she could do so again if necessary. But would she be able to grab a stick sturdy enough to be a weapon?

Unless she connected with Brian soon, they would be out of range. Would he even be able to hear her? What about the guys in the van? Weren't they supposed to be able to track her?

The only time she had used the pin was the other day in the library. He had instantly reacted, but they had been in the same room.

Should she risk making Sara angrier? Or should she take the chance?

She brushed her fingers along the side of the pin and pressed the button three times. Hopefully, one or the other would hear her.

"What did you do to Dixie?" Natalie needed to talk, and hoped her repeated question would distract Sara and keep her closer to the house.

Sara didn't immediately respond. "Like I said, she'll be asleep for a while," she finally answered.

"But is she alright?" Natalie asked, praying that Brian and Max would hear their conversation.

"Yes, damn it," Sara shouted. "I managed to get her to stop on her way up the drive and then I just hit her over the head. Just like I did Max the other day. Just like I'm going to do you, if you don't keep moving."

Sara nudged Natalie from behind, causing her to stumble on a root that snaked across the surface of the path.

The moon was full, but as they walked further into the woods, the shadows of the trees made movement more difficult.

Her pregnancy made Natalie's pace slower than usual, and she stopped altogether when she heard movement up ahead.

She prayed that it was the outside security, but sighed when a deer sprinted across the path.

Natalie worried that Brian might not hear her but knew she had to keep trying to talk Sara out of her plans.

The path was suddenly familiar, and Natalie realized they were on Brian's Therapy Trail, where they had taken many of their daily walks.

Natalie began voicing her apprehensions once more. "Sara, you really need to get help. You need to talk to someone. Get some therapy. Oh," she groaned and reached for a tree limb when the baby shifted.

The sharp pain was almost unbearable. This exercise was too strenuous for her very pregnant body.

"Shut up," Sara said as she nudged her forward with the gun in her back.

"Really," Natalie continued her campaign as she stumbled up the path, trying to ignore the pain. "Therapy is the best thing you can do for yourself."

"I said, shut up. I don't need any shrink."

"I'm not talking about a psychiatrist, Sara. I'm talking about therapy. A psychotherapist will listen to you and then help you to overcome your problems. I've researched it and found that therapy has worked wonders for many people."

Natalie wasn't sure she made any sense, but it sounded good. It was all she could do to keep talking. Her only hope was that Brian was listening and would come to her rescue.

Natalie had been gone for over ten minutes, Brian realized with concern. Good news or not, he wanted her out here where he could keep an eye on her.

He turned to express his concern to Max when he heard Natalie's voice in his ear. And then it was gone.

He looked at Max and knew he had heard it as well.

"Oh God," he groaned. "Sara's got her, I just know it. I know I just heard her and now there's nothing. I can't hear a thing."

"Wait, listen," Max commanded, as he concentrated. They could hear a faint voice, but the reception was weakening.

"Let's go outside, maybe we'll be able to get a stronger frequency. Marie," he turned to the woman at his side, but didn't have to say a word. She seemed to have read his thoughts, and moved to the opposite end of the room.

"Listen up folks. It's time for some action. I'm sure all of you will enjoy some karaoke."

While Marie moved to the opposite end of the room, Brian, Max and the security team raced outside.

As they approached the van, they heard Fitz barking from inside. One of the security team opened the door, and the dog bounded for the woods.

Everyone wore ear buds and once outside in the open, they all listened to Natalie's voice as she spoke to Sara. Brian could hear the fear in Natalie's words and prayed she would give them some clue as to their whereabouts.

Fury, frustration and disbelief raged through him when he realized that no matter how hard he and Max had tried to trap her, Sara had somehow managed to get inside and out again with Natalie

"Sara, you need to get help," he heard Natalie speak. He cringed at Sara's response, but continued to listen as Natalie talked about Sara getting therapy.

It wasn't until she had mentioned therapy several more times that he realized what Natalie was doing. She was really talking to him.

"She's telling us where they are. Therapy Trail. They're on Therapy Trail," he almost shouted as he ran in that direction.

"Brian, wait," Max said, running to catch up with his friend. Max's team was right behind him as he grabbed Brian's arm before he got too far. "We've got a plan, remember." He whistled for Fitz. "Now that we know where they're headed, we need to get into place."

Natalie kept talking even as she wondered if it was doing any good. The more she talked, the more it seemed Sara was getting distracted. But she felt that she might be getting through to Sara and had to keep trying.

They were nearing the end of the trail, approaching the cliff where she and Brian often stopped to rest before returning to the house. She desperately needed to rest now. Her back was beginning to hurt, and she was worried about the baby.

She was also worried about Sara's plans. The cliff was up ahead, and time was running out.

Natalie groaned, doubled over as another pain overtook her. "I've got to stop," she sobbed but Sara pushed her from behind.

"You can stop up ahead. That's where you get off anyway."

Natalie prayed Brian was listening. She was terrified that she wouldn't be able to stop Sara from killing her and the baby.

Her back was hurting, her stomach was cramping, and she was so tired. She doubted she could do anything but lay down and cry.

"Sara, I'm carrying his baby. Please don't do anything to hurt Brian's son."

"I should be the one having his baby," Sara hissed as she shoved Natalie ahead of her.

They were at the cliff now and it was all Natalie could do to stop herself from stumbling too close to the edge. She groaned and turned to face Sara.

"Please, I'm having some serious pains now. I need to stop."

Sara laughed. "Once you and the kid are out of the way, then it'll be his turn."

"Brian never did you any harm." Natalie defended Brian. "You're the one who's stalking him."

"Shut up!" Sara shouted. "He was mine until you came along. And now he has betrayed me. All of you must pay."

"Sara," Brian's voice bellowed from within the woods. "Let her go. I'm here. Do what you want with me, but let Natalie go."

Shocked, Natalie tried to search the woods for Brian, but Sara whirled and grabbed her arm, aiming the gun at her stomach. The two of them stumbled back a few paces.

"Don't come any closer," Sara warned Brian. "Or I'll shoot."

Brian stepped from the shadows of the trees but stopped when he saw Natalie within Sara's clutches.

They were so close to the edge the least little distraction would send them both over.

"Let her go," he pleaded as he began to inch his way closer to them. "She has never hurt you."

From the corner of his eye, Brian saw Fitz inched his way from the side.

"I mean it, Brian! Keep that mutt away or I'll shoot," Sara shouted.

Brian hollered, "Fitz, heel." The dog whined but sat. Brian raised his hands.

"Okay, I'll stay right here, but you've got to think about what you're doing. You don't want to harm her or the baby. It's me you want. Please, let her go. You can do whatever you want with me."

"It's too late. You betrayed me. I tried to tell you, but you wouldn't listen. Now, you both will pay."

Natalie groaned as another spasm shook her body. When she leaned forward to fight off the pain, she saw three red dots on the ground. Watched them move across her stomach.

She looked up quickly and met Brian's direct stare. She'd swear he was trying to will her to understand what was happening.

It took a second for the meaning of the dots to register. Sharpshooters were trying for a target on Sara. Unless she wanted to be shot accidentally, she needed to get out of the way.

Natalie sagged as much as she could.

"Stand up, you bitch," Sara complained.

"The pain," Natalie pretended to sob as she hugged her stomach. "It's getting worse."

Bracing for the fall, Natalie focused on making her legs collapse beneath her. She fell to the ground at Sara's feet.

Her original hostage no longer shielding her, Sara turned the pistol on Brian. Pure hatred flared in her eyes and her smile as she took aim. Brian dropped to the ground.

Muffled pops of gunfire sounded, and Sara's body jerked as she collapsed on top of Natalie.

"Natalie!" Brian shouted as he crawled toward them.

Both women were still. Too still. Oh, God—had Natalie been hit, too?

He pulled Sara's lifeless body away. He gasped when Sara's head bobbed back. Her eyes were wide open, but there was no life within them. The tiny hole in her forehead and chest assured him she was no longer a threat to him or Natalie. Or their son.

"Natalie!" He reached for her. She hadn't moved yet.

"Brian," he heard Max shout as he and the men raced from the woods. "Are you okay?"

Natalie wanted to scream but only whimpered when rough hands grabbed her shoulders and shook her.

It wasn't until she recognized Brian's voice that she knew the worst was over. She hadn't been shot. Or fallen over the edge. She was safe.

"I thought I had lost you," Brian murmured, as he settled beside her and held her tightly. "It's finally over."

Natalie glanced behind them and saw Sara's still body and blank stare.

"I must have blacked out. What happened?"

"We had you surrounded, but when she grabbed you, there was little we could do. It wasn't until you faked the pain that the sharpshooters could take her down."

Natalie hugged him once more. "Brian, she was so sick. I'm so sorry it had to end this way."

"Me, too, but at least this obsessive hell has ended. Now, we can get on with our lives."

EPILOG

HE ROSE FROM THE BED in the darkest hours before the dawn. Ignoring the lamps, he simply walked down the hall and stopped beside the crib.

The night light was all he needed as he placed a hand on his son's stomach to quiet his squirming. Hugging the high sides of the bed, he bent and kissed the ebony hair.

He no longer had to look over his shoulder. Sneak out. Screen his movements.

He enjoyed life once again.

His work still consumed him, but he now had a reason to work harder. His family.

Natalie had brought him peace. A miracle. And love.

He smiled. She might break his concentration, but she also inspired him, stirred him, encouraged him, and bewitched him.

She was his life and when he'd married her, he'd made a silent vow to never let her go.

He watched his son sleep. She had given him this miracle. A dream he'd never thought possible. And though she'd tease him occasionally about his original plan to have a son with a surrogate, he thanked his lucky stars that she had entered his life when she did.

Natalie watched Brian gaze down at their infant son. She knew about his fantasy and wore the red gown she had bought for their first night together as husband and wife.

She smiled as she recalled stepping into the bedroom. The only light was from the gas logs and helped to create the mood for his fantasy. Brian was already in bed and she watched his expression turn to awe as she drifted toward him. There was no breeze, but she knew the gown shimmered and caressed her body that was almost back to normal.

She slowly raised the hem of the gown and crawled to him from the end of the bed. She saw he was ready for her and as she mounted him, they both gasped, then shivered at the pleasure that tingled throughout their bodies.

"I've missed you," he whispered.

Natalie smiled then leaned forward to kiss his chest, shoulders and neck. "I've missed you too." While she was still snuggled around him, Brian flipped them so she lay beneath him, and stared down at her.

He kissed her, then slowly made love to her. "You are so much more than I fantasized. Thank you." For the first time, they enjoyed one another as husband and wife.

So much had happened since that fateful October night.

Two ambulances had been dispatched to Brian's chalet. One to carry Sara to the morgue and the other to carry Natalie to the hospital.

Sara's campaign of terror had brought on early labor pains, but it was too soon for the baby. The doctor had ordered complete bed rest and sedated her hoping to prevent the delivery. Brian wouldn't allow her to leave the hospital until she'd promised to marry him within the week. When the actual day came, only Marie, Max, and Dixie had been there.

Fitz too.

Three weeks later, Brian coached her as she delivered a healthy baby boy. A son who showed no after-effects of the trauma his mother had suffered during her pregnancy.

Nicholas Alexander Cato had arrived just six weeks ago, and it was as if he'd always been there. He was no longer a dream, but a reality.

A miracle she had created with Brian.

They planned to take an extended honeymoon later in the month, after Brian finished his testimony before Congress.

Since Sara's death, he had gone public about his harrowing two years as a stalking victim, drawing attention to the issue. He created a stalking awareness website that offered signs to look for, tips to cope, resources such as logs to track incidents for prosecution, and testimonies from others who had been stalked.

After his initial press release, they received many calls from other victims who searched for the same protections Brian had needed. Natalie hoped it would bring about some very needed changes in the laws.

With Sara out of the picture, there was no need for Max to be their protector. He and Fitz had moved to Fredericksburg to be near Marie, and Max had plans to start his own security company. Natalie smiled, sure there would be another wedding soon.

Her book was released two weeks ago and Brian's gift to had been a file folder. He and Max had researched her great uncle's murder and uncovered newspaper articles, police reports and court records. A sixteen-year-old boy had witnessed her great uncle being dragged behind a building but everyone questioned his credibility. Max researched the prominent man named by the boy and discovered a letter of apology written by the man's son to the teenager many years later. The man had confessed to the murder on his deathbed. All parties involved were deceased so there was little that could be done. More importantly, it deepened her love for Brian that he went to so much trouble to bring her closure.

"Isn't he beautiful?" She slipped an arm around Brian's waist, welcomed his warm hug.

"Handsome. Let's not give him a complex."

He smiled down at her before hooking a finger under her chin and kissing her lips. "We'll save beautiful for our daughters. They'll be as beautiful as their mother."

He kissed her again. "Happy?"

"Very."

"No second thoughts? I know I rushed you, but desperate men will do desperate things."

"I think I've loved you from the moment I saw your picture on the cover of your first book."

"My picture, huh? Is the real thing better than the image?"

"Most definitely," she laughed as she pulled his head down for another kiss.

Don't miss out!

Click the button below and you can sign up to receive emails whenever Kay Brooks publishes a new book. There's no charge and no obligation.

https://books2read.com/r/B-A-CCEE-ZQVQ

BOOKS 2 READ

Connecting independent readers to independent writers.

About the Author

As a teenager, Kay enjoyed reading Georgette Heyer, Daphne du-Maurier, Mary Stewart and Victoria Holt and treasured the ones she collected.

She discovered contemporary romance when she needed something light to read while the children were napping. She found herself wondering "what if" and decided to write a story of her own. She joined the Virginia Romance Writers and Washington Romance Writers DC and made many, many new friends while fine-tuning her writing skills.

Three small children, a full-time job as a Library Director, little league and civic obligations caused her put the pen away for a while, although she continued to write news articles and library newsletters. She became immersed in the community and made friends with many of the citizens through the library.

In 2013, she retired and pulled out her old manuscripts. Once again, she found herself wondering, "what if I make a change here? A change there? Update things?"

Spicer's Challenge Book 1 in **The Row Series** was released in 2014 in ebook format. *Dreams Fulfilled* followed in 2015 and *Newfound Love*, Book 3 in 2017. *Persistent Intruder* is the first of three books planned for 2018.

There are many more "what if" stories waiting to come alive.

Please enjoy her website, www.kaydbrooksauthor.com and like her Facebook page: Kay D. Brooks

She also welcomes comments via email: kaydbrooks.author@gmail.com

Read more at https://www.kaydbrooksauthor.com/.